The death of an Irish Sinner

BARTHOLOMEW GILL

wm WILLIAM MORROW 75 YEARS OF PUBLISHING *An Imprint of* HarperCollins*Publishers*

The deaTH of an Irish Sinner

A Peter McGarr Mystery

THE DEATH OF AN IRISH SINNER. Copyright © 2001 by Mark McGarrity. All rights reserved. Printed in the United States of America. No part of this book may be used or reproduced in any manner whatsoever without written permission except in the case of brief quotations embodied in critical articles and reviews. For information address HarperCollins Publishers Inc., 10 East 53rd Street, New York, NY 10022.

HarperCollins books may be purchased for educational, business, or sales promotional use. For information please write: Special Markets Department, HarperCollins Publishers Inc., 10 East 53rd Street, New York, NY 10022.

FIRST EDITION

Designed by Shubhani Sarkar

Printed on acid-free paper

Library of Congress Cataloging-in-Publication Data has been applied for.

ISBN 0-380-97798-2

01 02 03 04 05 RRD 10 9 8 7 6 5 4 3 2 1

For JONNA, whom I hear in the deep heart's core

PROLOGUE

1990

A GREAT WRONG was righted on a bitter spring day in 1990 when the German people rose up in outrage and sacked STASI headquarters in East Berlin.

For over three decades, 89,000 operatives of the *Staatssicherheitsdienst*—the State Security Service—and 170,000 informants had pried into the lives of East Germans, creating what many believe was the ultimate police state.

Children were paid to spy on their parents, householders were coerced into recording the comings and goings of their neighbors.

STASI records were so complete that body swabs were even collected from citizens and stored in hermetically sealed glass jars in case, later, fugitives had to be tracked down by dogs.

Most of the estimated 20,000 who stormed the hated fortress on that frigid day after reunification came to retrieve and destroy the data that had been compiled about them. Few entered the vast complex for any other reason.

One who did was not a German citizen, although she spoke and read the language well. A fit young woman of average height but powerful build, she spent three days inside STASI headquarters, making sure she had located and destroyed every last reference to a certain Josefina Maria Stanton-Hopf.

She also noted down the name of the only other foreigner who had requested and been allowed to view STASI files, nearly a decade before, undoubtedly for a price.

On her second and final night in the STASI complex, the woman was accosted by two men who tried to rape her.

She left one dead and the other paralyzed from the neck down.

PART I
IMMANENT JUSTICE

Christians, even as they strive to resist and prevent every form of warfare . . . have a right and even a duty to protect their existence and freedom by proportionate means against an unjust aggressor.

POPE JOHN PAUL II

Our life is a warfare of love, and in love and war all is fair.

JOSEMARIA ESCRIVÁ DE BALAGUER
(*founder of Opus Dei*)

DUBLIN, 1990

TWO WEEKS LATER in Dublin, the same woman who had visited STASI headquarters used a master key to enter the office of Francis Xavier Foley in fashionable Fitzwilliam Square.

It was a quiet Sunday afternoon, and she assumed nobody would be about.

But she had only begun her search when she heard a key in the lock and in stepped Foley himself, she knew from the photographs she had been given of the man.

"You there!" Foley roared. "What the devil are you doing in my files?"

"What does it look like to a devil?" she replied, continuing her search as though his presence did not matter. "Aren't you supposed to be on holiday?"

"Get out of that! Get out of that now!" A big man who weighed over seventeen stone in his fifty-second year, Foley rushed across the small room and lunged at her, only to find himself quickly down on the carpet with her foot on his throat.

"I could kill you now, but I need you to answer a few questions. Pick yourself up, close the door, and sit in that chair." The foot came away.

"Those files are protected by law," Foley complained as he rose to his feet unsteadily. His groin and neck were now galling him. "I'm a solicitor."

"No, you're not. You're a blackmailer."

"I should call the police." Foley managed to reach a chair.

"Go ahead. Here's the phone."

It landed on the floor by his feet.

"Wouldn't they be interested in what's in here?"

As the pain eased, Foley took in the woman—late thirties or early forties with close-cropped blond hair, blue eyes, and a brace of gold rings pierced through the edge of one ear.

It was hot in the tiny office that Foley leased mainly for the upmarket mailing address, and she had removed her jacket.

Wearing only a tank top and tight slacks the same pale color as her eyes, the woman was either an athlete or some class of weight lifter, he judged. Her shoulders and arms were taut with muscle, and the rest of her looked just as fit.

Not a stupid man, Foley quickly considered his options. He could ring up the police, and surely they would arrest her for illegal entry. But she could—and probably would—bring Garda investigators down on him as well. Foley did not want that.

It had taken much hard digging into the private lives of the country's elite to get him where he was. Now Foley had a house on Killiney Bay, another in the Azores, a trophy wife and two young children, a mistress, and the sure knowledge that a steady flow of untaxable readies would come streaming in to him for the rest of his life, with nothing more for him to do than to keep his identity hidden. And his threats frequent.

Of course, all that was on hold, at least for the moment. At the very least, Foley would have to move his office and sequester his files, in case she both took what she needed *and* informed the police. Wasn't it now wiser to discover whose dossier she was after? And how she had found him out? Then he would decide what to do.

"Can I help you with anything? What is it you're looking for?" he asked.

"Is the information in these files on your computer as well?" She pointed to the machine on a table behind the desk.

"If you mean, do I back up my files? I do, surely. Here and elsewhere." Hearing the sound of his own deep voice emboldened Foley, and it now occurred to him how completely the woman would disrupt his life if he allowed her to leave the office.

"Mark me, woman," he blurted out. "When I discover who sent you, I'll double what I'm owed or expose them. Just for the fuck of it."

As though smitten by the word, she stopped her search, closed the filing cabinet drawer, and turned to him with a brittle smile creasing the corners of her mouth. "Never, *ever* utter that word again in my presence."

Fuck off, Foley wanted to say, but something fierce and final in her light blue eyes made him hold his tongue. It was as though, suddenly, her face had become a mask.

"You're a thoroughly despicable human being," she continued in an even but unnatural tone, stepping toward the computer. "For the better part of twenty blessed years you've been preying upon people for their weaknesses and indiscretions. It's disgusting and totally un-Christian the way you've behaved. Have y'never heard the word *work*?"

Foley tried to suss out her accent, which was neutral but with now and again a certain flat twang, as though Australian or American.

Unplugging the monitor, keyboard, and printer, she picked up the central processing unit and turned to him. "Tell me, how'd you get on to Mary-Jo?"

Foley's head went back, and a wave of adrenaline surged through his large body. Christ Almighty, he thought, it's them. Little wonder she had found him out and got a key to the office. The bastards were so well placed, and they were everywhere.

For months after Foley had flown to East Germany over a decade ago and paid the equivalent of twenty thousand pounds Sterling to copy the Hopf woman's file, he had agonized over blackmailing Mary-Jo Stanton just because of what was happening now.

Over and over, had told himself there were simply too many of them, and it was impossible to know who they were.

And with God on their side and their entire history of claiming to be . . . what?—the successors to the Knights Templar—they would murder him without compunction if they found him out. So his reason had told him.

But the more information Foley gathered, the more bloody money he discovered they had. Billions, in fact. And the sorry truth was—Foley now admitted to himself—he had been unable to resist making the initial phone call and what he had thought then was an outrageous demand.

Which they had met in spite of Foley's periodic and arbitrary increases for over ten thoroughly gratifying years. As well, he'd been careful, using three double-blind trusts instead of the usual two.

But now he was in the broth, big time. Could he talk or buy his way out? He didn't think so, not in a thing like this, not with them. No apology and no amount of money would suffice. They could not tolerate somebody who was not one of them walking around with the knowledge of who Mary-Jo Stanton actually was.

Conclusion? Allowing the woman to leave the room would be tantamount to signing his own death warrant. He had no choice but to squelch her and flee the country as quickly as possible with whatever he could get his hands on. Foley had killed before; it was not hard.

He smiled. "Why not—I'll tell you how I found Mary-Jo out. *If you tell me how you got onto me.*" Foley straightened up in the chair, his eyes scanning the room. He needed something big, heavy, and near at hand. "Is it a deal?"

Still holding the computer as if it weighed nothing, the woman shrugged. "The Berlin Wall?"

Foley nodded.

"Perhaps you haven't heard—it's down."

"And you were with the crowd that stormed STASI headquarters?" The brass desk lamp, he decided. He'd snatch it up and bash her head in.

"If you remember, they made you sign the cover of the dossier. Name, date, and your reason for viewing it. You said, 'Next of kin.' You should have used an alias."

"I wanted to, but the agent I bribed was a right bastard. He made me show my passport."

The woman nodded. "Which made my job easy. I suspected Mary-Jo's blackmailer was Irish, somebody known to her. There are several Francis Xavier Foleys in the country, but only you knew her, albeit through your wife.

"And then, you're a lawyer with no clients, a lavish spender with no known source of income. A liar, an adulterer, and a cheat.

"Now, your turn. You tell me how you formed your suspicions about Mary-Jo."

"*Suspicions*?" Foley asked, placing his hands on his knees and bending his head, as though chuckling. "Let me begin with the most obvious suspicion. First, there's the painting."

"The one in Mary-Jo's study?"

He nodded. "You only need two eyes to see the resemblance. And then the name."

"Josefina Maria and Mary-Jo."

"Aye." Foley guessed it would take him about a second to heave his bulk out of the chair, maybe another to snatch up the lamp, and yet another to lunge across the desk and smash the bitch's head in.

"Also, there was the eternal biography she'd been writing for decades before I met her and is still, I'm told."

"Of Escrivá?" The woman meant José Maria Escrivá de Balaguer, who had been the founder of Opus Dei, the most successful and—some said—the most ruthlessly self-serving religious order in the modern Roman Catholic Church.

Foley nodded, easing his weight onto the balls of his feet. If only he could get her angry and debating him. Why then he might have a chance. "She's written big thick revelatory books about everybody else—why couldn't she bring that project to fruition? I asked myself."

"Because she's waiting for Father Escrivá to be beatified, then sanctified," the woman complained. "With an already completed manuscript and given her reputation as a biographer, she stands to make millions."

"What does Mary-Jo need more millions for?" Foley scoffed. "Doesn't the *Times* list her name as one of the country's ten richest people, year in and year out? What number is she now—four? Or is it three? And that's only what's known about her wealth. Her *advisers* keep the bulk of it hidden.

"No," Foley continued. "The reason she hasn't completed that manuscript is because she either can't bring herself to tell the truth about the thoroughly Machiavellian and unholy character that Escrivá actually was in his lifetime and how he's related to her. Or your crowd won't let her, which explains why there's always clergy about the house. Especially the boyfriend, Fred."

"You don't know what you're talking about. Father Fred is not Mary-Jo's boyfriend, he's a man of the cloth," the woman objected.

Foley glanced up to sight her in. "Right you are—the bed cloth. How can you ignore the facts and lies? Speaking of lies, Mary-Jo is down on record as telling the press and magazines that she was born here in Dublin in 1932."

Foley shook his head and placed his hands on the arms of the chair. "What's *true* is that Escrivá, whom your order calls *The* Father, is also Mary-Jo's father, who in 1931—"

"Stop! I won't allow you to derogate—"

But Foley, raising his orotund courtroom voice, spoke over her. "—who in 1931 was appointed chaplain of Madrid's Patronato de

Santa Isabel. At that time it was a church, a convent for Augustinian Recollect nuns and also a women's college. One of the students there was a certain Beatrice Stanton—a beautiful parentless Irish girl of sixteen—who was expelled when it was discovered that she was pregnant.

"Some generous soul, it was assumed, took pity on her, and she was whisked off to another convent in Leipzig. There she gave birth to a daughter, listing the father as José Maria Escrivá."

"A figment of a young girl's imagination," the woman objected. "Father José Maria was her confessor. She idolized and fantasized about him. And nothing more. Beatrice Stanton was an Opusian acolyte who was raped by a drunken socialist, and Father José Maria did, in fact, take pity on her. End of story."

"Don't be so naïve. Do you think that Escrivá—that paragon of piety who was busy building the most ruthless and militant order in the recent history of the Church—would suddenly single out one young pretty pregnant Irish girl to take under his wing?

"Escrivá," Foley continued, his eyes falling on the letter opener on the desk blotter, "the priest who's responsible for countless thousands of deaths, murders, and torture victims in South America and elsewhere?"

Would it be sharp enough? No. And too messy. He had to kill her quick and get out of there fast. "Escrivá—the priest who orchestrated the deaths of more than a few who wished to leave your order."

"You don't know that! Those are old charges, brought by corrupt journalists who have since been revealed for what they are."

"Quite the contrary—it's *you* who don't know and don't want to know. Who do you think put Perón back in power in Argentina, Pinochet in Chile, and Arana in Guatemala, to mention only Latin American involvements? Who do you think assassinated Salvador Allende—the CIA?

"The American government had no real presence in any of those countries, but José Maria Escrivá's order, your order, Opus Dei, did, with its army of zealous lay supernumeraries who could and did kill in God's name. Admit it, you're one of the assassins yourself."

Still clutching the CPU to her chest, the woman was now visibly nettled. Her eyes had widened, and her jaw was clenched.

"And that same José Maria Escrivá is responsible for Beatrice Stanton's incredible luck in Germany during the height of the Depression. There she was in 1933—sixteen years old, pregnant, penniless, and bereft in a country where she didn't even speak the language.

"Suddenly she makes a brilliant marriage to the aged Karl Hopf, a wealthy landowner and devout Catholic, who felicitously dies within the year. Apoplexy, the death certificate says, leaving Beatrice Stanton-Hopf his entire estate. You can call that providence, but it was not divinely inspired providence. It was Opus Dei taking care of business.

"And no fool Beatrice." Foley gestured with his right hand, in order to get it closer to the desk and lamp. It was the only object close by and heavy enough to do the work.

"In 1939, just as the war was beginning and the German economy was booming, Beatrice sold out her Leipzig holdings for a premium and came back here to Ireland, where for a song she snapped up what amounted to the western flank of the Wicklow Mountains.

"How did she know to do that?" Foley asked. "Instinct? Or was it that all along Beatrice and Mary-Jo have had a series of excellent advisers, interested parties who have steered them to one good thing after another. The same advisers who have made Opus Dei by far the richest order in the Catholic world. Why, you even bailed out the Vatican in the 1970s, when the Church was awash in debt. Now you're the Vatican's banker."

"That's balderdash! Mary-Jo is a self-made woman. Her books have sold millions. Why, the film rights alone—"

"Are peanuts," Foley cut her off, the right hand up again, "compared to what is known about her wealth. But the question is—the question that compelled me to investigate her past, since you asked—is *why* were she and her mother afforded such advice and protection."

A cast had fallen over the woman's light blue eyes, the very same pall that Foley had observed earlier. "You tell me, but I warn you—make it the truth."

"I utter nothing but," Foley demurred, both hands up now. "It's because Opus Dei is conflicted."

He watched her blink, which he saw as a sign of agreement.

"On the one hand, you could never let it be said that your founder—that most pious man, to whom God, he's told us, has spoken, could ever have had knowledge of the flesh.

"But on the other hand," Foley also raised his own left hand higher, "if he did, perhaps Opus Dei should continue to protect the flesh of his loins, as he had himself throughout his lifetime.

"The reason? Because Opus Dei considers itself not merely an institution of the Church but the Ideal Church for the new millennium. The Better Church, if you will. Therefore, he who founded the Better Church—José Maria Escrivá—must have been, like Jesus Christ himself, an incarnation of God here on earth."

"That's cock!" she protested.

"You said it, not I."

"All cock! Which we categorically deny. José Maria Escrivá was just a man, a very good man who devoted his life to God."

"Then why did you pay to keep me quiet all these years, and what are you doing here?"

"Protecting—since you brought up the word—the good name of Mary-Jo Stanton, José Maria Escrivá, and Opus Dei from a scandalmonger, known blackmailer, and probable murderer, like you."

Foley's laugh was hollow, but he had succeeded in disturbing her.

Color had risen to her cheeks, and she now lowered the computer to the desk.

"Don't give me that," he continued. "Look who's lying now? You paid me and you searched me out here for two reasons. One"—with arms still raised, Foley peeled off a finger—"everything I said is true. Two—and this is the delicious irony—nobody in your ruthless sect, which has propounded the deaths of so many innocent others, has got the guts to snuff her and end the problem that she represents.

"Why? Because if José Maria Escrivá is another and more modern Jesus Christ because he sinned, then the flesh of his loins is holy too. Pity Mary-Jo and Fred, for all their hanky-panky, didn't toss up a brat or two to carry the wholly unholy dynasty into the new millennium."

Just as the woman barked "Enough!" Foley lunged across the desk, one hand grabbing a corner for leverage and the other seizing the neck of the lamp, which he swiped across the side of her face.

"But I've got the guts!" he roared, cocking back the lamp and whipping it down at her head.

Instead it struck the computer.

Again and again Foley flailed at her, moving around the desk as she retreated.

Until he raised himself up on his toes to maximize his leverage, and she buried her foot deep in his groin. As he crumpled up, she slammed the heavy machine down on his head.

Foley fell to his knees.

She struck him again.

Foley toppled over on the carpet.

Holding the CPU over her head, she whipped her body and crashed the tower into his face, before turning to the mirror behind the desk.

The sharp bottom of the lamp had gouged her cheek, which was now bleeding profusely. She'd have a long scar if she didn't get it stitched soon.

But there was much work still to do, both here and at Foley's home on Killiney Bay, as well as in the mistress's flat in Dun Laoghaire. No trace of Mary-Jo could be allowed to remain.

Now that he was dead and would be missed, the files here in the office would have to be removed quickly and destroyed. But safely, in a manner that would leave no trace.

It now occurred to her where—a building on the quays that was owned by a friend who, in fact, might find some of the information in the files useful. She would enlist his aid.

But she fervently hoped Foley hadn't told either his young wife or his stylish mistress about Mary-Jo. It would be a pity if there were any evidence that he had.

PART II

MORTIFYING THE FLESH

2

DUBLIN, SPRING 2000

LITTLE COULD CHIEF Superintendent Peter McGarr have known that the investigation into the unsolved murder of Francis Xavier Foley—solicitor and blackmailer—would resume over a decade later with another killing on the evening of the first fine day in spring.

Winter had been desperate altogether, with torrential, wind-blown rains and coastal flooding in many parts of the country. Early spring proved little better.

Then, one Friday night in the middle of April, the winds ceased with an abruptness that was startling. Stepping out of the headquarters of the Serious Crimes Unit in Dublin, McGarr noticed a change in the air that had to do more with texture than temperature.

A gentle yet steady breeze was blowing in from the southwest, and now and again through thinning clouds he could see stars overhead. The climate had finally relented, and the morrow would be fair.

Pouring himself a drink in the pantry of his house in Rathmines, McGarr took a sip and glanced up at his reflection in the glass cabinets that ringed the small room.

In his mid-fifties now, McGarr had a long face, clear gray eyes, and an aquiline nose that had been broken more than a few times and now angled slightly off to one side.

He was balding, but the hair that remained was curly and a rich red color that had only begun to gray at the tips. But it was the contrast between his still-vibrant hair and the pallor of his skin that disturbed McGarr. He looked pasty, winter-worn, and gray.

Although an avid fisherman and gardener, he asked himself when he had last spent a full day out of doors. Sure, there was the weather to blame, and the caseload of the "Murder Squad"—as the press had dubbed his agency—had never been more onerous.

But how many more truly active springs did he have? In the last few years McGarr had found himself going to funeral after funeral, with not all of the deceased older than he.

Topping up his drink, he called out to his wife, Noreen, saying that it was time to take their annual spring pilgrimage to her parents' country house in Dunlavin.

"You mean it's that day again?" she said from the Aga, where she had been readying dinner—a piquant *osso bucco*, McGarr could tell from the aroma. While they had been at work, it had bubbled in the least-hot oven of the ornate stove that dominated one wall of their kitchen.

"I've already spoken to Bernie about the truck," McGarr continued, carrying his drink out into the kitchen. "You two can take the car."

Turning from the cutting board where she was slicing greens, Noreen pointed her chef's knife at him. "This year, I want you to remember—none of that stuff comes into this house in any way, shape, or form, no matter the excuse.

"Everything from your boots to that coverall thing you wear—hat, gloves, the works—gets left in the shed at the end of the garden. I won't have Maddie and me sneezing for months because of your . . . preoccupation." She turned back to the cutting board.

A trim woman nearly twenty years younger than McGarr, Noreen had removed her skirt—so as not to spot it while cooking, he assumed—and had donned a bib apron over her slip. From the back, like this, the angular flow of her body with her good shoulders and legs but narrow waist appealed to McGarr in a way that was beyond words. Her stockings were turquoise in color, her hair a tangle of copper-colored curls.

"You don't seem to mind what my *preoccupation* yields," he complained.

"That's different. I love the vegetables. But can you tell me one other gardener in the entire city who has to resort to such a vile substance to make his garden grow? Dermot across the square seems to do just fine with whatever he can find at the garden shop."

Ach, Dermot D'Arcy's vegetables couldn't hold a candle to the plump juicy tomatoes or big glossy eggplants that McGarr grew yearly in a climate that was usually inhospitable to such species, he thought, taking a sip of malt. All the aptly named D'Arse-y could raise were spring lettuce, radishes, and ground vegetables. Turnips were his specialty, and in a sunny year he might come up with the odd zucchini courgettes.

Yet McGarr held his tongue, knowing that it was wiser to engage his young wife in debate only *after* she had eaten.

Also, she had a point about the "vile substance" that would be the object of McGarr's quest on the morrow—rare, aged chicken manure mined from a former commercial poultry farm that Noreen's father had purchased and appended to his country estate.

Having deteriorated to a near powder, the chicken droppings were so ammoniacal that McGarr was forced to wear a breathing mask when shoveling it out of the former chicken coops. Even so, the very odor of the stuff stung his eyes and burned his lungs.

But there was a payoff to his madness. Combined in the proportion one part manure to two parts of composted earth, the stuff was magic—the very secret to his garden—and proved such a fillip to growth that his garden flourished like none other in the neighborhood. Or perhaps even the city.

As for gardening itself, McGarr had dismissed all the standard explanations for digging in the earth, from reestablishing touch with his ecology to taking a direct part in the cycle of birth, growth, harvest, and rebirth. McGarr believed—and he would insist, if asked—that he gardened for simple pleasure.

Everything, from tomorrow's yearly trip down to Kildare for the magic chicken droppings to enjoying the snappy crunch of fresh vegetables and herbs in all seasons regaled him in a way that was beyond words.

He did it because he did it, he once told Noreen, for whom all urges required some explanation, and he couldn't think of anything else that would provide him with such pleasure. There was no other word for it.

"I think I'll go look at the plants," he said, moving toward the door to the cellar.

"Can I come too?" asked Maddie, who had heard his voice and now joined them.

"Of course. Let's see if the chervil has sprouted."

"Don't get distracted now. Your tea will be ready in a jiff," Noreen said, reaching for a pot on the speed rack above the cutting board in a way that spread the apron and firmed her lower back.

Mindful of urges and distractions, McGarr opened the door and allowed Maddie to precede him.

Down below in the darkness they could see the purple glow of the growing lights. "Wait." He put a hand on Maddie's shoulder, stopping her. "Smell that?"

"Smell what?"

"Just breathe in."

"Right—and what?"

"Can't you smell it? The oxygen? Plants take in carbon dioxide and give off—"

"I know, I know—don't you think we study that at school?" Now a confidant eleven and a miniature version of her mother, she switched on the lights and tripped down the stairs. "The only thing I can smell is that stuff in your glass. How can you?"

McGarr glanced down at the brimming glass of malt and wondered the same.

But not why.

3

SO, IT CAME TO PASS that spring arrived with the dawn of the next day in the form of a high sky and a hot sun.

Instead of taking the quick route along the dual carriageway southeast to Naas and then on to Dunlavin, the McGarr caravan of a battered old pickup and Noreen's Rover sedan journeyed due south, climbing to the tops of the treeless Wicklow Mountains, "Where we'll gain perspective on spring," McGarr enthused.

The air was so clear and the sun so bright that they caught glimpses of the dark blue and spangled waters of the Irish Sea in one direction and the rocky crags of Mullaghcleevaun in the other.

Even the usually bleak mountain moorlands were changing the dun colors of winter for the new green of spring, seemingly right before their eyes. McGarr opened the pitted window of the old pickup, the better to see, and was rewarded with the call of a cuckoo overhead and the sight of a pair of red grouse pecking at the edges of a mountain bog.

Drifting slowly down out of the mountains, they could see Dunlavin in the valley below them—a neat village at the junction of several country roads where the Wicklow hill country meets the rich limestone plain of Kildare. Unlike the treeless mountain barren, the land was rich here, and tall oaks and beeches—their boughs fringed with the chartreuse of new leaves—girded the hamlet.

As did a number of tall walls, built as make-work projects during the Famine. Some ran for miles on both sides of narrow country roads, ringing estates that were once the country manses of Dublin's Anglo-Irish elite. In most cases the holdings had passed on to those who could afford not only the purchase price but also the yearly expense of maintaining the walls, the acres, the stables and other out-buildings, and finally, the large main house. Some of those dwellings were truly stately, others merely substantial.

Noreen's parents' place—*Ilnacullin*, or "Island of the Holly"—mediated between the two conditions. No mansion, it was instead a large Georgian country house of three stories with a graceful facade that featured rounded corners and tall, arched windows. A complex of other structures, also constructed of white limestone, flanked one end of the house, and a wide patio leading down a hill into a formal garden complemented the other side. The brook with its island of holly lay in the distance.

Fitzhugh Frenche—Noreen's father—had made his fortune, it was said, mainly by being a clever man who had well-placed friends. He was also pleasant company, a good listener, wise when it came to advice, and utterly discreet. In some Irish circles, a timely tip over brandy and cigars was the currency of friendship.

A man well into his seventies, with an imposing paunch and rosy complexion, Fitz—as he was known to his many friends—accompanied McGarr to the former chicken farm mainly to get out of the house, McGarr judged. His father-in-law was at that stage in life where—after having given up his Dublin presence—he now missed the hurly-burly of daily life in town.

McGarr had noticed the same . . . itchiness, as he thought of it, in some colleagues who had said they couldn't wait to retire, only to show up in the dayroom every now and again, "Just to say hello." Or at crime scenes. Or they'd ring up McGarr with a tip or an invitation to lunch, where any scrap of gossip or inside information was coveted like a prize.

Packing a pipe, Fitz looked on as McGarr shoveled the precious powdered droppings out of the dilapidated chicken coop into a wheelbarrow and then to the back of the truck. "Janie—whatever are y'doing this for, carting it up to Dublin when there's perfectly good ground for a garden right here in Dunlavin? And plenty of it." Whenever the older man spoke privately with McGarr, he lapsed into the Dublin argot that was common to them both.

"How would I tend such a garden down here, and when?" McGarr asked, without stopping his work.

"Well—that's another matter altogether," his father-in-law huffed. "Nuala and me won't live forever, and the house is getting too big for us. Why don't the three of yiz move down here, where you belong, and leave the city to all them mots and bowsies from who knows where. You have enough of that in your work as it is."

During a recent visit to McGarr's house in Rathmines, Fitz had been shocked by how many of McGarr's neighbors were nonwhite—mainly students at Dublin's several universities. But others were political refugees or people with skills and talents needed by the new high-tech economy.

"Sure, it's no place to bring up a child," the old man went on, lighting the pipe."

On the contrary, McGarr had thought, Dublin was undoubtedly *the* place to bring up a child, since diversity would continue to mark the country and the rest of the world if free trade and the electronic revolution continued.

McGarr had only to think of the stultifying provinciality of his own upbringing in an overwhelmingly Catholic and working-class part of the city. There, Protestants had been looked upon with fear and scorn, like aliens from some unknowable and inconsiderable universe.

But McGarr said nothing, understanding it was pointless to debate the man, given his age and the fact that Fitz had been a child during the most insular decades of the country's history.

"You know—this place will be yours soon."

"No, it won't. Not soon and not mine. Noreen and Maddie's perhaps. I have me own digs up in Rathmines." McGarr closed the tailgate of the truck and began securing a tarp over his pungent cargo.

"But you'll look after it for them, won't you?"

"Of course. Now, are you coming up to town with me, or do I take you back to the house?"

With real joy at having been asked, Fitz reached for the truck door. "Cripes—I'm coming, of course. Wait—I don't have me billfold."

"What do you need that for?"

"Aren't we stopping at Floods for a pint?" His doctor had restricted his drink intake, and Nuala was making sure he kept to the regimen.

"You're all right," McGarr assured him, wondering if there would come a day that he himself would have to sneak off for a jar. "But I hope you know Floods has changed."

"In what way?"

"These days it's filled with mots and bowsies from who knows where."

"Ah, shit—haven't I drunk with politicians and solicitors most of me grown life? A few mere chancers won't bother me much."

Seven hours later—after completing the delivery with the requisite stop at Floods—the two men returned to Dunlavin. With the days still short, the sun was just setting as McGarr turned the truck into the avenue of beeches that lined the drive of Ilnacullin. A number of cars were parked near the well-lighted house.

McGarr knew what had happened. The inevitable houseguests from Dublin had arrived, and a neighbor or two—after having stopped in to say hello—had been invited to dinner.

Pulling the battered heap into the stable yard, McGarr had to nudge his father-in-law, who had slept through the return trip.

"What—here already? Amn't I a brilliant traveling companion? I hope I didn't snore."

"You okay?" McGarr worried that the older man—who had once been famous for his stamina—was beginning to wane.

"Tip-top. Nothing like a pint and a snooze to pick you up. Nuala have the usual suspects aboard?"

"It would seem so, from the cars in the drive."

"Good—we'll have a long pleasant evening with some old friends. It's what life's all about."

McGarr was unsure of how long the evening would last for him, since after a hot bath, a big meal, and all the physical labor he had put in, he would quickly nod off, especially if seated by the wood fire that Fitz kept crackling in the den.

It was there four hours later, after McGarr had "napped" for some time, that Fitz appeared by his side to whisper that he was wanted on the phone.

McGarr could not imagine who it could be, since an official call would have come through his cell phone or beeper, both of which— as always—he kept on his person. "Who is it?"

"One of our neighbors."

McGarr waited.

"Fred."

"The priest over at Stanton's?"

"He says it's imperative he speak with you yourself, nobody else. He wouldn't say what, but it sounds serious. You know Fred."

Indeed, McGarr did. While an affable dinner guest with many interesting stories about his days as a missionary in South America, the cleric was the soul of discretion.

Having to shake off his drowsiness, McGarr lumbered out to the phone in the hallway. "Fred—how can I help you?"

"Could you come over here?"

"Why? What gives?"

"A . . . catastrophe."

McGarr waited before asking, "Of what sort?"

"A catastrophe," the man repeated. "Please meet me at the gate." And he rang off.

Reaching for his cap and jacket, McGarr discovered that it was almost cold when he stepped outside. A brilliant half-moon lit the drive, and overhead banks of stars were layered so deep that the sky seemed opaque in patches.

4

LIKE ILNACULLIN, Barbastro—as a brass name-plate declared—was a walled holding. The difference was that its gate was two solid doors of what looked like bronze that were always closed.

"To keep passersby from peering in at our best-selling author," McGarr had once heard Father Fred say during a dinner. "It's not so much her *admirers* who wish to contact Mary-Jo. We deal with rafts of fan letters each week. But the *type* of person who would drive out here just to peer in. Not everybody cares for the truth that M. J. writes in her pages, and some, I fear, are envious of her success."

In the beams of the Rover's headlamps, McGarr scanned the coffered panels in the door, which presented the fourteen stations of the cross. The metal had recently been cleaned.

Instead of finials, small monitoring cameras had been positioned on the capstones of the gate, two beaming down on McGarr, two others focused on the interior drive. As though weighing tons, the gates now opened slowly. Father Fred was standing in the drive with something like a television remote device in one hand.

McGarr pulled in, and the priest aimed the gadget at the gate. Reaching over the gearshift, McGarr opened the passenger door.

"Thank you for coming," the man said, sliding in. "I'm glad you were here in Dunlavin. Alone. I wouldn't want . . ." His voice trailed off.

"Can you tell me what this is about?"

"Better I show you." He closed the car door.

Although nearing sixty, McGarr judged, the priest had a full shock of glossy black hair. He was a big man with wide shoulders who kept himself fit by bicycling in the Wicklow Mountains.

More than a few times McGarr had passed him either pumping up hills that seemed impossibly steep for a bicycle or catapulting down the other side at speeds that could prove fatal were a tire to puncture.

He turned to McGarr. "Straight ahead. At the house, take the lane into the garden." With a long straight nose, pale blue eyes, and a dimpled chin, he was a handsome man, and McGarr remembered some woman friend of the Frenches' dubbing him "the matinee idol of the Catholic Church" and adding, "It's a pity he doesn't take confessions." In the glow of the green lights on the dashboard, his shaven cheeks appeared flinty blue.

Again like the Frenches' estate, the drive at Barbastro was lined with towering beech trees, but the approach was much longer, with a series of graceful switchbacks, to a house that in every way justified the word *mansion*. Positioned on a knoll, the Georgian structure looked more like the main building of a college or a seat of government. Yet from afar, bathed in floodlights, the building did not seem outsized.

Serpentine walls compressed its apparent size, McGarr decided, as the headlamps of the Rover, following the sinuous drive, played over the facade. Surely it was one of Ireland's great houses, with wide lawns, a woodland park, and a formal garden where Father Fred now asked McGarr to stop.

"She's in here," he said, climbing out.

"Who is?"

But the priest had already passed beyond the car.

McGarr removed the pocket torch that Noreen kept in the glove box and followed the man down a pathway that repeated the serpentine motif of the drive and house.

In the achromatic light of the half-moon, the garden looked chalky and unreal. A rime of silvery frost had gathered on the shrubs and greensward.

They came upon her at the third turn of the pathway. Mary-Jo Stanton was down in a patch of daffodils, as though she had been on her knees gardening when she died. Her body was slumped on her legs with her forehead touching the dirt, the long white ponytail that she always wore having spilled forward onto the plants.

She was wearing jeans, tennis shoes, and an old twill shirt that was several sizes too large. With both arms splayed out behind her— one still grasping a garden trowel, the other wrapped in a glove—she looked almost as though she had assumed some position of supplication in her last moments of life. Like drawings McGarr had seen from Mandarin China, of the condemned offering their necks to the ax.

Because what struck him most about her corpse was the balance that it had achieved in death. He tried to remember when he had last viewed a body that had managed to remain even somewhat upright without the aid of a chair, car seat, or the like. He could not; for him, it was a first.

Nor was there any indication in the soft soil around her that she had struggled—attempted to rise up or flee—even though it was plain she had been murdered.

"What's that around her neck?" McGarr asked, pointing to a barbed metal . . . necklace, it looked like, that had been tightened around her neck with a large wing screw. Blood had flowed from where the points had bitten into her neck. But from the darkened color of her face, McGarr assumed the instrument had strangled her.

"A *cilicio*," said the priest. "Or at least, a type of *cilicio*."

"Which is?"

"Oh . . . I suppose it's an instrument of bodily mortification, a way of resisting the temptations of the flesh."

"Like a hair shirt?"

"Exactly. *Cilicios*, in fact, are hair shirts and were used rather commonly during the early ages of Christianity. Some orders—the Carthusians and Carmelites—still employ them by rule."

"Hair shirts," McGarr said again, because he had heard of the practice. But this was no hair shirt.

"Later on, I'm afraid, the practice was adopted by most of the religious orders, in imitation of the early ascetics, you know." The priest glanced over at McGarr. "Other devices were employed to increase the discomfort. That's where barbaric things such as that come from. Screw and all."

"I don't understand where it would fit. On one's body."

"Oh, the thigh, I would think. It would be applied at such times as when one was experiencing impure thoughts, the screw being tightened down as required."

"Could it be Mary-Jo's?" McGarr remembered that she had been a collector of unusual items—chains, whips, manacles, and the like. There was an entire large room in the house, where McGarr had once been a guest, devoted to the display of candelabra.

"I think this could be from her collection, although she kept the *cilicios* under lock and key on her floor."

"Which is where?"

"The top floor of the house. She alone lived there. Exclusively."

Exclusively of him, McGarr believed the point was, again studying the corpse with its curious balance. The frost had gathered on her body; it spangled her hair.

Half tempted to give the body a shove, just to test how stable it was, McGarr instead played the beam of the torch on the ground to either side. The dirt was patterned with a number of footprints, the most dominant having been made by a large foot that had been wearing cleats or toeplates.

"I'm afraid those are mine," Father Fred explained. "I was out wheeling well after dark. When I got back and couldn't find M. J., I looked to see if her car was gone, then searched the house and finally the grounds."

McGarr glanced at the priest, noticing that he had changed into his usual black attire, including the clerical collar.

"Between trying to find you—at your headquarters, your home, and finally at Noreen's parents'—I changed," Father Fred explained, as though having read McGarr's thoughts. And dispensing guilt, which ruled all in Catholic Ireland.

Had the man left a message at either Dublin location, McGarr would have been notified. He tried to remember just how long Father Fred had been Mary-Jo Stanton's . . . what? Confessor? Confidant? Companion? Years, ten at least that McGarr knew about. Certainly he had been her companion all of that time.

And didn't Father Fred, as a priest, have an "office"? as McGarr believed specific priestly vocations were called. Something to do? Work? If McGarr knew one thing about the Catholic Church, service was primary. Those who could serve, would.

As well—where were the man's feelings? Mary-Jo had obviously been . . . *assassinated* seemed the appropriate term, given her notoriety. The story of her murder would involve the world press.

"May I say something?" Father Fred now asked. "Everything I know, everything I've been taught and have believed all my life as a Christian, a Catholic, and most particularly as a priest tells me that this is the act of a madman. It has to be. Who would want, who would even conceive of murdering Mary-Jo, who was—in everything she said, did, wrote—a veritable saint?"

McGarr waited, now watching the larger man, whose features were shadowed in the moonlight.

"I can understand that there's no possibility of keeping this quiet, a matter between you and me." Father Fred let that sit.

As did McGarr. In the distant wood, an owl was hooting its plaintive oo-oo-oo.

"Consider, for a moment, the . . . travail this will cause, the pain for those who loved her—her friends, acquaintances, and her readers, even. Gone will be the remembrance of her accomplishments, all the charitable works that she was most proud of in her life. What people will remember is this . . . tragedy.

"Do you suppose that she could have done this to herself?"

What? How?

"You know—slipped it around her neck and tightened the screw quickly, then waited for the effect to take its course. In recent months, her health was not good."

Then why the gardening trowel in one hand, the glove on the other?

"I mean, academically speaking."

The school being murder. McGarr continued to wait. Beyond his thoughts, which were bizarre for a priest, the man had something to tell him.

"I don't imagine we could keep this between ourselves."

The warm west wind that McGarr had noticed the night before had returned. A jet bound for Dublin Airport was tracing the sky, its landing lights brilliant cones of luminescence in the distant heavens.

"I could have phoned a sympathetic doctor who would have ignored the *cilicio* and labeled this a death from natural causes."

Really? McGarr would like to know the name of such a caring person, although he understood that more than a few suspicious deaths of older people were simply attributed to age by inattentive physicians. The marks on her neck, however, could not have been ignored.

"I might still, without your ceasing your investigation."

There it was—why the priest had donned his clerical garb, why he had searched out McGarr and not phoned the local Guards or alerted McGarr's headquarters.

"You want to know who did this?" McGarr asked.

"Unquestionably."

"But at the same time, you don't want her murder to be reported."

"Exactly."

"Why?"

"I told you—to keep this . . . event from sullying her memory."

"How do you suppose I could go about that without involving my office?"

"I could help you. I have a cadre of acolytes at my service."

"And when and if we discovered Mary-Jo's murderer—what then?"

The priest only regarded him for a long moment before saying, "By which you mean, you can't do that."

Be a party to the cover-up of a murder, an illegal investigation, and the probable murder of an uncharged, untried suspected killer? With a priest as the literal *vice* in the plot?

McGarr would not acknowledge the possibility with a reply.

"You're sure."

McGarr ignored that as well.

The priest nodded once. "All right, that said—and forgotten, I hope—perhaps you'd like to examine the house and speak with the others who are here. Today only I left the premises, and we had but one visitor, who is staying the night. Or so say the log and the transcripts."

"Transcripts?" McGarr asked. It was a curious word.

"The logs we keep of comings and goings, the tapes that are made of various parts of the property."

"You mean there are more cameras than those at the gate?"

"Yes, of course. You don't know how many times Mary-Jo was

threatened. Attempts were even made to blackmail her." The priest turned, as though to walk away.

"Why would anybody have threatened Mary-Jo? Or blackmailed her?" Pulling out his mobile phone, McGarr speed-dialed his headquarters in Dublin.

"Because of her notoriety, because she wrote the truth. I'm sure that's who's to blame for this. Some . . . crazy who wished to settle scores."

"Were the police informed of the threats?"

"No—any publicity of that sort would just have encouraged others, I'm sure. And tipped off the press."

"Blackmail presupposes a cause for blackmail. What would that have been?"

"Oh"—the priest looked away—"scurrilous things really. I'm afraid I can't remember exactly what. Something to do with her mother, I believe, who was rather a free spirit."

When a voice came over the phone, McGarr explained where he was, what had happened, and then asked for the Technical Squad, who would secure the body and examine the crime scene.

Slipping the phone back into his pocket, he took a long last look at Mary-Jo Stanton, down on her knees, her forehead touching the ground in supplication, her long white mane now riffling in the wind, her arms splayed to either side, the curious *cilicio* around her neck.

To have grown so old and accomplished so much, he thought, only to have died in such a strange way for . . . *words*, as the priest had suggested? The very métier that she had practiced.

Seldom in McGarr's experience had he investigated murders that had been committed for words, unless the words had involved love, money, sex, or religion.

Surely the context of Mary-Jo Stanton's life had been religious, given the presence of the priest and her literary preoccupation with the lives of saints and religious scholars.

But what of love and money? Or sex? Who had loved her and how? And who would inherit her great fortune, the house and property?

McGarr stepped up the path. "The 'transcripts,' please. Would you show me the way?"

5

CLIMBING OUT of the Rover in front of the house, McGarr removed the Walther PPK that he kept in a holster that was fixed beneath the driver's seat. He inserted a clip of seven cartridges into the butt.

"Do you think you'll need that?" the priest asked. "Here?"

"Not if you think Mary-Jo's death wasn't murder. Here."

The priest could not have known that in the pocket of his jacket, McGarr also kept an Advantage Arms model 422, a derringer-type weapon that held four .22-magnum rounds in the four chambers of its one barrel.

Having been modified, the weapon fired all four cartridges with one squeeze of the trigger. It was McGarr's idea of an insurance policy, what any cop who'd made enemies of innumerable chancers over the years needed to stay alive.

Fitting the Walther under his belt, he buttoned his jacket over the butt and lowered the car visor, which was equipped with a Garda shield, so the Tech Squad, when they arrived, would know where he was. "How will my people get in?"

"When they pull in by the gate, an alarm will sound, and I'll be able to let them in from the control panel."

On his earlier visits to the house, McGarr had not noticed the other security cameras that were concealed at the corners of the building and by the door. "And this control panel is located where?"

"In the control room, of course," the priest said evenly, while sliding an electronic entry card over the lock of the stout but graceful front door.

The front door belonging to McGarr's parents-in-law only a half mile distant was locked only when the elderly couple was away on holiday. At other times, workers on the property, friends, and neighbors could open the door and shout, if knocking failed to rouse them.

What had Mary-Jo Stanton feared? Why the need for so much . . . control? "You locked this door?" After having discovered the woman's corpse and returned to the house to change into your priestly attire went unsaid.

"No—closing the door locks it." Having opened the door, the priest demonstrated by pulling it shut. "As doubtless you're aware, in addition to being known as a person of wealth, Mary-Jo was also a collector. After a robbery back in the eighties, I insisted that she install a security system, new locks, and so forth. Periodically, the system has been upgraded. It's state-of-the-art, as you'll see."

Having opened the door again, Father Fred stepped into an expansive foyer, McGarr in his wake. The electronic ID was again required to enter the central hallway, which contained a wide serpentine staircase that led to the upper floors and was lit by a crystal chandelier. Double doors to the main rooms of the mansion lined a wide hall.

"All residents and guests, of course, are provided with a new card every morning so they're not constrained in any way from coming and going. The cards open the doors to their bedrooms and most other doors in the house and around the grounds, including the front gate."

"But their comings and goings are recorded?" McGarr asked, mindful of the "transcripts" the priest had referred to earlier.

"It's one of the advantages of the system." Father Fred moved to a narrow door at the back of the grand staircase. Yet again having to use his electronic passkey, he led McGarr into a low, darkened room that was lit by banks of small video display terminals.

Each seemed to be monitoring some part of the estate—hallways and doors of the house, the main rooms, the kitchens, the front gate, garages, stables, greenhouse, even the pathways of the formal garden. McGarr could make out the shape of Mary-Jo Stanton's corpse bowed down in death—her white hair, the glint of the gardening trowel.

The small room was quite warm and stank of hot plastic and circuitry.

"What good is all of this if you need somebody in here to watch the screens?" McGarr asked.

"If somebody so much as touches one of the doors without using a pass card first, an alarm will sound both in here and on this." From the pocket of his clerical jacket, the priest removed the same remote device that he had used to close the front gate.

"As well, all of this is recorded." He swept a hand to mean the monitors.

"Recorded how?"

"To disk with a tape backup."

"You mean you have a recording of what went on here?" McGarr pointed to the screen with the image of the woman's corpse.

The priest's hand jumped to his jaw in a thoughtful pose. "You know, in the chaos of the . . . catastrophe, it slipped my mind. But yes! We should have it. What number is that?" He pointed to the screen that pictured the corpse.

In the darkness, McGarr had to squint. "Forty-one."

At a keyboard, the priest tapped some keys on the control panel and then pointed to the larger screen that obviously serviced the computer. "We'll see it here."

As the tape rewound quickly, McGarr and Father Fred appeared in the picture, then Mary-Jo Stanton's corpse alone for a while, followed by the priest dressed in his bicycling togs and bending over her. They then watched a long sequence of just her lifeless body, then a dark gap, and finally Mary-Jo herself, gardening while the sun was fully out.

"Shall I stop here?" Fred asked.

"Yes. Run it forward, please. Slowly, if possible."

The priest struck the keys once more, and they watched as the pretty, elderly woman with her white mane bound in a ponytail pottered around her garden in slow motion. She pruned a bush here, transplanted a seedling there, and paused now and then to wipe her brow and glance around her.

Once when a magpie kited down for a worm in a freshly dug section of garden, she paused and seemed to speak to the large, handsome black-and-white bird as it worried the ground, tossing bits of earth this way and that.

"Shall I speed it up?" Father Fred asked.

"Please."

The screen then showed Mary-Jo Stanton again moving from one spot to another and kneeling down to garden before the picture went dark.

"Stop," McGarr said. "Go back slowly from there."

Another series of taps backed up the tape, and they watched as suddenly the screen brightened again, and they saw her down on her knees exactly where she had been murdered, McGarr believed.

In reverse, it appeared that Mary-Jo Stanton had turned her head and said something to somebody behind her, then reached for the water bottle, which she raised to her mouth, before resuming her work. After that the screen went blank.

"Now roll it forward, please. Slowly."

Again they watched as she turned her head nearly to the camera and opened her mouth, saying something.

In silhouette, as she spoke and then drank from the bottle, Mary-Jo Stanton showed herself to have had a well-structured face with a long, thin, somewhat aquiline nose, prominent cheekbones, and a strong but not overly large chin.

Her skin was sallow, and her hair—brilliant in the full spring sun—had retained the pattern of waves that McGarr now remembered from the press portrait and the photos on the dust covers of her books. They pictured Stanton as a much younger woman.

The screen went dark again.

"How could that happen?" McGarr asked.

"I don't know."

"Could you slow it down, please?"

The priest complied, and for the next few minutes or so they watched the dark screen, until it suddenly brightened again, and there lay Mary-Jo Stanton's corpse as Father Fred had found it. And as it now was.

"They put something over the lens of the camera," the priest concluded. "Watch." Tapping more keys, Father Fred backed up the tape so slowly that they could make out the material of what appeared to be a jacket with a label being pulled over the lens.

"Where's that camera located?" McGarr asked.

"On the garden fence."

"What would it take to cover it up?"

"A tall person or a ladder. In back of the fence is M. J.'s gardening shed. There's a pruning ladder in there."

"I'll need this tape and all the others."

"Of course," the priest replied, leaning toward the bank of monitoring screens. "Oh, and look—the door into Mary-Jo's floor is ajar." He turned to McGarr with furrowed brow. "Do you think that whoever . . . could also have entered her apartment?"

McGarr did not know what to think, never having been in the apartment or even at the door. But he wondered if he was being led

on by the man who, only a scant quarter hour earlier, had asked him
not to report the cause of his longtime companion's death.

"Who else could get into her quarters?"

"Nobody, only Mary-Jo."

"Who could get in here?" McGarr meant the cramped monitoring room.

"Only Mary-Jo and I. Only our cards allow access."

"Who else has one of those?" McGarr pointed to the remote
device that had opened the gate and was, as reported by Father Fred,
also an alarm.

"Again—only we two."

"Where did Mary-Jo keep her two security devices?"

"The card she kept on a lanyard around her neck. You can't move
around the house or grounds without one. But about this"—he raised
his remote device—"she was most forgetful."

McGarr glanced toward the screen. "Did you notice either item
on her person?"

The priest shook his head. "I'm sorry, I didn't. I saw only the . . .
cilicio. As for this"—he waved the remote device—"it might be under
her, given the way she's positioned."

One thing was now plain: If Father Fred had not murdered her
himself, then the killer must have removed the pass card from the
body to have entered her quarters. At least if the facts were as
reported by the priest.

"How often did Mary-Jo leave her door open?"

"Never, not even unintentionally. She was most private. Leaving
her quarters, she locked the door. Always."

"Who else knows of her death?"

"Only you. That's why I could put forward the questions I asked
you in the garden. And ask you again now.

"Why do we have to sully the knowledge that the world has of
Mary-Jo? Can't we simply say that she died of natural causes, and

The Death of an Irish Sinner

then you and I can get to the bottom of this? I promise you, I'll give you every help that I can, and you won't regret extending the courtesy to us."

"Us?" McGarr asked.

"Opus . . ." Father Fred paused. "Let's just say those of us who loved her."

McGarr waited, but when no further explanation was offered, he pointed to the screen that displayed the open door. "Take me there."

6

AT THE LAST FLIGHT of steps up to what amounted to the third and attic floor of the large house, McGarr touched the priest's sleeve. "How long has she been living up here in—what did you call it?"

"Her quarters. Nine years, I'd say."

Before McGarr's marriage, over a dozen years earlier, Mary-Jo Stanton had thrown a large prenuptial party for Noreen, and McGarr had stayed on that very floor. It had been devoted to guest rooms, exclusively.

"Why did she move up here?"

"The simple explanation is that, as Mary-Jo got older, she became rather reclusive. She wished to be alone and closer to God— hence, the move to the top of the house."

Asking the priest to remain there, McGarr pulled the Walther from under his belt and mounted the steps on the wall side of the stairs.

The wide paneled door had been left enough ajar that he could squeeze through, and he paused there in the doorway to listen for any noise within the dead woman's living quarters.

Or rather, her aerie, he decided, as he advanced into the apartment. Even at night, like this, natural light from the half-moon and stars overhead spilled into the hall because of skylights that had been placed regularly along the ridgeline of the gabled roof.

A central hallway ran the length of the large building with—how many?—at least a dozen doors leading off into the rooms of the apartment. More than a few had been opened, but only one, near the west end of the building, was lighted.

Waiting at least a full minute to accustom his eyes to the darkness, McGarr slowly made his way toward the wedge of brilliance, pausing to listen before crossing in front of an open door. Oil paintings of religious scenes lined both walls.

From the clutter on the floors of the open rooms, he could see that somebody had already conducted a hurried search of the premises, which appeared to be continuing in the lighted room, where something now hit the floor with a thud.

With the Walther raised, McGarr was only a few feet away when he heard the muffled sound of quick feet on the carpet behind him. Swinging round, he caught a glimpse of somebody—a woman—rushing at him with something raised over her head that she now chopped down.

The blow sent the Walther skidding into the baseboard, and McGarr's wrist felt like it was broken. A second blow to the side of the head starred McGarr's vision, and he crashed into a painting that fell from its perch.

But before she could swing again—what was it? some sort of long heavy baton—McGarr's left hand darted out toward the center of her face and he felt her nose snap under his knuckles.

As she staggered back, McGarr took a quick step toward the woman and loaded his weight into a punch that he buried deep in her upper stomach. When she doubled up, he grabbed the back of her head and jerked her face down onto his rising knee. Her body snapped back, and she fell hard on the carpet with her arms splayed to either side.

Spinning around, McGarr searched the shadows for the Walther.

Not finding the gun immediately, he teased the Advantage Arms special-purpose pistol from the slit pocket inside his jacket before moving directly to the open door.

He saw a study or a small library that had been tossed. The drawers of a desk had been pulled out and dumped on the carpet, and books from the shelves lay nearby, as did the contents of a row of filing cabinets.

The central processing unit of the computer near the desk seemed to be missing; wires from keyboard, mouse, and monitor were dangling from the edge of a table in back of the desk. And it appeared that somebody had used a knife to cut a painting from a large, ornate frame with a gold nameplate that said, "F. José Maria Escrivá de Balaguer."

McGarr checked a small toilet off the room, and then moved to another door that led to a deep closet filled with other rifled file cabinets. But whoever had been in the room when the woman attacked him from behind had fled.

How? He glanced around. The large windows were closed, and it was a long fall to the ground. The person must have gone by him when he was reeling from the blow to the head, the one that had spangled his vision. Already his left eye was puffing, and only now did he feel the pain in his temple, cheek, and the side of his head.

Having come away without handcuffs, McGarr snapped off the chord from the wall connection and then a phone. After turning the unconscious woman over, he slipped the heavy six- or seven-foot stick between her arms and body and tied her hands in front of her. Even if she came to and gained her feet, she would never get through a door.

McGarr found Father Fred where he had asked the priest to remain—at the bottom of the stairs leading up to the dead woman's quarters. "Who went by here?"

"Nobody that I saw. But then I had to leave to let your people in the front gate. I've only just returned."

"Is there another way down from here?"

Father Fred nodded. "The servants' stairs. But again, you'd need Mary-Jo's pass card to open the door."

"To go out?"

The priest shrugged. "After the break-in, it's the way she wanted it."

"Show me, please."

As the priest led him down the hallway, McGarr asked, "How often were you up here?"

"Every now and then, when Mary-Jo wished me to help her with something—a sticking drawer, to get a book from a high shelf, that class of thing. But never"—his head turned to McGarr—"at night."

"Who cleaned this place?" As the pain rose, so too did McGarr's anger.

"She does. Geraldine."

They had come to the woman, who was still down on her back on the carpet, the baton protruding from under her arms. McGarr played the beam of his pocket torch on her face.

"She's the . . . manager here—of the house, the grounds, security. She holds black belts in several of the martial arts. Did she do that to your face?"

The woman's head was moving as she began to come around, and McGarr hoped she too was in pain. Her body weight on the stick behind her arms could not be comfortable, he imagined, noting through the blood that was flowing from her nose that she had a long, shiny scar on one cheek. A woman in her late forties or early fifties, she kept her hair, which was grayish blond, cut short. "Show me the stairs."

The door there was closed, and the small monitoring light on the yoke for the pass card was green. "Meaning that if whoever was up here went down those stairs, they did it either with Mary-Jo's pass card or yours?"

The priest nodded, before opening his black jacket and displaying a plastic card attached to an elasticized lanyard.

"Could there be a third or more such cards?"

"I don't believe so. They're issued by Avco, the security agency, only to us two, and when a card is lost or damaged, they come here and change the codes."

"Downstairs on the computer?"

"I believe so, but I don't actually know how it's done."

Could McGarr conclude that whoever had been in the library/study had Mary-Jo's card? No, not if the priest had been fully away from the door and was telling the truth.

Turning away, he again heard footsteps on the carpet and caught sight of a figure rushing at them. "Look out," he warned the priest, even as he crouched down to lower his center of gravity.

With her head down and her arms still bound in over the long baton, she was running at them while screaming, "Has it happened? Did it happen? Is that what this is all about?" She struck the two men at speed, knocking the priest off his feet.

Rising from his crouch, McGarr used his arms and shoulders to block her body to one side, where she tripped, slammed into the wall, and fell hard. With the barrel of the recovered Walther pressed to her temple, he asked, "Is there some reason why *it* had to happen?"

Sobbing now, she said nothing.

"Mary-Jo was murdered tonight. You seem to know why."

Still nothing.

McGarr stood. "If you get up again, I'll shoot you. Am I understood?" He prodded her ribs with the toe of his shoe, and she let out a wail.

"Am I?"

She cried out again.

"I'll take that for a yes."

Geraldine by name, she was the housekeeper and martial arts

expert who—along with the myriad electronic gadgets—had been in charge of security for a frail woman in her late seventies. And who had failed.

To the priest, McGarr said, "I need a list of everybody who was present in this house and on the grounds this afternoon. How many other people possess cards to the front gate?"

"Everybody."

"Everybody who has ever been in residence here?"

"No. The codes change daily, such that a card that can open the gate on one day can't on the next."

"How do your guests get these cards?"

"Geraldine slips them under their doors every morning, along with the *Times*."

Rather like a pricey hotel, McGarr thought. But a curious hotel, to say the least. Certainly Mary-Jo Stanton had been rich, and the house contained objects that had been the target of thieves in the past, according to the priest.

But the security precautions had been excessive and ultimately worthless.

"How many guests are there?"

"Today, only three, not counting me."

"You mean you consider yourself a guest here?"

"Yes, of course. Mary-Jo owned the house."

"How long have you lived here?"

"Oh"—Father Fred had to think—"nearly twenty years."

Which would have placed him in his early thirties when Mary Jo was in her fifties.

McGarr was about to ask if the priest had occupied some other religious office for all that time when he heard voices below them, loud and official—obviously the Tech Squad or members of his own staff. Which was good.

Suddenly his wrist and the side of his face were throbbing, and he sorely needed to take something for the pain. Preferably a large whiskey.

There had been a time—pain or no pain—when McGarr would have rounded up everybody in the house and interviewed them one by one—all night, if necessary—before the killer had a chance to formulate an alibi.

But McGarr no longer felt the need to be the chief operative as well as the chief administrator of his agency. He had trained his staff well, and Ward and McKeon—whom he could see in the hallway below him—could conduct the initial interviews, gather information, and deal with the Techies about the physical evidence.

Nor would he put up with banter.

"Would yiz look at him," Bernie McKeon, his chief-of-staff, said to Hugh Ward as McGarr stepped off the last stair. "Isn't he forever telling us, 'Lads—yiz've got to use your heads.' "

"But literally, like that?" Ward replied. "He asks too much."

"It's leadership by example."

"There's a woman up on the third floor who's to be brought in and charged with assault."

"On you?"

"Chief—say it ain't so. Could it be time for the gold wristwatch and the cottage in Tralee?"

"I want the whole thing worked out for me by the morning."

"After his beauty sleep."

"Bios of the residents and anybody else on the property today, possible suspects, the initial physical findings, and a rundown of the security system that you'll find underneath the stairs. Ring up the outfit that installed it. They must offer twenty-four-hour service.

"And finally, I want an inventory. Could theft have been the motive?"

Which quelled their comments. "But this place is huge, and there're only two of us."

"Get help."

Out in the car, McGarr eased into the contour seat that wrapped his back like two soft soothing hands. Bed, of course, would be better.

But it was not to be.

7

A CAR WAS BLOCKING the drive in the street outside the gate. With arms folded, a tall, thin man was leaning against the fender, his eyeglasses glinting in the beams of McGarr's headlamps.

As the gates closed with a solid clump, McGarr waited for the man to move, and when he didn't, McGarr flashed the car's brights and rolled a few feet forward.

Only then did the man step forward.

Gangly, mid-forties, he had a sprightly gait, more like a kind of lope, that McGarr believed he had seen before. But where?

Rolling down the window, McGarr reached for the butt of the Walther, which was again tucked under his belt. He had made mistakes enough for one night. "Help you?"

"Know me?" the man demanded, bending so his face was in the window.

McGarr said nothing, the face—like his odd gait—being only vaguely familiar.

"You don't know me?"

Still, McGarr waited.

"And there I was hoping you'd be the consummate Sherlock—

never forget a face and all that rot. You're Peter McGarr. I'm Dery Parmalee, publisher of *Ath Cliath*. Doubtless you remember me. We've met several times." His large right hand now accompanied his face in the open window.

Yet McGarr continued to regard the man. Named after the Irish language phrase for Dublin, *Ath Cliath* was a weekly tabloid newspaper that was distributed free of charge on streetcorners and dropped off at shops citywide.

But unlike so many erstwhile publications of the sort, *Ath Cliath* had flourished, if page numbers were any measure of success. The weekly tabloid was now the size of a thin book, and Noreen herself had taken to advertising her painting gallery in the rag.

"Why?" McGarr had only recently asked her, since the expense was nearly as great as advertising in one of the national dailies. Also, the quality of the stories was more than a little suspect. They were based mainly on scandal, innuendo, and gossip. Many began with the lead "Sources have revealed to *Ath Cliath* . . ." And Parmalee himself was often in the news fighting some slander charge in court.

"Ach, it's 'the word behind the hand,' " Noreen had replied, "what everybody in this town can't get enough of, and you know it. The inside scoop, what the other papers are afraid to print.

"Also, they cover all the films, plays, and concerts better than anybody, and the reporting about museums and galleries is the best I've ever read in Ireland. People pick it up to know what's going on. Add in a few gossipy exposés"—she had shrugged—"and it's a winner. Tell you true, I can't afford *not* to advertise in *Ath Cliath*."

McGarr now remembered that the cover exposés were nearly all written by Parmalee himself.

Who now withdrew the hand and straightened up. "To business then? I know what happened inside, what's going on, and why you're here." Parmalee waited for McGarr's reaction.

Seconds went by.

"I think there's several things you should know."

Removing his hand from the butt of the Walther, McGarr slipped the Rover into neutral.

"Mary-Jo Stanton? She was a numerary—an acolyte—of Opus Dei. In fact, this"—the hand gestured at the bronze gate—"is no mere private dwelling. It's an Opus Dei compound, their unofficial headquarters here in Ireland, with Fred Duggan in command."

"Father Fred?"

Parmalee nodded.

McGarr tried to remember what exactly Opus Dei was. In Latin, the phrase meant "the work (or works) of God," he knew from the years he had been forced to study that ancient language. Could it be a Catholic religious order? He seemed to think he had heard or read the name before. "Opus Dei?" he asked.

"John Paul the Second's reactionary shock troops," Parmalee said. "They fashion themselves as modern-day Crusaders, and they're zealots of the worst sort. They'll say and do anything to promote what they think is God's work. How did their thaumaturgic founder, José Maria Escrivá, put it? 'Our life is a warfare of love, and in love and war all is fair.'"

José Maria Escrivá was the name engraved on the brass plate of the painting that had been cut out and stolen from Mary-Jo Stanton's rifled study. But *thaumaturgic*? What exactly did that mean?

"*Pillería* is what Escrivá called the campaigns that Opus Dei has carried on around the world in the name of God's work. Dirty tricks, such as massive bank frauds with the money going into Opus Dei coffers, assassinations of political figures like Salvador Allende in Chile, and perhaps even Pope John Paul."

"The Pope?"

Parmalee nodded.

"But isn't he alive?" McGarr asked.

The man closed his eyes dismissively. "The first John Paul. The

John Paul who initiated all the liberal reforms in the Church, who championed Liberation Theology and birth control. They—the conservatives and Opus Dei—they thought of him as a mistake, an anomaly, and they got rid of him in thirty-three days."

Again McGarr waited, wondering if Parmalee were a bit off. Or perhaps he had something to tell him more germane to Mary-Jo Stanton's murder. Parmalee had a tic in his left eye; behind the octagon lenses of his eyeglasses it kept straying and darting back.

"They poisoned John Paul and claimed he'd suffered a heart attack, even though he'd just had a physical conducted by his doctor of over twenty years. It included an electrocardiogram. The man declared of John Paul '*Non sta bene, ma benone.*' "

"Not just well, but very well," the phrase meant. Before joining the Garda, McGarr had spent over a decade on the Continent, working for Criminal Justice in Marseilles and later for Interpol. "When was that?"

"John Paul died in September of 1978."

McGarr seemed to remember hearing or reading about some controversy regarding that Pope's death. But he also knew that the Vatican and the other institutions of the Roman Catholic Church had more than a few detractors. Claims of conspiracy and murder were floated whenever Popes died and were succeeded. "Wasn't there something about no autopsy?"

Parmalee's eye snapped to the side and remained there. "Not just no autopsy. No forensic tests of any kind, no official death certificate. The body was embalmed almost immediately.

"Only a few weeks earlier, the Russian Orthodox Archbishop of Leningrad, who was only forty-nine years old, also died of a massive heart attack, while waiting in a papal antechamber before meeting with John Paul about a possible softening of the Church's attitude toward Moscow. Opus Dei didn't want that either."

McGarr shrugged. "Why are you telling me this?"

"Because just as Opus Dei murdered Allende and John Paul when those two got in their way, they also murdered Mary-Jo this afternoon."

"Why?"

"To keep her from committing the ultimate betrayal by sending the manuscript of her biography of Escrivá, the Opus Dei founder, to her publisher in London."

McGarr sighed. It was getting late, and he would have a busy day on the morrow, handling the investigation and fending off the press. "I'm afraid I don't understand."

The slight smile had reappeared on Parmalee's face. "Because the manuscript contains the revelation that José Maria Escrivá de Balaguer may have been—and probably was—Mary-Jo's father."

"Her spiritual father?"

The man shook his head, the smile now almost gleeful. "Her fleshly father."

"You have proof of this?"

"No, of course not. Only a DNA match could prove that conclusively, and I'm sure Opus Dei would fight that with every resource at their command. But I was hoping you found a copy of the manuscript tonight, or it's still up in the study of her quarters on the third floor."

McGarr thought of the intruder who had cut Escrivá's portrait from the frame. There was too much . . . background—about Mary-Jo Stanton, the house and estate, and the Church—that he didn't understand. And how did this Parmalee know that she had been murdered in the afternoon, when McGarr had contacted his office only an hour or so ago. "Buy you a drink?"

"At this time of night?"

"Move your car and get in."

"But might I get towed?"

"Perhaps this might help. Fix it in a window." McGarr handed Parmalee one of his cards.

8

AT ILNACULLIN, McGarr turned the car down the avenue of beeches that lined the drive.

"Nice place—yours?" Parmalee asked, as they passed the house and parked in the stable yard.

McGarr only shook his head. "So, Dery—may I call you Dery?—how do you know all of this?"

"Mary-Jo was a close personal friend of mine. A decade ago we worked on a hagiography of Aquinas together."

McGarr added *hagiography* to his mix of verbal ignorance. Aquinas he knew of vaguely, having had to read excerpts of his writings while in school. "How did you come by your knowledge of the Church?"

There was a pause as Parmalee seemed to be phrasing a reply; they were out of the car now, walking toward the house. "I guess you could say that I'm a failed priest."

"What order?"

"Jesuit."

"Why did you leave?"

"Woman. Women."

"Anybody in particular?"

"After Mary-Jo, not really."

McGarr regarded the man, who could only be in his mid-forties. A decade earlier, Mary-Jo Stanton would have been in her early sixties. "How do you know Mary-Jo was murdered?"

"I intercepted your telephone message to your headquarters in Dublin."

"How?"

"A snooping device I have in the car."

"And you were where?"

"Just down the road in the village. I've been working on an exposé of Opus Dei's activities in Ireland, and I overheard your call to your headquarters. Felicitously."

"Which is illegal."

Parmalee hunched one shoulder and smiled. "Not nearly as illegal as what I've discovered about Opus Dei's 'warfare of *love*,' as they call it."

The others in the house had long since gone to bed, and after reviving the fire in the den, McGarr poured Parmalee a drink, then excused himself. "I'll be back in a jiff. Make yourself at home."

Well out of earshot in the kitchen, McGarr used the phone on the wall to ring up his headquarters. "There's a car outside the gates of the murder scene in Dunlavin with my calling card in the window. Impound and go over it bumper to bumper. I've been told it contains eavesdropping equipment. Copy any tapes or disks.

"I also want you to find out everything you can about a Roman Catholic order called Opus Dei—who they are and how important they might be in this country. I want that done by the morning."

"Where are you, Chief?"

"Home," McGarr blurted out, before adding, "In Dunlavin."

Asking the desk sergeant to switch on the tape recorder, he then recounted the details of what he had encountered at Barbastro. Typed up, it would save him the bother of writing a report in the morning and his staff would be a step ahead.

Back in the den, he found Dery Parmalee standing by the gun racks where McGarr's father-in-law kept his sporting weapons. Several times All-Ireland field champion, Fitzhugh Frenche owned a splendid collection of birding guns and had trained both of his children to be crack shots.

"Gorgeous guns," Parmalee said. "Any of them yours?"

McGarr shook his head.

"Handguns being more in your line of work, I trust. Don't I remember reading that your wife, Noreen, is some sort of champion?"

McGarr waited. It wasn't a question. The man was again letting him know that he was more than simply well informed, he was powerfully well informed with data that could be used in any way he chose—to ennoble or descry.

"All-Ireland skeet champ, isn't it? In her age group, that is."

McGarr poured himself a whiskey and took the seat on the other side of the hearth from where Parmalee had placed his own drink. "Tell me about Opus Dei. From the beginning."

"The very beginning?"

McGarr nodded. "I know very little about the Church."

"You're not a practicing Catholic, then?" Parmalee took his seat.

McGarr shook his head. In recent years he'd been inside churches and synagogues only for weddings and funerals. "And you?"

"No. Not anymore."

"You don't go to church?"

Parmalee shook his head.

"What about your former order, the Jesuits—have anything to do with them?"

"Individuals—my friends, a mentor or two—yes. The hierarchy, no. I've put all that behind me."

"But you're still interested in the affairs of the Church. Like this José Maria Escrivá."

"*Fixated*, I think, would be the better word." Parmalee's eye strayed toward the fire. "I'm interested in how faith plays out in the institution of the Church. The form it takes, how and why it becomes warped, and"—he sighed—"the grotesqueries that result."

"Like Opus Dei?"

"Particularly Opus Dei, which is the most pernicious and retrograde institution that has yet been created within the modern Church."

"Founded by José Maria Escrivá," McGarr prompted. "Who was?"

"A poor Spanish priest, born around the turn of the last century. He had a vision of how Church doctrine had misinterpreted a key passage in the book of Genesis. Or so they claim."

"They?"

"Opus Dei, the order that was created by him. They claim God spoke directly to Escrivá about the passage and other matters."

"Which key passage?"

"The fifteenth verse of the second chapter. It says, 'And the Lord God took the man, and put him into the Garden of Eden to dress it and to keep it.' After meditating on the text when he was only twenty-six years old, Escrivá decided that Aquinas's interpretation seven centuries earlier had been wrong."

McGarr canted his head, wishing to hear more.

"In the thirteenth century, Aquinas had formed Church doctrine in regard to the passage. He held that work—physical labor and toil of every sort—had become a part of man's life only *after* Adam and Eve's fall from grace and banishment from the Garden. Therefore, work, like death, was part of the price man had to pay for having sinned and been cast out of Eden.

"That interpretation was the official Church interpretation of Genesis from the Council of Trent in the sixteenth century right up to 1879, when Leo the Thirteenth restated Aquinas's position.

"Escrivá, on the other hand, reexamined the passage and held that work had been an essential activity in the Garden *before* man's fall from grace. Therefore, work was part of God's plan for man, work was a necessary part of the human condition, and—essentially—man could not be complete as God originally intended him without work's being an integral part of his life.

"Taking the interpretation a step further, Escrivá reasoned that one way man could honor and worship God was to work as well as he or she was able, not merely as a cleric but in all the occupations, whatever a person's abilities, be it street sweeper or brain surgeon. Hence, the name—Opus Dei, 'God's Work.' "

McGarr noted how animated Parmalee had become; two bright patches had appeared on his cheeks.

"Unlike Aquinas's medieval take on Genesis, which contended that work was punishment, Escrivá's interpretation was perfectly attuned to modern industrial and commercial society. Not everybody—in fact, few—can become a priest or a nun, given the present strictures of holy vows. With families, bills, debts, and so forth, most people must work and work hard.

"But didn't the *Bible* say that work had been an integral part of the state of grace that obtained in the Garden *before* man's fall? Escrivá reasoned. Therefore, humankind could honor and worship God through their labor by working as diligently as possible, preferably within the context of a new holy order that welcomed and respected lay vocations. Opus Dei members do not need to become priests or nuns. In fact, at present only two percent are."

"Out of how many?"

"Worldwide? Around eighty thousand."

McGarr's head went back; it was a large number. One of his brothers was a Jesuit, and he knew that order totaled only thirty thousand or so.

"Since the mid-seventies, at least, Opus Dei has controlled the Vatican bank and the Curia."

Which elected Popes. That much McGarr knew. "And how many Opus Dei members are there here in Ireland?"

"It's hard to tell, since Opus Dei would never divulge the actual number, but easily two to three thousand, all working for God among us. Not wearing clerical collars or habits. You'd never know who they were." Parmalee's slight smile had returned. "Shall I continue?"

"Please." If, in fact, Mary-Jo Stanton's Barbastro was an Opus Dei facility and not merely her residence, McGarr should know something about the order.

"Beginning immediately after his 1928 revelation, Escrivá proved to be not only an insightful thinker but also a consummate organizer and Machiavellian strategist. He may have written that *all* work was equal in the eyes of God, but he well understood that some types of work garnered more money and power than others, especially the work produced by graduates of universities, which is where he focused his recruitment efforts.

"Such that when the Fascist Francisco Franco rose to power in 1936, Escrivá's Opus Dei was perfectly positioned to assist Franco in rooting out suspected socialists from the universities and installing academics with fascist leanings.

"Opus Dei's tireless lay workers were so successful in eradicating the remnants of socialism in Spanish universities that, in 1947, Escrivá approached Pope Pius the Twelfth, who himself had fascist leanings. Escrivá was able to convince him to legitimize Opus Dei as an 'apostolate of penetration,' as he called it, to fight the spread of Marxist Communism."

Far from mere fascist leanings, Pope Pius XII had been the Pope who acquiesced to the Holocaust. "*Apostolate?*" It was yet another word McGarr was unsure of.

"Officially, I guess it's a group of lay brethren organized to promote some mission of the Church."

"Which is what Escrivá had established in Spain."

"Exactly. But by legitimizing Opus Dei, that Pope created the Church's first 'secular institute' and allowed Opus Dei to function on a world stage. Some lay members are required to take the sacred priestly vows of poverty, chastity, and obedience.

"Essentially, they're priests without collars and practice their chosen occupations or professions while living in Opus Dei residences, like Barbastro. Nearly all of what they earn goes into Opus Dei coffers.

"Other members, not as fully committed, live with their families, wives, and husbands, while focusing their life on God's work through Opus Dei.

"And still others simply worship with and help the order succeed in the world, knowing that every little boost they give Opus Dei is a way of promoting godliness in the world. Or at least their interpretation of godliness, which is the bottom line.

"Because"—Parmalee moved up in the chair, plainly exercised now—"*because*, like other zealots and true believers, they're convinced that God is with them every moment no matter what they do, which allows them to do just about anything. No, *anything*—topple governments, murder Popes or, as here, anybody else who poses a threat to 'God's Work.'

"Beginning in 1949 with Pope Pius the Twelfth's imprimatur of legitimacy, Escrivá succeeded in creating the most heinous religious army since . . . well, since Cromwell, to put things in an Irish context.

"But as I said, a covert religious army, open warfare being passé and not their style. Rule 191 states, 'Numerary and supernumerary members must always observe a prudent silence regarding the names of other members; and never reveal to anyone the fact that they belong to Opus Dei . . . unless expressly authorized to do so by their local director.' "

"*Numerary, supernumerary?*" McGarr questioned.

"The two highest levels of lay commitment. Also there are *cooper-ators*—people who contribute to God's cause either materially or through their offices. People like Eamon de Valera and Charlie Haughey here in this country, François Mitterrand in France, the Kennedys and William Casey, the onetime CIA chief, in the States."

McGarr glanced at his watch. Without proof, Parmalee's charges—if that's what they were—were scurrilous in the extreme and journalism at its worst.

"I know, I know." Parmalee raised his palms. "It's getting late, and all this is rather much to take in at first blush. But I think you'll find you'll need to know more, as your investigation proceeds. And I'll be at your service, of course."

Really, now. That Parmalee believed he knew how the investigation would proceed rather interested McGarr. "What was Mary-Jo Stanton's status within Opus Dei?"

"As I mentioned earlier, she was a numerary, the highest category for a woman. *But*"—Parmalee raised a finger, his brows arching, his eyes still bright—"she was in many ways a disobedient and self-willed numerary who wrote the truth as she, not they, saw it. And it was in this last project—writing the biography of Escrivá, her father—that she transgressed the boundaries of Opus Dei. They could not allow that."

"*They?*" McGarr asked.

"The priests who control Opus Dei. They're only two percent of the membership, but they control and direct all."

"Father Fred being one of them."

Parmalee nodded. "On permanent—how shall I phrase this?—guard duty at Barbastro. His assignment was to keep Mary-Jo happy, since she was so important to Opus Dei in two ways." Parmalee raised two fingers. "First, as a steady source of significant money. Everything—trust me; the house, the money, the collections and archives—will be left to the order, if the lot doesn't already belong to them.

"And second—to make sure she didn't go public in any way about her family history, given her direct fleshly connection to Escrivá."

"Who has been beatified?"

Parmalee's eye darted to the side; he nodded his head. "The first step to sainthood."

It was a major charge—that a man who had been vetted for sainthood could possibly have fathered a child. "You have proof of this?"

Parmalee shook his head. "As I said—in the house, perhaps. Unless, of course, they got to it before you and your staff arrived."

"They?"

"Again—everybody else in residence there. All are Opusians of one form or another."

Reaching into his jacket pocket, McGarr drew out the list that Father Fred had given him. "What about Geraldine Breen?" She was the woman who had attacked McGarr on the third floor of Barbastro.

"She's an assistant numerary."

McGarr glanced up.

"It's a subcategory that reveals the essential misogyny of Opus Dei. You must keep in mind that the order is a product of Franco's Spain, and among women numeraries are assistant numeraries, who 'dedicate themselves to the material administration'—I believe the phrase is—of Opusian residences and centers. That means they're scullions who clean, cook, and cater to Opus Dei priests and the fully fledged numeraries. No such category exists for men."

Which corroborated what Father Fred had said about Geraldine Breen—that she was the housekeeper. "What about Delia Manahan?"

"She's an associate member. Generally, associates live outside Opus Dei residences. The Manahan woman arrived at Barbastro last night, as she often does on weekends, rather like a retreat, I should imagine."

McGarr wondered just how long Parmalee had been engaged in

his research of Opus Dei and if the residents of Barbastro had been aware of his surveillance.

"Father Juan Carlos Sclavi?"

"Like Fred Duggan, another Opus Dei priest. He's been there for about a fortnight, got there the day after Mary-Jo announced that she had finally finished her biography of Escrivá and was about to send it to her publisher."

"Announced to whom?"

Parmalee hunched his shoulders. "Her friends, I guess."

"You among them."

"She rang me up and told me."

"Why would she do that?"

"Because we're friends. *Were* friends."

Curiously, from his first words to McGarr, Parmalee's mood had seemed anything but funereal. In fact, he appeared even now nearly—was it?—gleeful that he knew what had occurred at Barbastro. But, of course, Parmalee billed himself as a reporter. "Did she know you were researching Opus Dei, and you planned to write about the order?"

Parmalee smiled. "She encouraged me."

"Why would she do that?" If one of Opus Dei's tenets was utter secrecy, even within the confessional.

"Because she was afraid for her life."

"She told you that?"

"I have it on tape, if you care to hear."

McGarr nodded. "Oh, I do. I do." He pushed himself out of the chair. It was late. "What are you going to do with your information?"

"About the murder? It depends."

"On what?"

Parmalee's slight smile had returned. "I can imagine a scenario in which, after you cracked the case and were about to make an arrest, I'd get an exclusive."

McGarr waited for the other shoe to drop.

"My running what I know in Monday's paper will only make things more difficult for you, I should imagine, especially with what I could fold in about Opus Dei. And would. Will.

"You'd have the international press crawling all over this town and Dublin. And you'd have whatever pressure Opus Dei will bring to bear on your investigation cranked up to the max. They might even"—the eye twitched to the side and back again—"take a shot at you. Literally. I think you should be aware of that. You'd be foolish to view Opus Dei as a benign religious order. They're ruthless. Utterly.

"Add to that, in the former scenario, you'd have me as a resource, a guide, somebody to answer questions about Opus Dei, the Church, and your list of likely suspects." His hand flicked out at the piece of paper that McGarr was folding into his shirt pocket.

"Can we discuss it tomorrow?" McGarr asked.

"Of course. But I have a four o'clock deadline for the Monday paper. When will you release the notice of her death?"

McGarr hunched his shoulders; the more time his staff and he had without intrusions from the press and public, the better.

"You'll have to at some point, won't you? Late Monday, after you've had a chance to go over the crime scene and house more thoroughly?"

McGarr canted his head. It was possible, no, probable. Parmalee was no fool; he understood how things worked.

"You know—I could rush what I have now into the press, scoop the dailies, and make a big splash for *Ath Cliath*. But I'd prefer to wait for the full story. And the exclusive."

Why? thought McGarr. Journalists that he knew ran scoops as soon as they could, understanding that the shelf life of any story was unknowable. Sooner or later, all stories became public. He held out his hand. "Tomorrow."

Parmalee took it. "By noon?"

"Since you have the back story already written," McGarr probed.

The man's smile became more complete. He released McGarr's hand and tapped his forehead. "In here."

"But on paper as soon as you get back to town."

"Speaking of which—how do I get there, since I'm sure you've impounded my car?"

Again McGarr was surprised at Parmalee's prescience. "You have a choice. I can ring for a car now, which will take an hour to get here. Or"—McGarr checked his watch; it was nearly one-thirty—"I can give you a bed and have somebody take you in on the morrow."

Parmalee chose the latter, and McGarr showed him to a guest room at the back of the house.

As McGarr slipped into bed, he woke Noreen.

"What happened?" she asked in the darkness.

The bed was blessedly soft and warm from her body.

"Mary-Jo."

"Dead?"

"Yah."

"And Fred called you?"

Exhausted and still sore, McGarr wanted most simply to sleep, but he knew she would not rest until he told her. "It looks like she was murdered."

"Mary-Jo? You're coddin' me."

"Can I tell you in the morning?"

"Sure. Of course. You must be knackered. But"—there was a long pause during which McGarr nearly fell asleep—"who were you just speaking with in the den? I could hear the rumble of your voices."

"Dery Parmalee. He's staying over."

"The journalist from *Ath Cliath*?"

McGarr made a low noise in the back of his throat.

"Down here to cover the story?"

McGarr again assented.

"Quick, isn't he?"

Which was the question that McGarr fell asleep on and woke up wondering about.

PART III
WHO RULES

9

BUT PARMALEE was gone by ten the next morning when McGarr got down to the kitchen.

Seated at the long table were Bernie McKeon, Hugh Ward, and Ruth Bresnahan, Murder Squad staffers, who were being served a killer Irish breakfast, McGarr could see as he walked in: crisped rashers, sausages of several kinds, a mound of eggs scrambled with cream and cheese, grilled tomatoes, chips, and buttered toast.

None of which McGarr could have. His cholesterol was sky-high, a Garda physician and friend had told him, after a mandatory testing of everybody in the unit. Well into the two hundreds. "Add to that, Chief Superintendent, you don't seem to be able to do anything about your smoking, so something has to go.

"May I suggest fatty foods? I could put you on a strict diet. You'd lose weight, feel better, be more active. How much younger is Noreen than you? A fair few years, I'd say. I'd hazard she'd like you around as long as possible." Worse news was—a copy of the physician's report had been sent to the house.

Some friend.

The diet proved to be simple in the extreme; anything and everything that tasted at all good was verboten. "Not to worry," the cruel doctor had assured McGarr confidently. "You'll get used to the regimen. Once you start losing a few pounds and feeling better, you'll turn up your nose at all those bloating things that you formerly hungered for."

It was now day eleven, and McGarr's nose was pointing at the platter of eggs. Add to that, he had never actually felt unhealthy, he decided, raising a hand in greeting to the others, as he advanced on the table. It had been the physician who had predicted he would possibly feel bad sometime in the future.

"We're talking about the big one here, Peter," the man had carried on. "Myocardial infarction. A heart attack. Bang, and you're dead. Or some major surgery followed by an equally major change in how you conduct your life. Perhaps you might have to change your occupation. Could you handle that?"

At the moment, McGarr believed he could handle a smallish dab of everything on the table.

But before he could even sit down, a bowl of stirabout was placed before his chair, along with a cup of black coffee, a glass of orange juice, and a small heap of pills—vitamins mostly, but also one to lower his blood pressure and another to combat the cholesterol.

"You should keep in mind," the preachy doctor had continued, "that growing old successfully requires abandoning unhealthful practices one by one."

Until oatmeal mush was all that was left, McGarr decided, looking down into the gluey mass.

"In addition to tobacco and rich foods, I also mean alcohol," the man had ranted on, scanning the questionnaire that McGarr had foolishly filled out truthfully. "Do you really drink this much every day? What hour do you begin?"

Reaching for the butter, his eyes shied toward the pantry where the liquor was kept.

"Allow me to remove that from your sight," Noreen said, her hand whisking the butter dish off the table.

Not in the best of moods before breakfast under normal circumstances, McGarr only glared at her. Earlier, when looking in the mirror to shave, he had been shocked at how swollen his face was, and he could scarcely tie his shoes, his left wrist was so sore.

"Shall I begin?" McKeon asked, shaking out a sheaf of papers. "Chief—that report that you asked for on Opus Dei is there by the side of your plate."

A rotund middle-aged man with a thick shock of once-blond hair but dark eyes, McKeon pushed aside a plate that had only recently contained not a little bit of everything, McGarr deduced from the remains.

McGarr cleared his throat. "Tell you what. I'm not in the greatest form this morning, and I'd like what Bernie had," he said in a small voice, feeling very much like a character out of Dickens.

"Now, now—that'll pass once you get something in your stomach," Noreen said in a motherly tone of voice. "You know what the doctor recommended, and you agreed to."

"Ah, let the poor man have what he wants," her mother, Nuala, put in. "You can see for yourself, he had a hard go of it last night. I hope you gave as good as you got, lad. Let me freshen that cup for you now."

"And me," said McKeon. "You shouldn't use me as a model, Chief. Didn't the sawbones say I had the cholestorol level of a pregnant woman? You saw the numbers yourself."

"Maybe that should tell you something," Bresnahan observed, reaching for the teapot. "Have you been by a mirror lately?"

"If he starts wearing a nursing bra," Ward muttered, "I'm filing a grievance."

"I can et anything I wish," McKeon continued.

"Including the occasional platter of crow." Again it was Bresnahan, banter being the usual tone of morning meetings. She was a tall, statuesque redhead who, as a recent mother, was herself on a slimming diet.

"Whereas some of us just don't have the numbers. Didn't the doctor explain it all to me in a phrase?" McKeon pushed the half glasses down his nose and paused dramatically. "Genetic superiority."

"Bad doctor, bad science," said Ward, reaching for the platter of sausages. Like Noreen, Ward was a trim person who would never be heavy. A former amateur boxer, he still spent a few hours in the gym every second day, working the bags, lifting weights, and sparring a few rounds with younger fighters. His dark eyes avoided McGarr's as he forked a few sausages off the platter.

Noreen now cut a thin slice of butter and dropped it into the oatmeal. "It'll taste almost the same, trust me."

McGarr's eyes flickered up to hers, which were turquoise in color and bright. She had slept well.

Meanwhile, he could hear her mother in the pantry, where she had gone with his cup. There was a squeak, as of a cork being twisted from the neck of a bottle, and then a few good glugs as his coffee was being freshened.

McGarr relaxed. At least that part of his day was proceeding according to form; he'd not missed an eye-opener in decades. "Where's Fitz?" he asked, not having seen his father-in-law.

"Down in the village," Nuala said, placing the brimming cup before him. "He thought he'd put an ear to the ground, given what happened. Maybe the locals will loosen up for him what they wouldn't say to the police.

"There, now—you drink that while it's hot and good."

"Mammy—you're just abetting him," Noreen complained.

"What? Nothing of the kind. You've read the reports that say a little touch now and then is spot on for the ticker. You could do with a drop yourself."

"And Maddie—where's Maddie?"

"Schoolwork. I thought it might be uncomfortable for her to hear whatever details Bernie's got for us this morning."

McGarr raised the blessed drop to his lips and allowed the hot, peat-smoky liquid to course down his gullet. There now. That was better. "Bernie?" he asked, reaching for his spoon.

"Not all the news is good," McKeon began. "In fact, two items are altogether troubling. First is, our chief here might consider treating himself to the odd steak or two of an evening, for strength if not for taste.

"Geraldine Breen—the woman who put him in the condition we see him in this morning and whom he put in hospital—she absconded last night, replacing herself with the Guard who was securing her room. And a big fella, by all accounts.

"It's thought his back might be broken. The nurses assumed we'd removed the Guard, and seeing a form in the bed, they didn't realize she was gone until a few hours ago.

"We've issued an 'all points,' of course. But no trace of her yet.

"As for the second revelation—preliminary findings indicate Mary-Jo Stanton was murdered around four in the afternoon. That coincides exactly with the event that was taped on the security monitor, the one that views the section of garden where her corpse was found by the priest, Father Fred"—McKeon turned to another page.

"Duggan," Ward put in.

Mary-Jo Stanton's "keeper," if what Dery Parmalee said about Opus Dei and Barbastro was factual, McGarr thought.

"However—and this is the big however—Mary-Jo Stanton was not killed by the device that was found around her neck. At least not directly, since the wounds and pattern of bleeding indicate that the punctures from the barbs occurred before her death." McKeon glanced up over his half glasses. "The wounds from the—I'm going to call it—'silly-sea-oh.' "

"Thee-LEE-thee-oh," corrected Ward, who spoke Castilian rather well.

"Exactly. But that device was not the cause of death, it says here. What killed her was a myocardial infarction."

"A heart attack?" Bresnahan asked.

"Then she died of natural causes?" Noreen asked, taking a seat at the table.

"Natural enough, if you dismiss the—"

"*Cilicio*," Ward supplied.

"Which could have brought on her death," Bresnahan mused.

"Well, certainly Mary-Jo didn't wrap the blessed thing around her own neck and tighten it until it drew blood." Noreen reached for the platter of eggs.

"The postmortem is by no means complete, of course. But perhaps we should view it like that, until we receive the final report." McKeon glanced over at McGarr, who nodded.

"Moving on to the guests and residents of Barbastro . . ." McKeon glanced up from his notes. "What is it about the sound of that name that gives me the willies?"

"That's easy," Bresnahan put in, now doodling on her notepad. "You find the *bar* part enticing, given your proclivities. But one letter further, it's ouch. Then there's the *a, s* part that's pronounced 'ass,' which, of course, never applies to you, Bernie."

"Yet," Ward muttered. "Give him time."

"*Bast*, of course, is half of *bastard*. But again, that's not you. And finally there's the *astro*, which is five-eighths of *castrato*. Little wonder you're concerned about your willy."

"Barbastro, I'll have you know, is the small city in Aragon where José Maria Escrivá—the beatified priest who founded the Opus Dei order—was born," said McKeon, shaking out his notes. "Father Fred Duggan told me that. He was and is a resident in the house, along with Geraldine Breen, who is a member of the sect—"

"Order," Bresnahan corrected. "In a Catholic context, *sect* implies heresy, and from what I know, Opus Dei is more than simply mainstream. They're at the very center of the Church, since they control the money."

Spooning up some stirabout, McGarr took note of Bresnahan's knowledge of the—

"Order," McKeon repeated. "Father Juan Carlos Sclavi, who has also been resident in Barbastro for the last month and was there yesterday afternoon, is a priest of same. Little English, we were told by Duggan, less it seemed when I spoke to him and, later, Hughie in his native lingo."

"Wouldn't say anything without Duggan in the room," Ward added. "Kept looking at him for a wink or a nod, whenever I asked the question."

"As well," McKeon continued, "one Delia Manahan spent the day and the night at Barbastro. She too claims an affiliation with the Opus Dei order, although she told us she lives and owns her own house on Killiney Bay."

Another monied person, thought McGarr; property values on Killiney Bay had skyrocketed in recent years. Many of the houses were large, the view of the bay and Bray Head to the south were magnificent, and the commute into Dublin by high-speed train was quick.

"Duggan claims to have been away from the property at the time—around four in the afternoon—when the surveillance camera was obscured, which the pathologist estimates was the time of Mary-Jo Stanton's death.

"Finally, we have the gardener, the aptly named Frank Mudd, who on first blush appears to be a three-monkeys kind of guy."

"See no evil, hear no evil, speak no evil?" Noreen asked.

"No. If you groom me, I'll groom you. If not, I'll go to the third monkey, who'll pay for the pleasure."

"I don't get it." Noreen reached for McGarr's coffee cup.

Said Bresnahan, "He wants to know what's in it for him."

" 'Without Miss Stanton, I'll be put out of here by the priests, who'll bring in one of their own,' " Ward put in. " 'It's time for me to start thinking of meself.' "

"Could be he's afraid of something." Noreen sipped from the cup. "Us, maybe."

"How can you?" she asked McGarr, her hand rising to her throat. And yet the cup remained in her hand.

"Otherwise, the videotapes that we watched?"

"Interminably," said Ward.

"They show nobody else on or about the property at the time the 'silly-sea-oh' was clamped down on the poor old crone's neck, maybe or maybe not causing her death."

"But at least we can assume she was attacked by somebody she knew and did not fear," Noreen mused, obviously having perused the reports that now sat in the middle of the table. "There's the tape of her turning around to see somebody approaching her, then somebody or bodies placed something over the surveillance camera, and when that thing was withdrawn, there she was, dead, with the device wrapped around her throat."

"God bless us and save us from all harm," Nuala whispered, turning away to the sink with tears in her eyes. "To think that such a thing could happen to an elderly lady—and very much the lady—tilling the soil in her garden."

"Any other surveillance cameras malfunctioning?" McGarr asked, finishing the porridge and reaching for the cup, which Noreen handed him.

"Yes."

"Where?"

"One along the wall that borders the main road into the village. Another in the kitchen."

"Focused on what?"

McKeon glanced at Ward.

"What had been the servants' staircase, when there were servants. It leads up to the quarters of the victim on the third floor."

And it was the staircase down which whoever ransacked the victim's apartment could have fled, thought McGarr.

"But there was a servant—the mannish woman, Geraldine Breen," Nuala managed. "She waited hand and foot on Mary-Jo, day and night now for . . . at least for a decade that I can remember. There was even talk that the two might be a, you know, couple."

"Although there was talk like that of Mary-Jo and Father Fred."

As well as a statement from Dery Parmalee that he had been involved with her romantically in the past.

Nuala flapped a hand. "Ach—people talk. Yap. We know that."

"Finally, the car you had us impound, Chief?" McKeon continued. "The one registered to a Dery Parmalee. It's just a car—no electronic equipment, no tapes, not even a cell phone."

Lie one, thought McGarr, now curious to learn how Parmalee had otherwise known of the woman's murder. He pushed back his chair and stood. "You two get some sleep," he said to McKeon and Ward. "Ruthie—you work on Parmalee. I want to know everything possible about him, including your personal assessment."

"Meaning I don't need to identify myself."

Why, to a liar. McGarr wondered how much Parmalee had misrepresented Opus Dei; perhaps a second opinion would be helpful in viewing Duggan, Sclavi, and the Manahan woman. "I'm especially interested in how he found out about the murder."

"What about me? What do I do?" Noreen asked. "Remember, I grew up here. I know the turf and the players."

Which was a point, McGarr decided, as he picked up the report on Opus Dei. "What about our daughter?"

Said Nuala, "Sure, that's what grandmothers are for."

"Give me a moment to freshen up," Noreen said. "You'll have a chance to read your report there."

"But I hope you'll remember—you're with me as a resource."

"To look and listen but not be heard."

McGarr could not have it be said—and said in a court of law—that his wife had taken an active part in the investigation. "Agreed?"

"Agreed."

McGarr carried the report over to the window.

10

THE DAY WAS a spring ideal with wind and sun locked in a pitched battle for weather dominance, McGarr realized, as he stepped down the drive toward the stables and his car.

On his back the sun felt so warm he would have removed his jacket but for the gusts of wind—still cool off the nearby mountains—that buffeted him.

He had to hold on to the brim of his fedora to keep it from blowing off. Overhead, brilliant puffs of the purest cloud were tracking across a cerulean sky.

"So who done it, Chief?" Noreen asked, climbing into the car. Two patches of color had appeared on her cheeks, and her eyes were bright; she was enjoying herself.

"I would have thought you'd still be upset by the news of Mary-Jo's death," McGarr observed, wheeling her Rover down the drive.

"Oh, I am, sure. Mary-Jo was a saint. So good to all and sundry. Did you not read the bio Dery Parmalee did of her in *Ath Cliath* a year or so ago?"

McGarr hadn't, but he made note that he should.

"Mary-Jo was not merely a world-class biographer, she was also extremely generous. Didn't she build the school in the village and contribute to charities here and abroad, always anonymously?

"And she did all of that while living herself like a hermit, there in Barbastro, with that order of hers clinging to her money like a pack of avaricious leeches. They scarcely let her out of their sight."

"According to Dery?"

"According to everybody, if the village can be believed."

Who wished only the worst—which was the best—class of gossip, McGarr knew only too well.

"How difficult could it have been to dispatch an elderly woman kneeling in her garden? And how craven, since it's plain she knew her attacker and had no fear. As your report reads, it was as though she didn't resist at all."

McGarr raised an eyebrow; how did she know that? Noreen had obviously gone through McKeon's files closely.

"The murderer only had to draw a bit of blood with that horrific instrument plumbed from the depths of Dark Age zealotry, and she succumbed. Was it murder? You can bet your last farthing it was—worked by some heinous hypocrite in her immediate circle who espoused her heartfelt beliefs but whose true motivation was get-and-gain, you'll see when her will is read."

"A bit purple this morning, are we?" McGarr asked, as they drove through the village.

"You mean the jacket?" It was a plum-colored merino jacket over a puce jumper and black slacks. He glanced down at her ankles, which—like the rest of her—were finely formed, and his hand moved off the shift to her thigh.

"Please—I'm thinking," she complained, but she did not remove his hand.

McGarr rather enjoyed his wife's enthusiasms. She was, he decided, much like the day—blustery, visceral, yet warm and bright too. Apart from her beauty, what had attracted him was Noreen's capacity for life in all its forms.

And McGarr—without question jaded from his decades of police work—enjoyed the perspective that she often brought him. Mainly, it was her conception of humanity: that there might be, in fact, people who would never, ever resort to murder. Or anything else brutal and disgusting.

Yet, at the same time, she was attracted to his endeavors.

Turning his head, McGarr let his eyes play over her copper-colored curls, which had just begun to take on some gray now in her fortieth year. Her high cheekbones, the thin bridge of her nose, the angle of her head, which had dipped to one side as she pondered the few facts uncovered thus far. In that pose she looked like a pretty bird who had turned an ear to the ground.

"I know, I know," she continued, "I shouldn't rush on. But one thing is definite. Mary-Jo knew and did not fear whoever slew her."

Or at least, whoever had placed the *cilicio* around her neck and left her for dead.

Which could not be debated. At the murderer's approach, she had turned her head to him or her, then looked back down at her work in the garden. No worry, no perceived threat.

IT SEEMED ALMOST as though Father Fred Duggan were waiting for them just beyond the heavy metal gates of Barbastro, and he hadn't been there for long, McGarr could see. Steam was rising from the cup in Duggan's hand, and he was lightly dressed for the chilly morning.

Could he have known they were on the way? All it would take was a helpful villager seeing Noreen's car, which was well known, wheeling by.

"I thought I'd take the air this morning," Duggan explained when McGarr rolled down the window. A fit dark man, whose freshly shaven cheeks looked almost blue in the hard spring light, he squatted down lithely, so he could see into the car. "How ya, Noreen. Been a long time."

"Ah, Fred—I'm sorry for you. It must be difficult."

" 'Tis, 'tis—and to think something like this could have happened to Mary-Jo of all people. And here at Barbastro. Still and all, she was a devout, good woman, and I'm sure she's passed on to the reward that we all seek."

McGarr noticed that Father Fred appeared to have slept well. His eyes were bright, no bags or sags. And there he was, fully McGarr's own middle age or older by a year or two.

"Can we give you a lift to the house?" McGarr slid the Rover back in gear.

Duggan glanced at his mug of tea, then down the long drive. "Well . . . you can, sure. It's chillier than I thought this morning. There's a wintry edge to this wind."

Turning to throw the latch of the back door for the priest, McGarr noticed that tires had patterned the frosted dew on the drive. A car had driven down to the gate, turned around, and returned to the house. Only one person had got out on the passenger side; only one person had walked there since the rime had formed during the night. Fred.

"Did you get any sleep?" McGarr asked, after the man had climbed in.

"Not much with your two colleagues prowling about. But at least I got some. How about yourself?"

"Same. A chap name of Dery Parmalee was waiting for me here at the gate, rather like yourself this morning. Know him?"

In the rearview mirror, McGarr watched Father Fred's brow glower.

"Indeed. And you say he was here last night?"

"He knew what had happened. Case and point."

"How?"

"Said his car is equipped with eavesdropping devices that can monitor phone calls, both yours from the house and my cell phone. Said he was around here yesterday because he's doing an investigative journalism piece about Opus Dei."

McGarr watched Father Fred's clear blue eyes dart here and there. "And that Opus Dei is responsible for Mary-Jo's death, I should imagine," the priest said.

"Parmalee was with me . . . oh, I'd say the better part of two hours."

"Spewing out venom and hate, undoubtedly." Duggan tapped McGarr's shoulder. "Now *he's* an avenue of investigation—I believe you call it—that you should pursue. I don't think I've ever thought of anybody as purely evil. But Dery Parmalee comes close. Even the Jesuits couldn't tolerate him."

"He says you killed John Paul the First."

"And I suppose Salvador Allende, Roberto Calvi, the financier, and a host of other martyrs to Liberation Theology, pan-socialism, and abortion."

"He's not alone in those charges." The report McGarr had been handed earlier said that many respectable newspapers and periodicals had also either raised questions or made charges about the means that Opus Dei employed to achieve its ends.

They included *Corriere della Sera*—Italy's largest newspaper—*Newsweek* magazine, and both the *Sunday Times* and the *Financial Times* in England.

The report also said that, throughout his clerical life, José Maria Escrivá had reiterated to his faithful the maxim "Our life is a warfare of love, and in love and war all is fair."

Namely, *pillería*, as Parmalee had told McGarr and the report suggested was true. Nothing was beyond Opusians, it seemed, not even encouraging fiduciary sleight of hand by its members to enrich Opus Dei, and assassinations of convenience to further its agenda, which was one of extreme reactionaryism.

"I know, I know—just like Jesus in his time, we're not without our accusers, which is why we have to be doubly vigilant and strong. For the record—John Paul, God bless him—died of a heart attack."

"Myocardial infarction."

"Exactly."

Some critics, the report continued, charged Opus Dei with getting rid of its enemies by inducing heart attacks using colorless, odorless, and tasteless digitalis. The report referenced the death of the Russian Orthodox Archbishop of Leningrad—while waiting for an audience with John Paul—from acute myocardial infarction.

"Well—here we are," McGarr said, pulling up to the front door of the house. "Perhaps we'll see you later."

"I don't understand. Shan't I accompany you? I know the players, their backgrounds, their experiences with Mary-Jo, their histories here at Barbastro."

It was the argument that Noreen had made not even an hour earlier. "Problem is, Fred—they know you."

In the rearview mirror, Duggan's eyes flashed up at McGarr. "What's that supposed to mean? Of course they know me. I hope you're not taking Parmalee's scurrilous and libelous carry-on seriously. The man is delusional, I'll have you know. When he was here working with Mary-Jo, he admitted to her he was taking tablets to treat paranoid schizophrenia, which gives you some idea where his papal-assassination and worldwide-conspiracy theories are coming from."

"*Working* here? Parmalee led me to believe that he was having an affair with Mary-Jo."

"*What?*"

"That's what he told me."

Plainly perturbed, Duggan flung open the door, spilling the tea on himself. "Damn." He swung his legs out of the car and batted at the milky stain. "I hope that gives you proof of Dery Parmalee's insanity. I knew Mary-Jo throughout the year or two that she collaborated with Parmalee on that project, and I can attest to the fact that there were no relations of that nature between Mary-Jo and that . . . ingrate."

"Attest? How can you attest?"

"I was her confessor. And I know she would wish me to break the bonds of confidentiality to tell you this. As well, Mary-Jo was old enough to have been his mother."

"Or yours," McGarr observed in a quiet voice.

Duggan closed the door and stepped up to the driver's window, which McGarr rolled back down. Again the priest squatted to peer in.

"Peter—I'm going to assume, even through this trying time, that you'll continue to be our friend and our neighbor. Am I correct in that assumption?"

McGarr only considered the man.

"You've spoken to Parmalee, at length, you said. May I ask you this? What are his intentions? Is he planning to make a mockery and a . . . circus of Mary-Jo's death? Is that what he intends?"

McGarr continued to hold the man's gaze.

Finally, the priest looked away, before raising himself up. "Pity he owns that rag he writes for. Otherwise . . ."

Otherwise, what? McGarr wondered. Otherwise, Duggan and Opus Dei would squelch him?

"The irony is—Parmalee began *Ath Cliath* with funds that Mary-Jo herself advanced him. 'Seed' money, she called it. Some seed, that will now vilify her life, which was holy and above reproach in every regard, I'm here to tell you."

Again the priest glanced down at his splotched trousers. "Be sure you take Mary-Jo's life—and not just the manner of her death—into consideration, Peter. You wouldn't want the opprobrium of a smear campaign to fall on your head."

There it was—guilt, which ruled all in Ireland. McGarr raised a hand and allowed the car to drift down the drive toward the gardens.

"What does he mean that you're *our* friend and our neighbor? Who's us? Opus Dei?"

McGarr hunched his shoulders.

"Do you still have that report on them Bernie gave you?"

From inside his jacket, McGarr removed the folded report and handed it to her.

"And amn't I right in thinking he just threatened you?"

McGarr looked over at Noreen and smiled. "Could it be you're catching on?"

STOPPING THE CAR at the murder scene, McGarr got out and described to Noreen how Mary-Jo had been found there in her garden—prone, in a position of utter subjection as though bowing down to whoever had wrapped the *cilicio* around her neck and tightened it until it drew blood. *Before* she died of a myocardial infarction, McGarr reminded himself.

"She still had the gardening trowel in one hand," he mused.

"After having recognized whoever approached her and even having said a few words," Noreen added.

"Before the security camera was covered up."

"Where's that?"

Walking back toward the corner of the garden haggard that a tall, cedar-pole fence enclosed, McGarr wondered if Father Fred was watching them. By his own say-so, he was now the only person who possessed a passkey to the monitoring room.

McGarr pointed to the camera lens, which had been concealed so cleverly it looked like the shaft of an intersecting cedar pole.

"Whoever obscured it was well enough acquainted with the property to know it was there and to know there was a blind spot where he or she could approach Mary-Jo and yet not be recorded."

That there were probably blind spots in other parts of the property now occurred to McGarr, and he was glad Noreen had insisted on tagging along.

Yet as they stepped back to the car, he had a feeling he was missing something right there at the crime scene. But what?

Like the other outbuildings at Barbastro, the gardener's cottage was concealed in a sizable copse, not far from the haggard if you walked through the wood, McGarr reflected. But the road itself wound around tall beeches on the periphery of the small forest until it entered an avenue of—could they be?—giant sequoias that cast deep shadows.

Surely the towering trees from the Pacific Coast of North America had been planted as a curiosity in other gardens and demesnes in Ireland, and the species had thrived in the damp, mild climate. But only within this vale, where the service structures of the estate were located, was their great height apparent.

"Magnificent, aren't they?" Noreen said, as though reading his thoughts. Which she could, she sometimes insisted and McGarr always denied adamantly on the grounds that there had to be some limit to intimacy.

"That must be the gardener there," she added.

Before them was a tall, thin man loading sacks of fertilizer onto the bed of a wagon yoked to a tractor. Catching sight of the car, he moved toward an outbuilding, which was where McGarr found him on the phone.

The man covered the mouthpiece with a hand. "Moment, please. I'm on the phone."

McGarr nodded but did not move, Noreen now entering the small office behind him.

"I said—I'm on the phone. It's personal and private."

So is murder, McGarr thought.

"I'll be out in a moment."

McGarr scanned the cramped room, which had one small window and an interior door leading farther into the building. It was open.

The desk was heaped with bills and brochures from gardening suppliers; sacks of grass and other seed sat on a pallet in one corner.

Not cleaned in years, the floor was caked with a meringue of dried mud from the door to the desk, and the tight space reeked of both the barnyard and the ashtray in front of Frank Mudd, McGarr assumed, the more than aptly named gardener, who was an old thirty-five.

A rather ordinary man with a bulbous nose and a windburned face, Mudd had not shaved recently, and his face was stubbled with a reddish beard. A battered fedora shadowed his brow.

Removing his hand from the phone, Mudd said, "They're here right now." He listened, then, "Oh, aye. Aye. I will. Be sure of it." His eyes, which were some unlikely shade of blue, flashed up at McGarr, taking in—McGarr could tell—the swelling on the side of his face, the eye that was turning black-and-blue from the blow he had received the night before. "He'll not railroad me."

Which was a term McGarr had not heard in some time. *Railroad*, the verb, was an American term and at one time prison slang, he believed. Otherwise, Mudd's voice was deep and raspy, because of the cigarettes, and carried a slight Northern burr.

Mudd slid the receiver into its yoke. "You're Peter McGarr?"

McGarr nodded.

"That was my solicitor. He'll be right over, and he says I'm not to speak to you until then." Mudd reached into his jacket and took out a packet of smokes.

"Really? Why?" McGarr pulled back the only chair, so Noreen could sit. "I'm interested." Easing himself onto a corner of the desk, McGarr watched the man light the cigarette—the fine blue smoke jetting toward the ceiling—and he could feel a kind of anger welling up. "Are you afraid you'll tell us the part you played in Mary-Jo's death?"

Mudd's head jerked back slightly, and he opened his mouth, but he said nothing. Surely a gaunt man, Frank Mudd nevertheless had wide, well-muscled shoulders, and his hands—now cupping the cigarette that was snaking smoke toward the ceiling—were large and gnarled from work. One thumbnail had been injured sometime in the past and was black and cracked right down to the cuticle.

"I said, I'm not to say nuttin'."

"Have you something to hide?"

The hand with the cigarette came up to his mouth. "Me? No."

"Perhaps you've been to prison."

As though needing something for the other hand to hold, Mudd now reached for the stub of a pencil, and his eyes, which seemed almost purple in the shadowed light, snapped toward the window. Body language, telling all.

"Of course we'll check," McGarr continued in an easy, confidential tone of voice. "Today. Count on it. Here, the Continent, over in the States. Mudd your real name or just something . . . generic, I'm betting. Know what?"

The man's eyes returned to him. "I'm also betting Mary-Jo gave you this job when nobody else would—here behind the walls and gates of this place where few would ever see you."

McGarr let that sit for a moment. Above Mudd's head, an old clock in a wooden case was ticking loudly. Silk Cut, the face said. It was a brand of cigarettes. McGarr slipped a hand into his jacket pocket where his own were kept. But for Noreen, he would have lit one up.

"And here she's been murdered in her old age, and you've got nothing to say."

Mudd again drew on the cigarette and looked down at the pencil in the other hand. The tiny office was now a fug of smoke. "Aye, but she's dead and I'm here. Like I told yous last night, like my solicitor just said—it's time to think of meself."

McGarr had suffered through this conversation countless times in the past but seldom with so much gorge rising—he could feel it—because of his need. For what? A cigarette, of course. "Think of yourself and what's in it for you?"

Mudd—or whatever his name was—only eyed him.

"Apart from a clean conscience and knowing you've done the right thing, perhaps a little sympathy, although"—McGarr raised a hand—"I promise nothing. If it's murder or kidnap you've done—over there, here—I can't help you. Bank robbery, felonious assault, anything with a gun." McGarr shook his head. "Was it any of that?"

Mudd said nothing, but he looked suddenly relieved.

Turning over the cigarette packet in his coat pocket, McGarr noticed the rime of dried salt around the band of Mudd's fedora. "Tell me, now—you work hard around here. Maybe too hard. Because mainly you're alone. Sure, Fred lets you hire in some help now and again when a big tree comes down or there's a washout or to cut all the lawns in summer. But—"

Stubbing out the cigarette, Mudd shook his head. "No, not the lawns—I do the lawns myself."

"What about the gardens?"

"Them too."

"And yesterday you were doing the gardens."

Mudd shook his head. "Like I told yous, I'll not say a word about that. My solicitor—"

"What else would you be doing now in spring?" As a stratagem, McGarr told himself, he pulled out his packet of cigarettes and offered one to Mudd, who took it. McGarr lit his own and slid his gold lighter, which had been a present from Noreen, across the desk.

Breathing out the blessed smoke that tasted—as only the first cigarette of the day always did—of fresh fields, toast, and taffy. "And then, of course, your solicitor's right—you don't have to say anything. Not a word. Since we have it all on camera."

McGarr watched as Mudd's head went back and his eye again shied toward the window.

"So, after you took care of the animals, you went up to the garden where Mary-Jo had asked you to meet her." Here McGarr was guessing, but in spite of her good health, he could not imagine a woman of her age having turned over the soil in the large patch of garden where she had been found. "You carried up the flat of peonies, you tickled the beds, then smoothed them for her."

Now smoking steadily, Mudd only regarded him.

"An hour went by, maybe two, while she made steady but slow progress planting the bed. She asked you for this or that, but mainly you busied yourself with other work—pruning rosebushes or pottering around in the haggard there.

"Did you break for lunch?"

Mudd closed his eyes, as though agreeing.

"When did you see her next?"

The eyes opened. "You'll remember this?"

McGarr's hand—the one with the cigarette—swung to Noreen. "With a witness."

Shaking his head, Mudd began: "I had no lunch, none at all. I had to go hunt up some mulch. Sure, we've got plenty of perfectly good mulch here, but for the Miss it had to be peat mixed with vermiculite and nothing else. And I had a hell of a time finding the premix, since she wanted it now, 'With no excuses,' says she to me. 'We've got to get the annuals in the ground.'

"So, I got back around . . . three, I'd put it." His eyes met McGarr's. "And haven't I been thinking about it ever since? I covered what she'd planted and then came back down here for a quick bite and a cuppa. I'd a few calls to answer." Mudd pointed to an old dust-laden answering machine by the phone. "And"—he pulled on the cigarette until the head glowed—"when I got back up there, maybe three-thirty, there she was down where she was found, dead."

"How'd you know she was dead."

"I just knew it from the way she was bowed down. Nobody Miss Jo's age could lay like that."

"What did you do?"

"Well, I went right up to her, of course. I says, says I, 'Miss Jo, you okay?' a coupla times. And I think I was a bit scared, like—you know how you get when something's happened, and you've got to do something, got to help, got to decide what to do?

"I crouched down and gave her a shove, like. 'Miss Jo?' says I again. But even though I couldn't see her eyes, I knew she was dead from the blue color of her arms."

"Then what?"

"Oh"—Mudd's eyes came back to McGarr—"I came back here as quick as I could to ring up Father Fred."

"You didn't go straight to the house?"

Mudd shook his head. "I been told . . . I can't count the times, not to go into the house. 'It's a holy place, and you're a heathen,' says she."

"Mary-Jo?"

"No, no—not Mary-Jo. Not her. She told me to disregard the bitch." Mudd swung his head to Noreen. "Sorry, ma'am. It's just—" Then to McGarr, "Gerry Breen, the housekeeper."

"Who answered the phone?"

"Father Sclavi, the other collar there. I told him what I thought had happened, but he didn't cop on, I don't think, even when he had me repeat it slowly. He's"—Mudd looked off—"Spanish or Italian, I think, and his English isn't good. And then"—he shrugged—"he just rang off.

"I figured I'd got the message across, and I'd better get back up to Mary-Jo, to keep her company, like. So I rushed back up there to find Father Fred crouched down by her side. And him and me . . . well, we don't get on. Haven't ever. I don't care to deal with him under the best of circumstances, so I just watched until he left, and came back here. Broke up, don't you know. Mary-Jo"—as Mudd reached to stub out the cigarette, his eyes met McGarr's—"was everything for me here. And without her I'm . . ." Mudd shook his head.

Back in the drum, McGarr imagined, wherever it was he was on the lam from. Which could be the reason he thought he needed a solicitor. "What was Father Fred doing when he was kneeling beside Mary-Jo?"

Mudd shook his head. "Dunno. Seeing if she was dead or alive, I guess, although . . ."

"How was he dressed?"

"The bike togs. Just got back, I'd say. Goes to hell-and-gone, he does, pumping up and down the mountains." Again Mudd shook his head as though disapproving of the practice.

"Then what?"

"He jumps up and runs toward the house. He can do that too, despite his age."

"And you?"

"I kept my vigil, there in the copse. Wonderin', like."

"Wondering what?"

"Ah, well . . . you know"—Mudd's hand moved toward his packet of cigarettes but thought better of it—"what was going to become of me. Selfish?" He nodded. "Yah. I figured Mary-Jo had a long life, but me? Without her, well, I'm . . ."

"Was there anything around Mary-Jo's neck when you found her?"

"Like what?"

"Like . . . a kind of necklace."

"Mary-Jo didn't wear necklaces. Nor jewelry. She was very plain and simple. A saint."

"You didn't see something that looked like barbed wire around her neck?"

Mudd suddenly looked puzzled.

"Or blood?"

"I don't get it. Is that the reason you're here?" His eyes moved from McGarr to Noreen and back again.

McGarr stood. "Show me the path to the garden."

"Through the wood?"

Passing by the cottage, Noreen asked Mudd if she might use the facilities. "Too much coffee, don't you know." Of course, she drank only tea, and her eyes met McGarr's when Mudd pointed to the door.

The distance between the cottage and the patch of garden where the corpse had been found was a good three hundred yards, McGarr guessed. Paved with wood chips, it was a direct line, sheltered by towering beech trees, from Mudd's dwelling amid the compound of maintenance buildings to the garden haggard near where the corpse had been found.

"It's my daily commute," Mudd said, attempting a semblance of levity.

"And a tough go, what with all the birdsong," McGarr replied, playing along. "But somebody's got to do it."

Which opened the interview to chat mostly about gardening, with Mudd knowing more about horticulture than the average gardener, McGarr judged.

At the haggard, McGarr pointed to the surveillance camera at the corner of the fence. "What do you do with that when nature calls? I suppose you're the porn star of Barbastro."

"Not a bit of it. I duck behind a tree"—Mudd pointed to the big trees at the beginning of the path in the copse—"or I do this when I can't."

Pulling off his hat, Mudd, who was a tall man, hung it over the barrel of the camera. "Ta-dah! And I'll tell you this—sometimes I do it just to send a bit of wind up Fred's shorts. He'll come out here huffing and puffing, saying, 'Don't you know that we've paid thousands of pounds for security here, and you're defeating our measures?

"And I say to him, says I, 'What do you mean, defeating your measures, your honor?' 'Your blasted hat, you oaf,' he'll say, or something like that. And he'll pluck it off and chuck it down.

" 'I had no idea, sir,' says I to his back as he tromps off.

" 'The hell you didn't, you bloody thug,' says he."

Bloody? McGarr rather doubted that Duggan—the consummate priest—would use the word.

"This is the good part—because then I shouts to him, I shouts, 'Please, your honor—please don't tell Mary-Jo.' Because, you see"—Mudd lifted his hat off the camera—"she *hated* them things worse than me.

"We'd be out here or some other part of the garden working away, and she'd notice one was on us. 'Francie'—it's what she called me—'where's your jacket?' she'd say. I'd cover it up, and we'd wait for Fred to come storming down on us."

"How long would that take?"

"Sometimes right way, like he really had been watching us. Other times, an hour or so, I'd say. But Mary-Jo would let the bastard . . . you know, the man speak. And then she'd say something like, 'I'd like to remind you whose premises these are. Now, go back to your prayers, we've work to do.' Which drove him crazy."

And which sounded very much like the feisty Mary-Jo Stanton that McGarr had known. "You're religious yourself?" McGarr asked, as they moved back into the wood toward Mudd's cottage. Above them a murder of crows were contesting a roost, their cries raucous and shrill.

"Jaysus, no. Not a bit of it, which is what bothered them up there most, you know. I'm from the North—Antrim Town—and don't I know the problems religions like theirs brings."

"You're not Catholic yourself?"

"Born and bred, like. But I've had enough for a lifetime, I tell you. Which is why"—Mudd stopped and offered McGarr a ciga-rette—"my days are numbered here, I'm sure."

Accepting the cigarette, McGarr waited.

"The minute the will is read and they take firm control of this place, I'm out on me arse, count on it. They'll put one of their own in here, not minding if he don't know a lily from a daffodil. It's the believing that matters to them, their style."

"And their style is?"

"Total, like. You do as they say, work like a divil, and turn over what you make to them. They had one yoke in here—a bloody numerary, which is like a priest without the collar. He was a surgeon, he was, with an office and all in town. And didn't they come and demand he turn over his wristwatch, saying he'd become too attached to worldly possessions. It had been a birthday gift from his family.

"Well, sir—didn't he do the right thing and tell them to feck off. After he left, they tried to ruin him altogether, I'm told."

Heard tell from whom, McGarr wondered. "Ruin him how?"

"By spreading stories, having him up before some medical review board. They hounded him right out of the country, and it continues over in the States, I'm told."

"You're well informed, Francie. May I call you Francie?"

"Anything but late for last call," Mudd quipped. "And them— they think just because I'm a bloody agricultural man out here in the bloody wood that I'm a bloody ee-jit. Well, sir—there's advantages to being out here in regard to the wind."

And which way it blows, McGarr suspected Mudd meant. "Tell me—who did this thing to Mary-Jo?"

"You mean—you think it's murder?"

McGarr nodded.

"Them."

"Why."

"Her money. Bags of it, the papers say. And then there's this place, which they'll never leave. Like rats, they are—once in, never out."

Back at the cottage, they found Noreen out front, sitting on a bench in the sun. "It's so pleasant here, really warm and springlike."

"No wind," Mudd remarked. "Sure, I wouldn't trade this she-bang for the best room in the big house. More's the pity."

In the car, Noreen said, "Bachelor digs with a few exceptions—a rather capacious push-up bra and bikini tights drying inside the press. Condoms in the med cabinet and a rather large variety of shampoos and conditioners in the shower for a rural swain such as he. And I found this in the litter bin."

It was a monthly lid of birth-control tablets, all of them having been removed. "Either your man is a mighty convincing cross-dresser or he has a constant visitor."

"Or visitors."

"Him?" Her turquoise eyes flashed at McGarr. "Please. A yoke like him should dedicate daily novenas to any woman, no matter how ugly or old, who would share his bed."

But surely not old.

McGarr swung the car up the drive toward the big house.

11

BY LUNCHTIME, Ruth Bresnahan had returned home to Dublin to nurse her new baby and to change into something that would catch Dery Parmalee's eye more completely than slacks and a jumper.

A full but shapely woman before her pregnancy, Bresnahan had discovered to her delight that—after losing the pounds she'd put on before delivering Fionnuala—she'd only added a little padding to her hips.

Standing in front of a full-length mirror, she asked, "Well, then—how do I look?"

"Altogether smashing," said the nearly gray-haired woman who had a baby under either arm.

Ruth's smoky eyes flashed at Lee Sigal, wondering if she was having her on. Apart from their relationship being new, it was . . . well, different, to say the least, and the two women were still getting used to each other.

Tall and statuesque with good shoulders and shapely legs, Ruth Bresnahan understood that she had probably never been more appealing. Gone were the jejune teens, when she'd felt a bit gawky, and the twenties, when she'd taken little care of her appearance and put on a bit of weight.

Now, at thirty-two, standing five feet eight and weighing a hundred and thirty-two pounds, Ruth knew how to dress her angular frame, and with her auburn hair, which she kept long, and exotic eyes, she knew she could "stop traffic," as Hughie Ward—her colleague/lover/shared husband—put it.

"What about the skirt?" Bresnahan was wearing a chrome-yellow retro miniskirt and a white tube top that wrapped her torso like a second skin. Her legs, which she'd tanned during a long weekend holiday in Madeira, were bare.

On her feet were a pair of white sandals with block heels. Her nails—fingers and toes—she'd painted the very color of the skirt. "Isn't it a bit short?"

"Not for the task at hand. I swear, as you stand there you have to be the most gorgeous woman in all of Dublin."

And you the most compassionate and understanding, Bresnahan thought, stopping at the babies to kiss them before departing.

"What time will you be back?"

"Hard to say. Depends on how much of a ladies' man ex-Jesuit Parmalee is."

"You take care of yourself. Somebody murdered Mary-Jo Stanton, and certainly Parmalee was on the scene from what Hughie tells me."

"Is he asleep?" Ruth asked, glancing over the shorter woman's shoulder at the door that was open across the hall. She couldn't see into the darkness of Lee's bedroom, but she knew Ward was in the other woman's bed.

"Knackered. He was half asleep when he walked in."

"Well, good-bye, girls." Ruth gave each of them, including Lee, a bus on the forehead before turning toward the door.

Her "credentials" as a journalist would have to be devised first, before she approached Parmalee directly. But she had an idea how to accomplish that by happy hour at the Claddagh Arms, where—she'd been told—the *Ath Cliath* staff hung.

†

    ON THE FIRST ring, Father Fred Duggan answered the door at Barbastro.

"Been here by the door long?" McGarr asked. "Or did you avail yourself of the technology?" He pointed at the surveillance camera concealed in the eyes of a plaster nymph, that decorated a corner of the foyer.

"I hope you didn't place any credence in anything that . . . gardener, or whatever he is, said. Mudd's a chancer altogether, and he'll be gone from here soon. Mary-Jo sheltered every class of blow-in, he being the worst by far. Do you know his past?"

McGarr and Noreen had moved into the front hall with Duggan at his elbow. "You mean about prison?"

"He *told* you about that?"

"Perhaps Fred couldn't read our lips," McGarr said to Noreen. "Someplace in the States, wasn't it? He wasn't specific."

"Attica. In New York. Hard time for an armed robbery in which a policeman was shot and killed."

"By him?" McGarr stopped at the stairs to the upper floors.

"Who knows? Could be." Duggan's dark eyebrows, which formed a continuous line across his forehead, were now hooded. "Didn't he grass on the others to save himself. Got off with a six-year sentence reduced to less than two. And then he fled back over here."

To hide out from those he'd sold out, here in a walled and gated compound with security cameras and a daily regimen as strict as any jail, if Dery Parmalee could be believed. "What's the connection?"

"Delia Manahan." Duggan glanced up the stairs. "His sister."

"Where's she?"

"Top of the stairs, take a right, last door on the left. Here—I'll show you."

McGarr put out a hand. "No need, Father, thanking you just the same. We'll find our way."

"But perhaps you'd like me to introduce you."

"We'll manage."

At the top of the stairs, McGarr and Noreen couldn't find a light switch, and they had to wait a moment until their eyes adjusted to the darkness.

"This place is vast," Noreen said as they approached the door, behind which they could hear a woman speaking or praying. The voice was rhythmical, almost a chant.

McGarr knocked. And a second time, harder.

"Do you think this place is bugged?" Noreen asked.

"It wouldn't surprise me."

"Wouldn't it be better to interview people down at the barracks or in town?"

Perhaps. But that might encourage the parties to arrive with a solicitor, which was never helpful. "We'll see."

The door opened an inch or two, and a deep blue eye appeared there. It took in McGarr and then Noreen. "Yes?"

McGarr pulled back the placket of his coat to expose his Garda ID, which was fixed to the lining. "We'd like to ask you a few questions."

"About what?"

"Please." Putting a hand on the door, McGarr pushed it open.

"And you are?" she demanded.

"Police."

"I've already spoken to the police."

Delia Manahan was a rather tall woman with a narrow waist and an expanse of bosom. Her hair had either turned a brilliant shade of white prematurely or she took great care of her skin, McGarr judged. The contrast between her smooth and buff-colored skin and her hair—which she kept in a ponytail, à la Mary-Jo Stanton—was startling. How old could she be? McGarr wondered, as she turned toward a wing chair near the hearth.

Dressed simply in a white pleated silk blouse and slacks the same blue color as her eyes, the woman took a seat, crossed her legs, and twined her fingers. "I hope this won't take too long. I've my prayers, and Father Fred is to say mass in the chapel. I hope you can appreciate the importance of that. Today."

Thirty-eight, McGarr guessed glancing at the back of her hands, the skin of which had only just begun to wrinkle. Unlike her brother's, Delia Manahan's nose was not pugged nor her chin weak.

With a slightly aquiline nose and chiseled features, she had the sort of classic good looks that McGarr not infrequently viewed in the art of museums that Noreen dragged him to.

McGarr had the feeling that he had seen the woman before, but it was some time ago, and he could not remember where or in what regard.

Noreen sat on a love seat opposite her, while McGarr moved to the window and looked out at a sweep of terraced lawn ending in a sculptured lily pond. A fountain there was jetting mist into the morning sunlight, while two fat robins tested the wet grass for worms.

In the far distance was the garden where Mary-Jo Stanton had died, and on a table near the window stood a pair of binoculars. McGarr picked them up and held the glasses to his eyes.

And there was Frank Mudd in the haggard that was used as a staging area for the garden, pottering about.

"Do I know you?" McGarr asked, moving back to the two women.

Delia Manahan only glanced at her wristwatch.

Beyond her, the hearth was patterned with small chips of multicolored tiles in the manner of majolica. The scene pictured Christ with his disciples on the pinnacle of some mountain. It reminded McGarr of his own ignorance of matters religious.

Reading the Bible and knowing its stories had never been part of his education, not in church nor in the church-run schools that he had attended. Only knowledge of prayers and some knowledge of the several rituals was insisted on, which, he supposed, all celebrated some aspect of Christ's life. But because they had been in Latin and only partially explained in English, he remained ignorant of the full canon of biblical belief.

"Please tell me about yesterday. Where were you? What did you do and see?"

"Don't you have it in your reports? I spoke to Superintendent Ward—at length."

McGarr sat next to Noreen. He had this information, of course. The Manahan woman said she had spent the day in prayer, rest, and reflection, as she always did on Saturdays at Barbastro, because—in her words—there was a "necessary ritual to the day."

Said ritual had involved—on the night before Mary-Jo Stanton's murder—sleeping on boards covered only by a blanket, which she did once a week, "as prescribed." When Delia Manahan awoke, she resumed the Major Silence that she had entered into during the evening, and she kissed the floor.

A half hour was allotted for washing and dressing, and another half hour of silent prayer that prepared her for mass in Barbastro's chapel on the main floor at the east end of the house.

Throughout that time, the Major Silence was still in force but was broken after mass when a communal breakfast was served in the "refectory," by which Manahan meant the large formal dining room of the house.

"Since on Saturdays I have no work apart from the duties I'm assigned here, I spent the day saying the rosary, reading from the gospel for the commentary I was to give in the evening," she had told Ward. "Of course, there was the Angelus at noon."

When questioned about the commentary, the woman had

explained how days usually ended at Barbastro and other Opus Dei residences. "After we return from the *work* day, we finish whatever spiritual reading we're unable to get through during the day, and we spend another half hour in silent prayer. It's then our apostolic duties commence."

In the margin, Ward had written "spreading the word, recruiting new members," as though to suggest that McGarr—heathen that he was—would not know the meaning of the word.

To fulfill her recruitment duties, Manahan presided over a circle of younger men and women who met with her weekly in the library of Barbastro for about an hour and a half.

After that, Manahan's day ended in the chapel, where the collective conscience of the group was examined through a reading from some sacred text and a commentary given by a different member each night. "It's important that the commentary be spiritually appropriate," she had told Ward, so she usually discussed it beforehand with the director.

"And the director is?" Ward had asked.

"Father Fred."

After the reading, the Major Silence began again, and the Opusians passed upstairs to their respective rooms for further reflection and prayer before bed.

All on a weekday.

Yesterday being a Saturday, however, instead of commuting into Dublin and her work as a solicitor for the poor and disabled, Manahan had passed the day in prayer and meditation focused on a "spiritual problem that I have discussed only with the director and do not wish to divulge."

And she had remained in her room until informed by Father Fred about Mary-Jo Stanton, whereupon he had advised her to stay in her room. "So, you see—I was here all day long."

"Did you leave for any reason?" Ward had asked.

"No."

"Not even to eat?"

"No. I have not eaten since lunch."

"Who might have wanted to murder Mary-Jo?"

"I have no knowledge of other people's unspoken wants, most especially in that regard."

"Did you speak with Miss Stanton at any time during the day?"

"Yes—I believe we passed pleasantries during breakfast, as was our wont."

"And she seemed . . . ?"

"Cordial, as always."

"Then do you know of any unpleasantness in her life recently?"

"If you had known Mary-Jo, you would understand that she did not allow unpleasantness into her life. And if perchance something untoward were to happen around her, she would never so much as acknowledge it, much less speak about it."

And so the interview had proceeded on the night before, with Delia Manahan taking what McGarr feared would be the "company" stance on the "unpleasantness" of the *cilicio* that had been clamped around Stanton's neck and tightened down until it drew blood. Before the elderly woman died of a heart attack.

"You reside here?" McGarr now asked.

"Obviously."

"And you told Superintendent Ward that you did not leave this house at any time yesterday, is that right?"

Manahan nodded.

"Not even, say, to take a turn down the driveway or around the lawn."

"If you mean did I go into the garden, no, I did not."

"What about those binoculars? What do you use them for?"

"Birding. I'm an avid birder."

"Did you bird from these windows yesterday?"

"Not that I can remember. When I pass by the window or hear birdsong in the gardens, then I use them."

"But not yesterday."

"Not that I can remember."

"Not even when the police arrived?"

"That was after dark, after Father Fred informed us of what had happened and ordered . . . *advised* us to remain in our rooms."

"How do you know he spoke to the others? Did you discuss Miss Stanton's murder amongst yourselves?"

Delia Manahan only regarded him, which was as much of an admission as he was likely to receive, McGarr suspected.

"Who do you think could have done such a thing?"

Again she only stared at him.

"I conclude you have an opinion."

Her blue eyes neither wavered nor blinked.

"I would surmise, from your involvement in Opus Dei, that you are committed to God and the truth." McGarr let that sit for a moment or two then. "Well, are you?"

She nodded. "I'm committed to God, Who is the truth."

"But you're declining to help me discover the truth in this matter."

"God knows the truth, which is all that matters."

"And you're content to allow Mary-Jo Stanton's murderer to go unpunished?"

"No sin goes unpunished. Ultimately."

McGarr had heard this very woman utter that statement before, he was now certain, but where? "Do I know you?" he asked again.

Her eyes began to shy, but she pulled them back and held his gaze.

"We've met, I'm sure, and it's only a matter of time before . . ."

Again the woman glanced at her wristwatch. "Really—this is becoming tedious. And may I ask, who is this woman?"

"My wife, Noreen."

"Should she be here?"

"The formal interview was last night. I'm just trying to piece things together, and Noreen was a longtime friend of Mary-Jo."

"My parents own Ilnacullin," Noreen put in. "I've been coming here all my life. Mary-Jo was a friend of my parents."

In the silence that ensued, McGarr wracked his brain trying to remember just where, when, and under what conditions he had met Delia Manahan.

It was the problem with police work, he had been telling himself for . . . oh, the last decade; he met, interviewed, talked to, and observed so many people in the course of a single day—to say nothing of the decades of his career—that it was impossible to remember them all. His brain neurons were simply overloaded with stimuli, was all it was.

Yet if truth were told, he also knew that there had been a time when he forgot nothing, nobody, not a face or a statement. He could still remember telephone numbers from his youth, the number plate of his father's first motorcar, the name of every boy in his school.

But the number plate of his own car? At the moment, he could not remember it for the life of him.

Deciding on a different tack, one that would keep Delia Manahan talking until he could remember where he had met her, McGarr asked, "At what level are you involved in Opus Dei—numerary, supernumerary, cooperator?"

"Really, now—I've important things to do. As I told your assistant last night, I'm a numerary."

"Which is the highest level."

"No. Being an actual priest is the highest level of involvement in the work."

"The work of God."

The woman did not respond, but her nostrils flared in pique, McGarr supposed, at his obtuseness.

"Therefore, you've dedicated your life to God."

Having twined her fingers at her waist, Delia Manahan firmed her upper body, as though steeling herself. "To the *work* of Opus Dei, which *is* the work of God."

Because Delia Manahan either did not possess or had plucked her eyebrows, her face—unrelieved by cosmetics of any kind that McGarr could see, and set off by her brilliant white hair—presented a severe appearance. But for her blue eyes, it was colorless, although, like the rest of her, well formed. "Work being one way to honor God," she added.

"But do you serve Opus Dei directly as a solicitor?"

She shook her head, then touched the band of her ponytail, which raised her significant breasts, which were encased—McGarr could see through the diaphanous silk blouse—in a lacy brassiere. "No, I serve the poor and those who are oppressed, and in that way— as well as through the work of being a solicitor—I serve God."

"But again, I don't see the purpose—"

"Do you receive compensation for your work? A salary? Fees?"

"Both, depending on what basis and for whom I work."

"What happens to that money?"

The hand came down from the back of her head, and her eyes flashed. "Oh, I see where you're going with this. Do I fork over my earnings to Opus Dei and live here on virtual—that's wrong, on *spiritual*—air, whilst my earnings flow into the coffers of avaricious priests?

"The answer is yes. That's why I drive a new Jag and have a closet full of expensive clothes, one child at the Sorbonne, the other at Brown. Really, now." Placing her hands on the arms of the chair, Manahan pushed herself to a stand on the strength of her biceps, rather like a gymnast. "I am neither the murdered nor the murderer, and you're disrupting the spiritual rhythm of my day. And I won't have that on this of all days."

Noreen moved forward on the love seat, as though to stand, but McGarr stayed her. "Sit down, please. You can answer my questions here or in Dublin. Your choice," he said, addressing Delia Manahan.

Hands again clasped at her waist and breasts militant, she regarded him. "Really, I should have a solicitor present."

Which would do what to the spiritual rhythm of your day, McGarr wondered. "Your choice. We'll wait. In the meantime, tell us how you came to be involved in Opus Dei."

The woman glanced at the clock on the mantel, then strode to the window and looked out. In spite of the flare of her shoulders and the expanse of her chest, she was a trim woman and fleet.

"Expecting somebody? Or are you looking for your brother."

All in one motion, she turned to them. "How did you know Frank is my brother?"

"We could begin with his patent pseudonym," McGarr replied, if only to shatter the high seriousness of the interchange. "Whoever gave him the surname has a sense of humor. And your last name before you married was . . . ?"

Her wrist came up; she glanced down at her watch. "Really, now—you must go. I have to finish my prayers before the mass."

McGarr kept his hand on Noreen's knee. "Tell me your maiden name first. And then how you came to be involved in Opus Dei."

"If I do, will you leave?"

McGarr now stood. "Obviously, you were married. Are you still? I have it that Opusian numeraries take a vow of celibacy." And poverty and obedience, which vows are renewed yearly, according to the source that Ward cited in his report.

The woman was fingering the gold ring on the fourth finger of her left hand, which was, McGarr assumed, the ring she was given when, after having served five years as a novice, she swore an oath of fidelity to Opus Dei in the presence of the order's regional vicar and two witnesses.

"It implies that the oblate, who with the ceremony becomes a numerary, is now married not to the Church but rather to Opus Dei," the report said.

Delia Manahan turned her back to them and spoke to the window. "True, I was married. I have two children. But I was always religious. My father had been a priest, my mother a nun before . . . Suffice it to say that after my husband died suddenly, leaving me with two young children, I needed some emotional and spiritual support." A hand moved to her eyes.

"Which was when . . . which was when Gerry helped me out enormously with . . . with everything, including my spiritual needs, and I decided it was time for me to turn to Christ."

"Through Opus Dei."

She nodded and pulled a handkerchief from the pocket of her bright blue slacks. "Thank God for Opus Dei."

"Geraldine Breen, the . . . house manager? Is that what she is here?"

Again she nodded. Before blowing her nose. "Really, you'll have to excuse me. I hope you realize how . . . extraordinary all of this is for me. For us."

"Us, who?" You and your brother? McGarr wondered. Or you and Opus Dei? If Dery Parmalee was right in his claims about the history of the order, murder and other forms of *pillería* were standard operating procedure.

Slowly she rounded on him, her eyes filled with tears. "Opus Dei, you fool. Do you think all of this is mere sham?" A hand gestured to the walls, as though to mean Barbastro itself. "Do you think we're pretending here and that all of what we profess is just a . . . ruse to enrich ourselves and obtain power over others?

"See this ring? When I swore my oath of fidelity to this order, I swore it before an empty cross. The cross was empty because, as our founder wrote, 'When you see a poor wooden Cross, alone, uncared for, and of no value and"—she sobbed—"and without its Crucified, don't forget that that cross is your Cross . . . the Cross which is waiting for the Crucified it lacks, and that Crucified may be you.

"Now, get out! Your—your disbelief reeks, I can smell it on you! And I won't have caviling heretics in my presence on this of all days!"

"Your maiden name, please."

"Manahan," she shouted, rushing at them. "Now get out, before I ring up Brian Doherty!"

Who was commissioner of the Garda Siochana, and McGarr's ultimate boss.

"And your brother's first name is actually Francis?"

"Yes, dammit, yes it is." Wrenching the door open, she shoved Noreen into the hall. Her face was distorted with fury. "And if you report his whereabouts to *anybody*, I'll see—*we'll* see—that you suffer for it."

McGarr stepped out of the room.

"Remember, the Cross and your soul, if you have one. You'll be on it sooner than you think."

Delia Manahan slammed the door, having uttered a lie in failing to reveal her maiden name.

McGarr had seen the woman before, but where? "Do we know her?"

"Now? She wouldn't allow it."

"No—before. I've seen and spoken to her . . . and as part of an investigation." At least that much had returned.

"Well—Chief Super or Super Chief—I'm not always gracing your forensic presence, am I? And I hope that only once in my life will I be forced to clap eyes on that piece of holy work. Severe is not the word for her. Did you catch her eyebrows? It takes planning and skill to look like that."

Lost in thought, attempting to spool back through the compendium of cases that he'd investigated over the years, McGarr turned down the hall toward the door of the Opus Dei cleric with the Italian last name.

"And by the by," Noreen asked, taking his arm, "where do you stand on the issue?"

"Which issue?"

"God in particular, religion in general."

Well away, McGarr thought, if Barbastro and its occupants were any measure of those who stood close.

12

RUTH BRESNAHAN knew from the moment she walked into the Claddagh Arms that she was a sight for sore—no, aching—eyes.

The barman had a face, as the saying went, like a plateful of mortal sins. Not only was his nose in rosy ruin, but his eyes were downright patriotic in color. Buried in two pouches of deep bruise, they were—like the flag—a mix of green and white but mostly orange/red.

Yet Bresnahan could not fault the man on his taste. He knew rare, somewhat aged beauty when he saw it, she concluded from his fractured smile.

"Haven't I told ya'—when was the last time I told ya'—yeh'r' me heart's desire," he barked in the pancake accent of a true Dub'. "Yeh'r' altogether the darlingest girl to set foot in this kip since . . . well, since I t'rew open the doors in 1787 or thereabouts."

"My sentiments entirely," Bresnahan replied, sliding onto a bar stool. "Have I told *you* I enjoy candor in a man. And plain old good sense."

She crossed her legs, which were much exposed courtesy of her chrome yellow miniskirt. "May I confide in you? Do you have a name?"

"That's Jam."

"Jam?"

"No, *That's* Jam. It's what me father uttered at the moment of my conception, and what me mither—never seeing the darlin' man again—*preserved* in me name."

"Her own being Crock-et, I suppose."

The twin pouches of bruise widened, and his smile appeared again. "I like that. You have wit as well as beauty."

"Make that *great* beauty, and you have me on toast, Jam. Because—come closer while I tell you—it's not easy being beautiful. In fact, it's a curse. Men ogle me, women are jealous of me, and barmen, such as yourself, come on to me so brazenly that for a moment I thought we might be old friends. Or lovers. Do I remember you? Or you me?"

Jam was aptly named. His slack jaw having dropped open, he looked only stunned.

"Now then—" Bresnahan placed her purse with its Glock and Garda credentials on the bar and squared the armament of her significant chest. "Repeat after me—'Oh, great mistress' . . . say it."

Together, they said, "Oh, great mistress."

"Possessor of the packet entire."

"Possessor of the packet entire."

Bresnahan continued, "What are you having to drink this fine afternoon? A brimful glass of Chablis, thank you very much. Then, the bill of fare. As you noticed when I walked in, I'm nothing but skin and bones."

Jam's moiling eyes dropped down her body again. "I like you," he managed.

"No, no, no—you love me. Say it."

"I *love* you."

"No, with more feeling, since you truly mean it."

"I *love* you."

"That will have to do for the moment. Now, my wine, Jam man. On the double—hip, hip, hip."

Smiling slightly, Jam trudged toward the wine cooler at the other end of the bar.

Bresnahan looked around the pub/restaurant with its exposed-brick walls, checkered tablecloths, and framed front-page copies of history-making events on the walls. Plainly an eatery that hoped to attract journalists. Only a few tables were taken now at half past six. And no Dery Parmalee.

"*Ath Cliath* crowd come in here?" she asked, when the brimming goblet was placed before her.

"You mean Dery and his lads? Like clockwork. Be here"— Jam checked the clock in back of him—"in ten minutes, I'd hazard."

"What—no lasses?"

"Tell you somethin'?"

Bresnahan leaned forward, knowing that her black scoop-neck jumper would afford the barman a peek at her breasts.

"I don't think he fancies lasses."

"You're coddin' me."

Jam swallowed. "Well, they say he's a bit of a poof. Ex-priest and all."

Who claimed he had an affair with Mary-Jo Stanton, Bresnahan remembered from the morning briefing. "No—now you *are* coddin' me."

"Gets a little jarred now and then, after they've put the paper to bed, as they say. And he cruises the bar here, leaving as often with trousers as skirts, if yeh catch me drift."

Which made Bresnahan's own odds fifty-fifty. She reached for the glass.

A few minutes passed by, the bar began to fill up, and Jam again appeared by her side. "Are you ready now?" He pointed to the swing doors that gave entrance to the pub. "Foive, four, t'ree, two, two,

two, two"—the doors opened, and in stepped a man who could only be Dery Parmalee, followed by several other, younger men.

"One," said Jam. "Shite, call it a rehearsal. I'll give out to them about it now. Just watch me."

The group took a corner table near the window that possessed, Bresnahan gauged, a clear view of her legs. And throughout the first round of drinks, eyes flashed her way, Parmalee's—framed by his octagonal glasses—as often as the others'.

After pints were emptied, Parmalee rose to order more and worked his way into the now packed bar. Wearing a white turtleneck jumper and straight-leg jeans under a blue blazer, he was a good-looking man of around forty with a square face, a straight nose, and thinning sandy hair. Tall, thin, and angular, he moved lithely, athletically, in a way that suggested he worked out. He glanced at her once more as he entered the bar crowd, and she smiled in return.

Handing back the change, Jam muttered something and canted his head toward Bresnahan, obviously saying that she'd been asking after Parmalee and perhaps he should chat her up.

Consulting her wineglass demurely, Bresnahan waited.

At length a hairy wrist appeared on the edge of the bar, and she looked up.

"You've been asking after me, have you?"

"Women do, surely."

Behind the donnish spectacles, his light blue eyes closed pointedly and reopened. "But a woman of your . . . er, kindly disposition. What *possibly* could be your interest in me?"

"Well"—Bresnahan uncrossed her legs, and in turning to face him, her knees brushed across the front of his jeans—"as it happens, I'm seeking employment. I need a job."

A smile appeared. Nearly as white as his jumper, Parmalee's teeth were even if rather widely spaced. "Are you, now. In what capacity, may I ask?"

Bresnahan was prepared. "Staff writer. I admire your publication—how different it is from the stodgy rags in this town, how you're willing to take on the thorny issues. And I'd like to"—reaching for her purse, she aimed her smoky eyes at Parmalee—"throw my weight into the mix."

Pulling out the résumé that she'd had a friend in Los Angeles fax her, Bresnahan handed him the several pages. At a Dublin employment agency, she'd had another friend scan the document onto his letterhead, so the packet looked somewhat legitimate and could be checked, at least on the Dublin end.

It said that Sonya Stephens had graduated from Trinity College in 1986, emigrated to the States that year, and begun a career as a journalist, working for underground and small weekly presses. After taking a master's in journalism at the University of Missouri, she then began writing for a succession of large, well-regarded papers, such as the San José *Mercury-News* and the *Star-Ledger* of New Jersey.

It included three letters of recommendation from editors and a list of journalism awards.

Sonya and Ruth were the same age, looked rather alike, and Sonya, having left journalism to pursue other interests there in the States, would not be located easily.

Parmalee scanned the pages before sliding them onto the bar. "Great résumé, and I'd hire you in a heartbeat, were it yours.

"Charles," he called to the barman, "could we have a round over here?"

"He told me his name was Jam. Or *That's* Jam," Bresnahan offered, sensing that the jig was up.

"And that you're the darlingest girl to set foot in this kip since he opened it a few centuries ago, I should imagine. Don't feel complimented. He tells that to all the girls. It's his shtick. Like yours, Miss Bresnahan. Or shall I call you Detective Inspector Bresnahan? What are you having—another glass of wine? Or—"

"A large whiskey," Bresnahan muttered glumly.

"While nursing?" Parmalee asked, his eyes dropping down to her breasts. "Is that advisable? And while we're on the subject of contra-marital bliss, how are you handling your . . . novel arrangement there in the Coombe with your colleague, Superintendent Ward, who is the father of your child, and his—Ward's—common-law wife, Lee Sigal, and the two children he has by her?"

Parmalee had raised his voice, as though addressing those around them. "You know, I'm glad you came here this afternoon. I've been meaning to ask you if we might do a feature on your unique living situation. I think my four hundred thousand readers here in Catholic Ireland would be fascinated to know that polygamy, unknown since the days of Brian Boru, is staging a resurgence right here in Dublin City.

"And here she sits amongst us, gentle persons, the perpetrator of such viciousness. To look at her with that short, tight skirt and all her"—Parmalee swirled a hand—"accoutrements hanging out, you'd think . . . what?" Parmalee asked a man standing next to him. "Tart, right? But you'd only be half right."

The drinks had arrived and Bresnahan reached for hers.

"Because what you see before you is a tart with two big differ-ences, and I'm not talking strictly glandular, although she'll do—and does—in that department, as you can see."

Bresnahan gripped the glass, wondering if she could contain herself, as she knew she must. If ever it became public knowledge how she and Ward were living, both of them would surely have to resign their posts. In gossipy Catholic Ireland they would be marked for life.

"The first is that she's a cop tart," Parmalee now went on, glass in hand. His eyeglasses winked as he tilted back his head to declaim, "What's that, you ask? Pop tart? Nay, nay, nay—not *pop* tart. *Cop* tart.

"That's a cop who gets herself all tarted up, like this, and comes in here representing herself as an agent of the Fourth Estate in the attempt to land an undercover surveillance job not *for* me and *Ath Cliath*—but rather *on* me. This woman, this cop tart sitting here before you, actually wanted to spy on me!

"Why, you ask? Will murder do?"

Now the bar crowd had quieted.

"Shhhh!" somebody in back of Bresnahan hissed. "Dery's a gas character, and he's having 'Big Red,' there, off."

"You, you, and even you too"—Parmalee pointed at some of the others—"you thought she was just another journalistic bimbo who'd do any little *thang* at all to join in the business at *Ath Cliath*.

"Truth is, she's been doing some rather nuanced little *thangs*, including the business with one of her colleagues and her colleague's common-law wife."

Now the silence in the crowded bar was nearly palpable, and Bresnahan could feel the weight of their eyes on her bowed shoulders.

"And what a story! An amazing story, one filled with lust, perhaps love, two betrayals that we can count, two further pregnancies, and now two common-law wives with two young children, all of whom have set up literal shop with their betrayer.

"Will you hear more, gentle persons?"

"Go, Dery!" one exhorted.

"It seems that this woman's paramour of three years had a checkered past. And after a three-year liaison with her, it was revealed to him that, miraculously, he already possessed a ready-made family with a wealthy, handsome, eligible woman right here in Dublin City. *Who*"—Parmalee raised a hand—"quickly became pregnant by him again, after he moved in."

Bresnahan glanced at her drink and then the door. Sliding off the stool, she reached for her purse.

"Now, now, Miss B.," Parmalee advised, "this really isn't the class of party where you'd want to be the first to leave. I could name names, and then where would you and your ménage à trois be?"

Bresnahan eased herself back onto the bar stool. In spite of its over half-million inhabitants, Dublin was still a small town, and any hint of scandal was circulated with the speed of a wildfire, especially concerning the police, whose personal lives were supposed to be above reproach.

"So, with her lover not merely admitting to fresh betrayal but also having left her for another woman, what's a poor girl to do? Pine for a while, then lose herself in lust? She tried that for . . . how long was it, dear?"

Under hooded brows, Bresnahan glared at the man. Yes, she and Ward had maintained a three-year relationship, sometimes living together in his digs, other times in hers. And yes, Ward—in the course of an investigation—had stumbled upon an old flame who had revealed to him that fourteen years earlier she had given birth to his child.

Then, after he had been shot and nearly killed, the woman—Lee Sigal—had both the time and the money to nurse him back to health, during which time one thing had led to another, and she had become pregnant by him again. Bresnahan could understand that—how it could happen and why.

But, yes, she had also felt grossly betrayed, even as she had pined for Hughie Ward—his love, his warmth and companionship. But she had not lost herself in lust. In fact, she had been rather repulsed by the other men who had taken her out. She had become so used to his presence and body that it was as if she had lost the other—and in many ways better—part of herself.

"Run away? Flee? Not this woman," Parmalee went on. "Not 'Big Red' here. Do you like that moniker, Rut'ie?"

Bresnahan's eyes flashed at Parmalee. If he mentioned her surname, she didn't know what she would do, but she'd take her vengeance there, while she had him in her presence.

"No—she took a completely different and creative tack, she did. Instead of acting the part of the woman scorned, she seduced her betrayer, got herself pregnant by him, and moved in with the lucky gumshoe, who up until a year and a half ago was a confirmed bachelor.

"Now the three of them and their three children live together in common-marital bliss. The wives are buddies, the kids great pals, and everybody loves their da-da. Tell us, 'Big Red'—how do you handle the sleeping arrangements, or do they just work themselves out?"

Rather perfectly, Bresnahan believed. After the initial torrent of rage and jealousy—when she realized that she still loved Ward deeply and perhaps it might be possible for him to love two women equally and at once—all else became possible.

Now together they had three incomes, all the day-care they could want, intelligent, mature companionship, and much love, since Ward was attentive to the needs of both on that score.

The only quibble with the arrangement that Bresnahan had found was that Ward smiled too much. She had never seen him happier, which had made her wonder if all men were actually repressed bigamists.

And why not, she thought, again sliding off the stool and stepping into Parmalee so their noses were only inches apart. Dublin was a potentially cosmopolitan city with good schools and universities, cultural institutions, and even journals, Parmalee's tabloid excepted.

Why couldn't—no, why *shouldn't*—alternative living situations, based on love and mutual respect and in which children were also loved and cared for, be explored? Certainly the model nuclear family was in serious disarray in much of the world, if statistics could be believed.

And now to have this—what? ex-priest-turned-scandalmonger—not merely poking fun at but also threatening their excellent arrangement enraged Bresnahan. Low, so only Parmalee would hear, she said, "You don't know me, you don't know us—"

"Oh, but I do," he began to say through a thin smile. "I do. I have touts—"

"No. You. Don't. And what you don't know is—you push this thing to the max, we will too. Our way. Count on it. And you won't like our max, not one bit."

Parmalee stepped away from her, his smile muting to one of wonder. "I can't believe it! The bitch is actually threatening me with bodily harm."

Bresnahan only regarded him.

"Did you hear it?" he asked one man. "Or you? I want you to be my witnesses—just in case this curious person can find the . . . er, *balls* to act on her threat."

Some of the others now began laughing.

"Do I say your name now, or will you spare us the burden of your loathsome presence—pistol-packin' adulteress that you are?

"Now, be off!" Parmalee pointed toward the swing doors.

The laughter was general and sustained as Bresnahan made her way through the pub.

"Ah, c'mon, Dery—tell us her name. D'ya have her number?"

"He's got that, all right."

"Great *craque*! The best!"

"No, no—great *rack*. Will you look at the prow on her. Wouldn't mind a bit of that meself."

Bresnahan knew it was wrong, but for the first time since having her baby and moving in with Hughie and Lee, she felt different and . . . unhappy about who she was and how she was living.

Which made her angrier still.

THROUGH MUCH OF the afternoon, McGarr and Noreen had waited for Father Juan Carlos Sclavi to complete a "Confidence" with his "spiritual director," Father Fred Duggan.

"From what Father Sclavi has already revealed to me, you won't be disappointed," Duggan said, when offering them lunch in the refectory of Barbastro.

"Truth is, we have some spiritual issues to clear up. Sclavi is a . . . hugely caring and sensitive human being, and divulging information about somebody, no matter how accurate or important, is most difficult for him. I hope you understand."

McGarr checked in with his headquarters, wondering if any leads to the whereabouts of Geraldine Breen had turned up. "Not a one," said John Swords, the desk sergeant on duty. "It's as if she simply disappeared, and I can't see how, the way she looked—the busted nose and all."

McGarr did. She had obviously been hidden by her cohorts in Opus Dei, and he was half tempted to declare her wanted for murder and have a before-and-after artist's rendering published in the country's newspapers.

But would she have attacked him in Mary-Jo Stanton's headquarters had she murdered the woman? Perhaps not. Still, a case could be made that she had attacked him to allow whoever it was who had been tossing the place to escape.

"How many staffers do we have on her?"

"Five, including myself."

"Add two more. Concentrate on known Opus Dei residences. Try to get inside. Watch for any medical attention—physicians, nurses, trips to the chemist. That class of thing."

Throughout lunch and then later, in a walk around the grounds of the estate, Noreen and McGarr discussed the subject she had broached earlier in the day—faith and religion.

"And you mean to tell me you don't believe in anything at all?"

"I didn't say that, exactly."

"Yes, you did. You said you didn't see a sign of God anywhere in the universe."

McGarr looked away at an expanse of sloping lawn that led down to a large pond framed by the twin stands of magnificent, immemorial linden trees that graced the bank.

He remembered how Mary-Jo Stanton once spoke to him, gardener to gardener, of her theory of planting. "I like making vistas at every turn, in a way that will lead the visitor from one picture to another." They had been walking along this very pathway in spring, like this.

"Of course, this sends people who like great panoramas completely mad," she had continued. The three islands on the pond—or "lake," as she had called the maybe forty-acre impoundment—were thickly planted with pampas grass and New Zealand flax "to provide the architectural element" among the waterside plantings. As he remembered, those consisted of candelabra primulas, fair-maids-of-France, lilies, hostas, foxgloves, and dicentra, which had only just begun to show themselves.

"Well?" Noreen demanded.

McGarr felt his brow furrow. Conversations like this, which supposed the multiplicity of life could be reduced to simple statements, were difficult for him. Often he considered himself just not clever enough to sum up his feelings, as could Noreen and many of the other people they knew.

Which could be why he had become a policeman, right and wrong being the one concept that he understood thoroughly. "No," he replied. "I said I see no sign of a god at work anywhere in the universe."

"Well—where do you think the universe came from? And . . . *matter*? Us? You and me? And what does life mean? Are we just motes hurtling for an instant through time and space?"

"Well, take you, for instance." McGarr reached an arm around her shoulder. "I know where you came from. Heaven, surely. But the book's still out on me."

"Ah, go 'way now. Don't patronize me." She slipped out of his grasp. "I'm really disturbed that you're insisting on that class of tough-cop agnosticism that you dust off like a party piece whenever I try to speak seriously with you."

Agnosticism? Was she hoping? "Tell you true"—he managed to take her shoulder again—"this is the only heaven we'll ever know—you and me here in this garden. And we should enjoy it."

"You must be joking. Some garden, where a woman who sweated, slaved, and lavished her precious time on this patch of ground could be murdered in it in her eightieth year."

McGarr let pass the thought that at least she'd had the eighty years, less the day of her death, as gardener in one of the most beautiful places in the country, if not the world.

"Then do you think Mary-Jo has passed on to a final and eternal reward?" Noreen asked.

"Yes." Wherever she was, if anywhere, it was surely final and eternal.

"And it's some place like here in this garden."

"I would hope."

"See—you're just parsing this argument. Will you ever get serious with me? Or do you also take us, our marriage, our child, our lives as lightly as you view metaphysics? If the possibility of God means nothing to you, how can anything else?"

Rather simply, actually, everything else being serious in the extreme. "I hope you know I take you more seriously than any other person, place, or thing in the world," he said in a low voice into the fine auburn hairs at the nape of her neck. "Because I love you."

"Well, I *hope* that'll be enough. For you."

When his time came, he supposed she meant.

But it was. He was sure.

AROUND HALF PAST three McGarr's mobile phone rang, and five minutes later Noreen and he arrived at the door of Father Juan Carlos Sclavi's room. It opened at the first knock.

"Come in, *por favor*." The dark young man bowed slightly as they stepped into the large room. "I believe you know my spiritual director," he said in halting English, turning his head to Duggan, who was seated at a desk near one of Barbastro's tall windows. He was writing something on a piece of paper that he then folded and slipped into a pocket.

"Director?" Noreen asked. "Does a priest need a spiritual director?"

"Of course," Duggan put in. "We all need guidance in matters spiritual."

To ensure orthodoxy? McGarr wondered. In the packet of information he'd been sent, one item said that every Opus Dei member was required to attend a weekly Confidence with a spiritual director. Set topics were discussed, such as personal conduct, and faults in attitude. The "fraternal correction" that could be imposed might take the form of acts of contrition or some other punishment meted out by the spiritual director.

On other occasions, the spiritual director or other Opus Dei higher-ups might visit lesser members in their rooms and remove some personal belonging, like a wristwatch or a jacket, to which a member had become overly attached, "self-abnegation and sacrifice, discipline, and confidence in the strict sense (group secrecy) being the keys to membership control."

The report had continued: "This is a most secret, reactionary organization that views itself as the successor to the militant traditions of the Knights Templar. Opusians believe that in spreading their interpretation of Christianity, all means justify the ends of countering Communism, Liberation Theology, and radical Islam, and of defeating within the Church 'liberalizing' issues such as birth control and women priests. Insubordination is not tolerated."

Duggan now said, "As I mentioned to you earlier, Chief Superintendent McGarr—Father Sclavi has something he'd like to tell you. And would you mind terribly if I remained here while you interview him? His English is not perfect, and I believe I have evidence that will corroborate what he'll say."

Control again. Not only had Duggan orchestrated what the young priest would say, during the Confidence, now he wished to make sure the lines were delivered according to plan.

As though reading McGarr's mind, Duggan added, "Yes—we've discussed what he will say. But because of the details, which are particular, I think it would be wise to allow me to assist you."

McGarr shrugged. Why not learn what they had to tell them? He could always interview Sclavi in private later, and at least he'd have the Opus Dei position—forged during the Confidence—on record.

Or was he being entirely too cynical? Perhaps the young man with the dark hair and prominent widow's peak, the oval face and deep-set eyes, was sincere in what he was about to divulge.

Perhaps McGarr had been prejudiced against faith, religion, and priests because of his early brutal experience with the agents of religion. And more recently by what Dery Parmalee had told him about Opus Dei and what the quick inquiry into the order had partially confirmed.

"Work away," McGarr said to Duggan.

Sclavi half-bowed again and moved toward Duggan at the window. "I shall now speak?" he asked, turning his head from McGarr to his spiritual director.

Both men nodded.

"So, I was here at this window, looking out sometime after Pater Fred informed me that I should remain in my room. But I look out into the garden and see Miss Stanton, down on the ground where she was digging.

"Then I see a man pick something up from the ground and go into the wood."

"Do you know who that person was, Juan Carlos?" Duggan

asked didactically, his arms folded across his chest, his head cocked to the side.

"I do, Pater. It was the gardener."

"Francis Mudd."

Or Manahan. Brother of Delia Manahan. Informer and ex-convict.

McGarr moved to the window and looked out. Certainly he could see into the formal garden where the corpse had been discovered, but it was full daylight. At night, he imagined, the scene would be more difficult to see from the distance of—what?—easily a hundred yards. But then his own eyes were not what they once were.

On the blotter of the desk lay a pair of eyeglasses.

"More to the point, it seems that Father Sclavi's testimony can be documented," Duggan said.

McGarr waited.

"It's on the transcript—the security tapes. After the bit with the jacket being placed over the lens of the camera at the moment that Mary-Jo was being killed."

"How do you know that?" McGarr had ordered Ward and McKeon to seize the tapes as evidence.

"Oh"—Duggan closed his eyes and shivered his cheeks histrionically—"I neglected to tell you. I consulted my superiors, who inquired of a solicitor, who advised me to make copies of the tapes before handing them over. Yesterday, the day of the . . . crime."

"Why is that?"

"Well, as a simple precaution."

"Against what?"

"Against the possibility that they might be edited."

"By the police?" Noreen asked.

Duggan hunched his broad shoulders. "I was ordered to do it. I did it."

As a good soldier in Christ, thought McGarr. A modern-day Templar.

"But isn't that a curious attitude for a religious organization—not to trust the police?"

"Of course we trust the police. Implicitly."

But Noreen would not be put off. Two patches of red had appeared in her cheeks. "Then why make a copy?"

Duggan shook his head. "Perhaps to ease the mind of one of my superiors."

"And who might he be when he's at home?"

"I'm afraid I couldn't say."

"Yet that unknown—could he be unknowable?—person is orchestrating your actions here?"

Duggan only stared at her, rather balefully, McGarr judged.

"Take us to this tape," he said.

It showed what Sclavi said had happened, only minutes after Duggan and McGarr had left the murder scene. Mudd—or some figure that looked remarkably like Mudd—stole out of the garden haggard and, approaching the corpse, stooped and picked something up.

"It's the water bottle. The one that Mary-Jo always kept by her side when she gardened," Duggan narrated. "To 'hydrate,' don't you know. It's very important."

To hydrate? McGarr wondered. Or the bottle, as it related to the cause of her death—her sudden heart attack, when she had no history of heart trouble.

"And there's more," Duggan went on, backing the tape up to the events directly before the elderly woman's murder. "Remember how the jacket was placed over the camera?" Which was what now appeared on the screen. "I took the liberty of having a friend enhance the tape at that point—you know, enlarge and clear up the image."

Duggan removed the tape from the video player and replaced it with another. It showed a blowup of the label on the jacket, which said "Stafford."

"Your man Mudd has such a jacket."

McGarr turned to him.

"When it was new, I once remarked on it to Mary-Jo—where a man such as he had come by a garment of such quality and why he insisted on wearing it while performing manual labor."

McGarr held Duggan's gaze.

"So—I believe we have our murderer," Duggan concluded. "And a more ungrateful and heinous person there could not be on the face of this earth."

"What about the water bottle—did it belong to Mary-Jo?"

"I never saw it before in my life," said Duggan. "Usually Mary-Jo hydrated with commercial mineral water—Evian or Perrier—in the disposable containers."

"Would she drink from something that was just handed to her?"

"Why not?—if handed her by a trusted employee."

McGarr remained unconvinced. It all seemed so wondrously pat.

More so at Mudd's cottage in the copse of beeches where McGarr took Sclavi and, of course, Sclavi's spiritual director to confront Mudd/Manahan with the charge. And to secure the water bottle, if possible.

In the back of his mind, McGarr kept replaying Dery Parmalee's tales about the sudden myocardial infarction that had beset John Paul after only thirty-three days as Pope and had earlier killed an emissary of the Russian Orthodox Church, serendipitously for Opus Dei, if Parmalee—who seemed to have an ax to grind in regard to the order—could be believed.

"You three wait here until I ask you to join me." Removing his Walther from the sling under the seat of the car, McGarr fit the handgun into the right-hand pocket of his jacket.

It was dark now, and every room of the cottage appeared to be lighted. At the door, McGarr knocked and called out, "Mr. Mudd. Frank Mudd. It's Peter McGarr. Could you come out here for a moment?"

When he received no answer, he tried the handle and found the door open. Inside, a radio was playing, and all seemed rather neat, if not particularly clean. On the kitchen table lay an ashtray brimming with cigarette butts and a bottle of whiskey with only an inch remaining. A glass had spilled onto the worn lino.

There was a light in Mudd's stable office, which McGarr approached with equal caution. That door was ajar, but again he called out, his early interview with Mudd having been cordial enough, at least toward the end.

Another whiskey bottle, this one nearly full, was also in evidence on the desk, as was the odor of . . . human excrement, McGarr could only suppose.

The source of which he discovered in the adjoining room. There Mudd was hanging from a rafter. A noose of rope was wrapped around his neck, which canted off at an odd angle, and the other end was knotted to the hook of a come-along—a hand-operated winch that was used to hoist or move small loads.

Mudd was wearing the jacket from the videotape.

In death the man's bowels and bladder had evacuated, the effluent pooling around the toes of his work boots, which were only a few inches off the floor.

His weathered face had assumed a purple cast, and his light eyes were splayed and protruding from the pressure of the cinch, McGarr supposed. Could he have actually reached up and quickly winched himself off the ground and thereby suffocated himself?

How much easier it would have been to have taken a chair from the office, rigged the noose, fixed the other end to a short lead on the rafter, and then jumped. It was the way most every other hanging suicide had been accomplished in McGarr's experience.

But how many suicide victims are thinking clearly before their demise. And there was the evidence of the surfeit of whiskey. But no note—not in the stable or the house.

After using his cell phone to report the death and request a team from the Technical Squad, McGarr asked Duggan and Sclavi to return to the mansion, while Noreen and he went through Mudd or Manahan's effects, looking for anything that might explain the cause of his—was it?—suicide.

Or the water bottle, which McGarr found at length, stuffed into a plastic garbage bag in a van that was loaded with other refuse, evidently to be taken to the local dump on the morrow, which was a Monday.

"I'm surprised by what I didn't find," said Noreen. "The woman's clothes and underwear that I'd seen earlier?"

McGarr nodded.

"They're gone. And all other traces of a woman's presence in Mudd's life—the cosmetics and so forth."

Back at the mansion, Duggan yet again greeted them at the door. "Is there any way I can help you, anything I can do? Just name it."

"Your security tapes. Both those you copied and the tapes from today. All of them."

Duggan's brow wrinkled. "The copies, surely. I can give you those if you demand them, our solicitor says. But not any from today."

"Why not?"

"Because there are none."

McGarr searched the priest's dark eyes, the hale contours of his handsome face.

"Well, with Mary-Jo gone and you, your men, and your wife here wandering all over the property, I figured, what's the point? Why not conserve the expense? So I switched the system off, phoned the security company, and asked them to cancel the service."

"When?"

"When what?"

"When did you call them?"

Duggan's eyes shied. "Yesterday sometime. Or perhaps it was

early this morning. I . . . I've been . . . it's that I've been so devastated and distraught because of all this."

Yet he appeared to be sleeping well enough; that much was plain. Although roughly the same age as McGarr, the priest looked decidedly younger, the skin of his handsome face smooth and unmarred by pouches.

In the closetlike security room under the stairs, McGarr checked to see if the monitoring system had, in fact, been disabled. After receiving the copied tapes from Duggan, he used his mobile phone to contact Avco Security Systems in Ballsbridge.

The manager there revealed that the priest had phoned him about removing the system around one that afternoon, about the time McGarr had finished interviewing Delia Manahan and Duggan had requested the Confidence with Sclavi.

Could the two priests have used the time when McGarr and Noreen were walking in the garden to steal down to Mudd's with two bottles of whiskey and . . . ? McGarr did not think so.

After all, Duggan might be controlling and devious in order to protect what he perceived as the interest of Opus Dei. But his acolyte and he were still priests. Could they, *would* they murder and murder so . . . baldly as to get Mudd drunk and then string him up?

Said Noreen, "They certainly had the time, when, ironically, I was distracting you with all that carry-on about faith and religion. Sorry."

"Why be sorry," he assured her, since they both knew there was no stopping a murderer intent on murder.

At the car, McGarr drew her to him, and they embraced for a long moment. "The problem is—we don't really get the chance to see each other as much as we should," he said into her ear.

She nodded.

"We should go on holiday, someplace warm and away from all the bother—yours and mine."

"Santorini."

It was the Greek island where they had honeymooned. And where their daughter had been conceived.

"Maddie's never seen it. We can stay in that hotel that's been chipped into the top of the cliff."

With the breathtaking views of the deep blue Aegean and lesser islands in the distance. There was a wine on Santorini that McGarr savored more than any he had tasted since. Days there—filled with strong sunlight and cooling sea breezes—just seemed to flow into each other. And the fishing, which was another activity that McGarr practiced too seldom these days, was excellent.

"We'll set it up when I get a handle on all of this."

If I get a handle, he amended to himself. Could more than one agent be at play in the murder of Mary-Jo Stanton and the possible cover-up "suicide" of Frank Mudd?

"Your cell phone," Noreen prompted. It was vibrating in his pocket. McGarr released her and opened it up.

"Peter? Dery Parmalee here. Next time, send a true unknown to infiltrate my hateful rag. But not to worry. The only scars your Rut'ie took away are psychological and her own. With a correction of lifestyle and a dollop of contrition, she and her curious ménage à trois might escape righteous communal wrath. But no promises. Not one. You there?"

McGarr grunted. From the clamor in the background, it sounded as though Parmalee was calling him from a pub.

"On another, more sobering note—what about Mudd? Did he do himself there off the barnyard? Or do you suspect . . . foul play? Don't hang up.

"I called just to give you a heads-up, so to speak. I'm terribly excited by this recent development, and the staff and I are railroading the Opus Dei piece for a special edition we'll put out on the streets the moment you've solved the entire hugger-mugger of Mary-Jo and Mudd and grant us the exclusive, as promised.

"Talk about timing! Here I've been toiling—rather as you do and Mary-Jo did in your respective gardens—for a whole year to learn the ins and outs of Opus Dei. And just as I'm cobbling together the back story, along comes a double-murder cover story at the very locus of my inquiry. I call that downright serendipitous, don't you?"

"Where are you?"

"Ah, shit. I'm in town. You probably want to meet me for a gargle, pick my brain, gain some perspective on the unpleasantness out there in Dunlavin.

"Well, it can be arranged. What time do you think you can tear yourself away from the crime scene? I can come there, or you here. Makes little difference to me, although I am presently going over the proofs of the back story, as I mentioned. What's your pleasure?"

"How did you know about Mudd?"

"Touts."

"Touts where?"

"Do I yodel the first few bars of 'Here, There and Everywhere'? Written by John Lennon, another murder victim, as I remember. Christ, it's worldwide, isn't it? Sacrificial slaughter."

"You're in the Claddagh Arms, are you?"

"See—you have your touts too."

"Give me an hour."

"Granted."

McGarr rang off and dialed Hugh Ward at home.

13

FROM HIS LONG career as an amateur boxer, Hugh Ward knew that anger could be dangerous. It blinded you, made you drop your hands and lead with your head. It put what amounted to weights in your shoes.

And yet you couldn't prevent anger. You felt what you felt, and there was no escaping that. What you *could* do, however, was manage your anger, channel it, let the great surge of energy that came with it flow into proper places—the brain, the hands.

Problem was, the outrage he was feeling was personal outrage, not . . . professional outrage of the sort he felt on the job when confronted with a particularly ugly crime or heinous criminal. No.

The sort of anger Ward was feeling was more immediate and visceral. Dery Parmalee, who was holding forth at the end of the bar in the Claddagh Arms, had threatened the happiness of Ward's wives, as he now thought of Lee and Ruth, and the children he'd fathered with each of them.

And from what Parmalee knew about their living arrangement and what Ward knew about Parmalee, the man not only could, but one day would, make their lives front-page news. Which would destroy Ruth's and his careers with the Garda and make the lives of his children most difficult. Of that he was certain.

For not the first time in the last hour, Ward looked down at his hands, which any barrister worthy of his robe would denounce as lethal weapons in a court of law. All that needed to be mentioned was the fact that he had twice won the All-Euro amateur boxing title in the eighty-kilo weight class, which he had also dominated in Ireland for nearly a decade. Recently, in the gym, he'd had to pull his punches to keep himself from embarrassing the present champ.

Ward's dilemma was plain. He could do nothing, sit back, and watch the—scandalmonger was too delicate a term—at the end of the bar ruin their lives in a country where the collective mind forgot nothing the least bit compromising about a person. Especially a public person, as all police were in a direct way.

Or he could act and effectively give Parmalee additional evidence of his "way-Ward-ness" that would more immediately ruin their lives.

Ward's only option, therefore, was to impress upon Parmalee the fact that he was indeed a man who was good with his fists. And that in spite of his boxing background he was not afraid and would use them, regardless of the consequences, were Parmalee to print the slightest allusion to him or his family. He would make Parmalee's life a world of pain. There wouldn't be a morning Parmalee got out of bed that he wouldn't rue the day. *If* he survived. Ward's anger was that hot.

In a mirror, in the dining area of the pub—which was essentially one large room—he'd been watching Parmalee for over an hour. A tall man, at least six feet two or three, he was thin, with shoulders so square the ends seemed to function as mere hanging points for the blue blazer he was wearing.

Standing at the bar with hands inserted in the slit front pockets of his blue jeans, Parmalee was chatting up two much younger women, every so often throwing back his head to laugh at what appeared to be his own bon mot. The women were mainly listening and drinking, Parmalee every so often signaling the barman to provide further rounds, although he drank little himself.

Balding, Parmalee kept the steely hair that remained cropped close, and the skin of his pate, face, and hands was well tanned, as though he had recently passed a holiday in some sunny clime.

But as he rattled on—the octagonal glasses splashing light reflected from the globe lamps on the ceiling, his thin body bobbing as he "courted" the twosome at the bar—Ward decided that Parmalee did not live up to his billing. He was less the irreverent, successful publisher—"a kind of brilliant and restless scarab beetle adept at the most titillating and suspect form of quasi-journalistic coprology," said an assessment of him in a recent Sunday magazine—than a common barroom gobshite. Every pub had at least one—flap-jaw, motormouth, not interested in anybody's opinion but his own.

"We can't do *that*," one of the young women now said. "It's disgusting."

"Why not? As I said, I'll make it worth your while. If you're superstitious about the number three, there's always Bo over there." Parmalee snapped his head toward the largest man in the bar, who had been watching both Parmalee and Ward while nursing a pint of plain. "He's a man of daunting proportions in every way." With both hands, Parmalee chopped off fourteen inches of air. "I know for a fact that he could . . . handle all three of us, no problem, and still stand up and salute."

Plainly the two women were struggling to appear blasé, which could lead them down the garden path with Parmalee, Ward knew, having pulled his rap sheet earlier in the evening. A year ago nearly to the date, a woman had filed a complaint against him, alleging that, after meeting him there in the Claddagh Arms, she had accompanied Parmalee and two other men back to his flat. There he had drugged her drink and forced her to engage in group sex.

All three men, of course, swore they'd never seen her, and when a barman testified that she had left alone—Parmalee and the two others remaining until closing—the charge was thrown out. Outside of court, Parmalee told the assembled media gathered to report the out-come that he had found the entire experience "great *craque*, the very best advertising, which is free advertising, that *Ath Cliath* could get. There's nothing like living in a society protected by the rule of law. Don't you just love the way it safeguards the innocent?"

It was at that point that he turned his face directly into the cam-eras. "Therefore, I urge any other venturesome lasses who might have found my attentions excessive to come forth and file complaints. But this time, please, make it at least sporting. Bring witnesses."

Large, with weight-lifter muscles bulging under a blue blazer similar to Parmalee's that fairly shouted they were a team, Bo (or "Beau") Driscoll was the publisher's bodyguard, Ward assumed. And "bottom man," when needed in a pinch.

A pug in the super-heavyweight category who had once fre-quented the gym where Ward worked out, the large man had spe-cialized in baiting smaller fighters to climb in the ring with him. But no boxer, he waited until his opponents' arms tired, whereupon—usually—he'd flatten them with one punch. After a number of such incidents, the management barred him from the gym.

Yet Driscoll had never been foolish enough to fight on any level—amateur or professional—that would have paired him against somebody his size or larger. Which made him—what?—just another big, bloated bag of shite and a perfect match for a "brilliant scarab beetle."

And not as sure of himself as he had been in the gym. Now climb-ing off the stool to pass to the jakes, Driscoll fastened the middle but-ton of the blazer while staring over at Ward balefully. Could that slight bulge at the back of his spine be what Ward suspected it was?

Yes, he decided, as the "big fella" with the shaved head and soli-tary gold hoop in one ear returned to the bar a few minutes later. He had either not told his tailor about the cargo he'd be carrying, or the largest jacket off the rack was one size too small for the addition.

Ward stood and made his way toward the bar.

"Ah-sole," Parmalee said to the women, who turned to Ward as he passed.

"We have the heat amongst us tonight, ladies. Who will now entertain us mightily with his daring-do. But most probably don't, methinks."

Ward stopped well away from Driscoll. "Get off the stool and place your hands on the bar."

Driscoll turned his head slowly and regarded Ward, then turned back to the barman with the red face. "Know him?"

The barman shook his head.

"I do. A flyweight fook, he is. No fookin' balls at all. Boxes with headgear and big puffy gloves. 'Champ,' they call him where wee fellas prance and dance. Chump he is. And an arse-lickin' cunt."

The blow was telegraphed. Reaching a hand over to touch the shoulder of the other arm, Driscoll lashed out with a backhand chop that would have caught Ward in the side of the neck had he not dropped down. There in the shadow of the bar, he grabbed two legs of Driscoll's bar stool and jerked up with all he had, sending the large man sprawling across the bar. His pint glass splashed the barman before crashing to the floor.

The gold hoop came next. With one quick tug Ward ripped it from the ear, causing Driscoll to roar in pain and outrage.

Pivoting to swing from the man's blind side as Driscoll pushed himself off the bar, Ward darted a quick sharp punch into his upper stomach and felt the sternum collapse. Then, pivoting again on the ball of one foot, he kicked out at Driscoll's right knee, which collapsed under the blow.

As the man fell, Ward followed him down, making sure his bald head dunted squarely on the foot rail. Tugging up the jacket, Ward pulled what could only be a Tokarev from under Driscoll's belt. It was a large, heavy, Red Army–issue automatic of the sort that had been readily available for the decade since the collapse of the Soviet Union. Ward removed the clip, checked the chamber, and laid it on the bar.

Only then did he notice that Parmalee was gone. "Which way?" he demanded.

The barman hunched his shoulders.

"Which way!" he roared at the young women.

One pointed to the rear of the pub, where a door led into an alley.

There Ward caught a glimpse of Parmalee rounding a corner at a fast walk and lit out after him. Still quick after years of steady exercise, he caught up to Parmalee just as he was inserting a key into the lock of a tall commercial building.

"Yes, Inspector? Or is it Superintendent? I seem to remember you were promoted not so long ago. All the farther to fall, don't you think? Tell me, how is it that I deserve your suspect company?"

Ward waited until a car passed by before spinning Parmalee around and slamming him up against the door. "Spread 'em."

"Gladly. But wouldn't it be better upstairs?"

The pat-down yielded a cell phone, a miniaturized tape recorder, a reporter's notebook, a billfold, an electronic passkey on a spring clip, a ring of keys, and a Biro. The recorder was running. Ward switched it off and removed the tape.

"Should we call that a crime?"

Ward spun Parmalee back around. He wanted him to see the blows coming—the first up under the rib cage, the second slightly higher into the pectoral muscle, just to straighten the man back up. And then the other side. And again, both sides.

Ward knew how short, sharp punches hurt. Parmalee wouldn't be able to raise his arms for whole weeks without pain. Sleeping would be impossible, and even the very act of drawing breath would be a labor.

"Do your back for you?" he asked. " 'Big Red' thought I should. Sent me, don't you know." Yet again he spun Parmalee around and worked on his back—left side on the kidneys, and just under the blade of his left shoulder. And likewise the right. Two turns.

Without the punches to prop him up, Parmalee sagged to his knees.

"Tut-tut—try to keep the soot off your trousers," Ward admonished. "People might think you've been doing something naughty. And only you and I should know that you didn't slip and fall. How you had to pay for all these little items being found on your person."

From his own pocket Ward pulled a handful of glassine packets that contained two tablets each, stuffing some into Parmalee's jacket and letting some others fall to the ground. It was methylenedioxymethamphetamine, the euphoriant known as Ecstasy.

"Shall I ring up my colleagues in Drugs? I spared your face. You'll look just dandy on the front page of the legitimate newspapers. Think you can manage a smile? Which do you prefer—the *Times* or the *Independent*? Or don't you play favorites?"

"This is . . . illegal," Parmalee managed to say.

Which spiked Ward's anger—that Parmalee, who spurned and derided the rule of law at every turn, would seek its protection whenever necessary.

"Everybody knows . . . I don't do drugs."

"Do they? Not now. *Ath Cliath*, where you do your monkey business?" Ward waited until Parmalee opened his eyes. "How silly of you to keep part of your stash there and the other part in your flat. With the laws as they are, why—sure—you'll lose both."

Again Ward waited. Parmalee's gaunt but handsome face was a study in pain; his eyes were closed, his brow was knitted. Each labored breath was accompanied by what sounded like a whimper.

"Have I made my point?"

When he could, Parmalee nodded.

"And one other thing, you who know so much—who murdered Mary-Jo Stanton and Frank Mudd?"

"Gerry Breen," he managed in a small voice.

"Why?"

"Carrying out orders."

"From whom?"

"Duggan and Opus Dei."

"Why?"

"The biography."

"Which is?"

"Heresy. They just couldn't allow it to be published, because of Mary-Jo's . . . credibility."

"That he had fathered her?"

Parmalee nodded.

"Why Geraldine Breen?"

Again Parmalee paused to gather himself. "It's what she's been for Opus Dei over the years—an enforcer. Security. Muscle."

"Where is she now?"

He shook his head slightly. "You might try Delia Manahan's house in Killiney, the one she lived in before remarrying the Church. The two of them use it as a pied-à-terre."

"Why? What's Breen to Manahan?"

Parmalee tried to hunch his shoulders. "Maybe God doesn't answer all their needs?"

"You suggesting they're gay?"

"You've seen them—Butch and Biddy."

"You know that?"

Still leaning against the door, Parmalee raised himself up and opened his eyes. "Ah, go fuck yourself. You made your bloody point. Now piss off before I take both of us down."

A quick shot to the upper stomach buckled Parmalee up, and another between the shoulders slammed him onto the footpath.

Reaching up, Ward twisted the key and opened the door. By the collar of Parmalee's blazer and the belt of his trousers, Ward ran him into the darkness of a hallway and dumped him there.

Stepping back out, he closed and locked the door. But kept the key.

†

IT WAS FULLY NIGHT by the time Noreen and Peter McGarr arrived back at Ilnacullin. As usual there would be guests for dinner—they could tell from the array of house lights that winked at them through the avenue of beeches that lined the drive.

"Do you think my mother and father could ever live even a week without the company of others?"

"Sure, they'll have an eternity of that soon enough," McGarr blurted out, insensitively.

But he was tired, still sore and troubled by the events of the day— the death of Frank Mudd, or Manahan, the tape that seemed to show Mudd removing the water bottle, and finally, the way that information had been presented to him in such a . . . considered, no, such an orchestrated form by the two Opus Dei priests, Duggan and Sclavi.

More immediately, McGarr was hungry and in need of a drink.

"You believe that?"

He switched off the ignition and opened the door. The rich yellow house lights and the smell of burning peat beckoned.

"That in death we'll be alone?" she continued, climbing out. "And that my parents, God bless and keep them from all harm, are going to your oblivion sometime soon?"

McGarr could tell from the tone of the remark that she was as hungry and tired as he. "I didn't say that, did I?"

"Ah, but you did in so many words. I hope you're not . . . not wishing them gone?"

"You know better than that." But the truth was—they'd all be gone in what amounted to, and would be perceived as, a wee time.

It was as though, leaving school at eighteen, McGarr had blinked, and there he was, a fully middle-aged man, who was bald, running to fat, presently confused and out of sorts. Were he to blink again—well, he might never open his eyes.

"I don't know how I ever got involved with anybody with so little hope or vision" were her last words as they passed through the door into the brightly lit foyer.

Beyond, in the house, they could hear voices and laughter, and Maddie was coming down the stairs. "Well, it's about time," she scolded, one hand on a hip and her eyes narrowed, as her mother's would have been were the tables turned. "Nuala's been holding dinner for"—she glanced at her wristwatch—"twenty minutes at least."

Which was nothing in a house where entertaining was frequent and relaxed. McGarr could remember dinner being held for hours, when the conversation was lively or the guests had some pressing business.

The latter being the case, McGarr assumed, upon stepping into the sitting room.

"Well, there he is—the misnamed Peter McGarr," said a veritable bear of a man pushing his bulk out of the wing chair by the hearth. "H'ow are yuh, Chief Superintendent?"

McGarr reached for "Chazz" Sweeney's paw, which engulfed his own. "Misnamed in what regard?" he asked, if only to be polite.

Charles Stewart Parnell Sweeney—his complete and sardonically apt name—was a man whom McGarr thought of as more dangerous than any violent criminal in the street. Although only ever a Dail backbencher—and that time out of mind—Sweeney was said to virtually control the country through his contacts with the movers and shakers in commerce and industry. And connections with Fianna Fail, the political party that had exercised a virtual hegemony over the country since Independence in 1921.

Nominally the director of a private merchant bank, Sweeney had a small, drab office on the Dublin quays. But he was said to have been the bagman for an older group of politicians who had been exposed, publicly shamed, stripped of much of their known wealth and even— a few of them—placed in jail several years earlier. But not Sweeney.

The subject of innumerable articles, editorials, and supposed exposés by Ireland's media—including a long diatribe by *Ath*

Cliath—Sweeney was said to be so skilled at "engineering backhanders," in Parmalee's phrase, that "he would never be caught, no matter how well-conceived the sting."

Which had been tried and had failed. Sweeney had taken the Garda Siochana to court on an entrapment charge and won over a million pounds in damages, McGarr seemed to remember. Not much later, the investigating officer, who was a good friend of McGarr's, was sacked on a trumped-up charge of negligence in a matter where he himself had been entrapped. But could not prove it.

All the while, sitting behind a large desk in a dusty office with only one employee, Sweeney had maintained that he had nothing to do with the investigator's downfall and that his bank was his only source of revenue. Its privacy was shielded from public scrutiny by laws that his shamed cohorts had rammed through the Dail at his behest, *Ath Cliath* and other newspapers had noted. And because of that bank's holdings, which were unknowable but said to be vast, Sweeney still wielded great power.

And there he stood, as big as life, explaining, "Sure, your father should have called you Seamus instead of Peter. Because you're the veritable Seamus of Seamuses. The top cop in all of Ireland.

"Why the praise? Amn't I after being told—it's all over town— you've cracked another big one, and a nasty piece of business it was. Poor gentle Mary-Jo, a saint by any measure. And you bagged the villain before, *before* the crime was ever picked up by them gobshites in the press, led by that dung-beetle bastard Parmalee. Let's see what he'll write now about a holy order.

"Bravo, Peter"—Sweeney raised his glass—"you saved the country and the Church from a heap of not-needed embarrassment. Haven't we had enough of that lately?" Sweeney winked histrionically, obviously to mean some other of his acquaintances who were still being processed through the courts.

That Sweeney equated country and Church with his fellow

thieves and robbers, McGarr found interesting. But Sweeney was a guest, and McGarr had broken bread with the man during several large parties that his father-in-law had thrown in years past.

"Hello again, Chazz. But I fear you've been misinformed." McGarr glanced at Fitz, who raised both palms, as though to say—it wasn't me. "There's nothing conclusive yet."

Under bushy dark brows, Sweeney's rheumy eyes—reddened from whatever drink Fitz had already supplied—widened in disbelief. "Didn't the fella, the gardener there, the one that hung himself—it was him, sure, that done Mary-Jo, no?"

Noting Sweeney's grammar and his pretense of simplicity, in spite of degrees from Maynooth and some Spanish university, McGarr shook his head. "No. Or at least, we don't know yet. Too many questions left unanswered." Including how Sweeney, like Parmalee, could be privy to so much of what went on at Barbastro.

"Questions like what?" Sweeney asked, easing his bulk back into the chair.

"Peter—can I get you anything?" Fitz asked, playing the host and sensing McGarr's wariness of the man. "You must be knackered. It's been a long couple of days for you. Why don't I ask Nuala to draw you a bath."

"Why would you do that, when he has a wife who will do that for him?" Noreen said from the door.

Again Sweeney lumbered from the chair, to greet Noreen. After father and daughter had left the room, Sweeney said, "They care for you here."

As they should, being family, went unsaid.

"And we do as well." As befit a man of his size, Sweeney's voice was a low rumble.

McGarr studied the man's features—his nose, chin, and cheeks—which were also large. But his face was . . . meaty, McGarr decided—lumpy and ill-formed, as though some final smoothing process had been missed. Which only made the burn of his eyes, shadowed in deep sockets, seem more intense.

"We?"

"We who cared for Mary-Jo. Did you know that she was a close personal friend of mine and of many other prominent people—people like the former Taoiseach?"

Who had been disgraced but was still popular among the developers and large farmers whom he had enriched.

Leaning back, Sweeney twined his fingers over his significant chest. "And the less bloody bother we have about this, the better. We. Think." It was the message Sweeney had come to deliver.

"We might even just"—he shook his head and turned to the hearth, where the cracked red eye of a peat fire was hissing—"clamp a lid on this bloody thing. You know, limited press coverage. A simple release of the facts about this Mudd character, his criminal background and so forth. And have done with it. Finito. Over and good-bye."

Releasing information was McGarr's area of responsibility only when asked to do so by the commissioner. Otherwise, he stonewalled the press as a matter of policy.

Fitz appeared in the doorway with a drink for McGarr. "You okay, Chazz?"

He nodded.

"I'll leave you, then. Nuala needs me in the kitchen, don't you know." Fitz melted back into the shadows of the hall.

"What about the commissioner?" McGarr asked, meaning the head of the Garda Siochana. He sipped from the drink.

Sweeney flapped a large hand. "He's on board. I'll have him call you. Better—let's ring him up now." From out of a jacket pocket, Sweeney pulled a cell phone.

"Please yourself." McGarr wondered just how much *juice*—he believed the current term for influence was—Sweeney still had.

After listening for a while—his mottled eyes staring at McGarr unblinking, like the mask of a Gorgon—Sweeney lowered the phone. "Busy."

What—no voice mail, no message? No ring me back, please?

One take was: Sweeney's experience in the courts had chastened him, and he was wary of leaving his voice on tape. But it could also be that other politicians, of whom the commissioner was one—the post being a political appointment—were chary of such a controversial figure. Courtesy of Dery Parmalee.

But how to know that?

McGarr tugged on his drink.

A rather lengthy silence ensued, during which McGarr suspected he was supposed to avert his eyes from Sweeney's stony gaze.

"What about the *cilicio*?" McGarr asked, not sure that he had pronounced the word properly.

Sweeney had no problem with it. "The thing about Mary-Jo's neck? Ah, yes, that's your fallback position should the simplicity— and not the elegance—of murder/suicide trouble you and the other Seamuses on your staff."

Sweeney pulled his massive body up in the wing chair. "In that scenario—and I'm only putting this out here for discussion, Peter, mind?"

McGarr dipped his head once in agreement; he would hear the man out.

"In that scenario, which has a salient advantage over the first, one Dery Parmalee—bête noire, muckraker, nevertheless beloved by us all—is the perpetrator of both crimes. He worked Mary-Jo's death to implicate the larger us, about whom he was poised to write an exposé. All he needed was a 'hook,' or peg, as journalists say. A salient public event or occasion or—better yet—a murder to hang his excoriation of us upon.

"The second murder, then, the murder of Mudd? Why that?" Sweeney opened his large hands, before twining them over his paunch. There was now a kind of twinkle in his ravaged eyes.

"Why not? It only added proof of our capacity for blood and intrigue, that we would murder a perfectly—let us not say innocent—but an altogether agricultural sod to conceal our vicious and fatal attack on Mary-Jo.

"But would we as much as 'sign' her murder with a *cilicio*?" Sweeney's pronunciation of the word seemed rather more perfect to McGarr's ear than his own. "No—of course not. But Parmalee wanted to make it all seem patently obvious and"—the hands broke apart again—"journalistic. It's his game, after all."

Sweeney leaned forward. "Let's admit one thing between two men of goodwill, Peter. Parmalee is over the top. How much better we would be if he just . . . dropped off the face of the earth. Or some other great height."

McGarr took another sip. "How would Parmalee have got onto the property?"

"Barbastro? Hadn't he worked with Mary-Jo on writing projects in the past and maintained . . . ah, an amorous attachment to that comely person. Which was never, as he claims, mutual, I can assure you.

"Parmalee would have known the blind spots in the security screen, ways to conceal himself. Didn't he inform you himself, shortly after the murder, that he knew all about it because of eavesdropping equipment in his motorcar, which you later determined was a lie when you impounded the vehicle?"

How Sweeney knew that, McGarr could only guess. Was it possible that somebody on his own staff was an Opus Dei mole? Or could the commissioner or some other senior Garda official have taken a look at the daily reports, say, late at night when the desk sergeant was taking tea or otherwise occupied?

"Perhaps he had—*has*—such equipment in the flat that he has maintained over the chemist shop down in the village since his supposed liaison with Mary-Jo two decades ago.

"But one way or another, it puts him on the scene, doesn't it?" Sweeney looked into his now empty glass. "Fitz. Fitz!" he shouted, as though summoning a servant.

At length McGarr's father-in-law appeared in the doorway.

"Tell him what you told me about the flat Dery Parmalee maintains in the village."

Fitzhugh Frenche nodded sheepishly. "Chazz here and I were chatting, don't you know, about the whole Barbastro thing and how, this morning, I poked around down in the village, asking this one and that what they think went on. And didn't the chemist tell me your man Parmalee has maintained the flat over her shop since he worked on the book with Mary-Jo, the one about some saint.

"Now it's not like he lives there, mind. Over the years he wouldn't appear in a month of Sundays, the chemist says. But recently it's like he's moved in permanently."

Sweeney picked up from there. "The jacket that was placed over the lens of the camera in the garden? The one with the Stafford label. Parmalee could have nicked it from Mudd's cottage.

"The water bottle? Parmalee might have paid Mudd to remove it. What would it have taken? Twenty quid or a bottle of whiskey, I'm thinking.

"Or perhaps the two of them were in cahoots with each other until Mudd made some demand upon Parmalee, and Parmalee strung him up."

Sweeney swung his head to the fire.

Fitz remained in the doorway.

McGarr finished his drink and set the glass on the table beside his chair. "What strikes me, Chazz, is that you don't seem to care who killed either party or if, in fact, Dery Parmalee was responsible. Or if the murderer, the real murderer, will ever be caught. I could be wrong, but it appears to me that you're just looking for a convenient—"

"Solution to this mess?" Sweeney asked. "Right you are, Peter." Sweeney heaved himself to his feet. "Nothing can bring Mary-Jo or the gardener back. More's the pity. But as for Parmalee, if ever there was a candidate ripe for murdering or murder, 'tis he.

"Fitz, I won't be troubling you any longer, and I thank you for making your son-in-law available to my counsel, which, I trust, he'll value."

"But can't you stay, Chazz? Nuala's—"

"I'm afraid not. I'm expected at the Piggotts' instanter, and I can't be late, it being more business than pleasure, if you catch me drift." Lawrence Piggott was the chief justice of the Supreme Court. "Then it's off to Greece."

"Really, now? Ah, that's grand."

Sweeney handed Fitz his empty glass but turned his head to McGarr. "The wife is mad for the place, especially, I fear, all their bronzed gods."

"In the museums?" Fitz asked archly, playing the perfect host.

"Forget that—on the beaches, in the nightclubs. You know Breda, of course. A good Catholic woman. It's all imagination, I'm sure. But why she has to drag me through her midlife crisis is more than I'll ever understand."

"Don't you care for Greece, Chazz?"

Sweeney closed his eyes and passed some air between his heavy lips. "*Lawless* is the word. Do anything you want—drive on the footpaths, park on the grass. I don't think that country has felt a touch of civilization since they invented the concept a few thousand years ago."

The two other men laughed, and McGarr kept himself from noting that Greece, like every other civilization he knew of, proscribed murder and punished murderers severely. In the ancient world with stonings, he seemed to remember.

"That's a fine collection of weaponry you have there, Fitz,"

Sweeney remarked, passing toward the door. "But then, the lot of you are grand shots. Still have the skeet trap?"

Fitz nodded. "Noreen competes from time to time, but not me nor Nuala. Peter here is only interested in peashooters, but he does well enough with those."

In spite of the Georgian proportions of the doorway, Sweeney fairly filled the space. "I'll say good-bye to Nuala and Noreen, now. No need to see me out."

When Sweeney was out of earshot, Fitz explained, "I've no idea how long he waited for you. I was down in the village, and Nuala had gone riding with a neighbor. I walked in maybe an hour ago, and there he sat, larger than life."

They could still hear Sweeney's voice rumbling in the kitchen as he bade farewell.

"You know what this means, of course." Fitz's brow had knitted. "The fix is in, and I'd think twice about forgetting what was said here. If there's a piece of unlovely work in this country, it's Dery Parmalee, and in most circles you'd be judged a hero by putting him away. But"—he raised a palm—"who am I—or Sweeney—to tell you your business."

McGarr nodded and looked down into the sip that was left in his glass. Out in the hall, the phone was ringing. "Where's this flat of Parmalee's?"

"Down in the village? Shall I take you there?"

"After dinner." McGarr could not tell which was piqued more—his hunger or his curiosity—but the former, he judged, would be more quickly and easily satisfied.

Nuala appeared in the doorway. "Soup's on, gentlemen. And I've news for you, Peter—you've got a big bunch of company down at the front gate, Dery Parmalee just called to say."

"The press?"

"Television vans, klieg lights, the works."

McGarr wondered who, of the now many who knew of the double murder, had told them.

Parmalee? Why? Unless he was planning a special edition, *Ath Cliath* would not come out until Friday, which was three days off.

"Come eat your tea now," Nuala said, reaching for McGarr's arm. "You'll think better on a full stomach."

14

HUGH WARD'S ANGER had waned after his rousting of Dery Parmalee behind the Claddagh Arms. But the fear that had caused it—for his children and his "wives," he guessed you could call Ruthie and Lee—had not.

For himself, Parmalee's threat to expose them raised concerns only of what he'd do were he sacked from the Guards. He'd get by somehow—going into private or corporate security work would be easy, given his age and experience. Or he'd try something else entirely, perhaps even go into business for himself.

The spacious loft flat down on the quays that he'd bought for a song years ago was now worth a heap of money, given its drop-dead view of Dublin Harbor and its off-street parking. Apart from security checks, Ward had not set foot in the place for over a year. The sale of that alone would give him a good start in a new direction.

But that there were people like Dery Parmalee who preyed upon the foibles and—Ward supposed—the sins of others for profit and, in Parmalee's case, for perverse diversion still rankled.

Even if Parmalee exposed Ward, and Ward—in turn—set up and busted him, Parmalee's life would go on perhaps more agreeably, given the publicity. And with a high-priced barrister, Parmalee would spend only a short time behind bars and end up romanticizing himself, à la Larry Flynt.

Ward would probably never end up owning one of the select hillside houses that he could see through the windscreen of the darkened car that he had parked near the top of Killiney Hill. He'd probably never fully recover his public stature in a country where a word behind a hand was enough to damn a person, especially when the charge was sexual, and those matters were judged by unfeeling clerics who were self-consciously ignorant of the panoply of human emotion and experience.

No. He would only be the loser in any public dustup with Dery Parmalee, he decided, jotting down the make, model, color, and number plate of each of the three cars that he could see. But he would go out with a roar, not a whimper.

Switching off the dome light before opening the car door, Ward made sure the car was locked before ambling up the street, noting which of the adjacent houses had lights in their windows. What he was about to do was surely illegal, unless, of course, Geraldine Breen was presently in Manahan's house, as Parmalee had said.

At the top of the street, Ward paused for a while. It was a soft spring night. Out on the Irish Sea in the direction of Wales, a half-moon had just risen and was casting a fan of achromatic light across calm silver waters.

From that perspective he could see all the way south to Bray Head—a massive promontory—and the Big and Little Sugarloafs, two mountains that he had climbed often with Ruthie and would again with his entire crew, kids and all. He promised himself.

There was that, he now realized, which could never be taken from him. The mountains and the crescent sweep of buff beach that stretched out from the base of Killiney Hill, all the way to Bray. No matter what happened, he'd always be able to tramp the hills or bathe in that shimmering water. Which thought cheered him somewhat.

Walking back down toward the house that Delia Manahan owned, Ward pulled out his notepad once more and recorded the number plates of the other cars on the street. At the low wall that bordered Manahan's back garden, Ward vaulted the obstacle in one movement and found himself in the shadows of the house.

It had seemed almost modest from the street. But as he worked his way around toward the front, where he could see a light, he came upon a zigzag pattern of tall and wide windows that, he imagined, provided the front windows of the large house with a fractured 180-degree panorama of the sea, the bay, the wooded Shanganagh Vale, and the mountains in the distance.

What must the place be worth? Surely close to a million pounds. Had Manahan, as he had his loft, bought when prices were low? Or was her legal practice that lucrative and her financial commitment to Opus Dei not as complete as most critics assumed of numeraries?

The view from the wide deck that fronted the house was all that he imagined. The green port running light of a fishing boat that was motoring north looked like a brilliant emerald in a jade-colored sea. Now, as the breeze shifted, Ward could hear the gentle ticking of its engine.

Which was when Ward saw Geraldine Breen through a gap in a drape.

Wearing a housecoat, she was sitting on a divan with her legs folded under her in a position that resembled something from yoga. Yet she was watching the television.

The plackets of the garment had opened to display one decidedly taut breast for a woman of—how old could she be?—about Ward's own age, which was forty-two. The rest of her—emphasized by her erect posture and shoulder muscles that were testing the material—seemed similarly fit.

Even with the bandage plaster across her swollen nose, she was not an unhandsome woman, Ward judged, with regular features and blondish hair that had only begun to gray. What he could see of her stomach was a narrow washboard. She exercised regularly, he imagined. Strenuously.

The picture on the television changed to show McGarr in Noreen's Rover, politely but firmly declining to comment about anything, Ward could tell. One of the journalists pointed at his swollen face, doubtless wondering how it had happened.

While Breen was distracted, Ward decided to try the handle of the deck door. It was locked. But a strident klaxon began sounding at the side of the house, and in a flash Breen was up and out of the room.

Ward did not know what to do—smash his way into the house or rush toward the street to prevent her escape. She could hardly get down the mountainside with its nearly sheer drop to the sea. And now he was on firm legal footing, given the fact that she was wanted on a criminal charge.

But could she be armed? Is that what she had gone for? Could he have precipitated a gunfight or, worse, a standoff that would further involve the press? Ward did not want that.

Stepping back, he raised a leg and with three well-placed thrusts shattered the frame and was into the room, his Beretta 84 held before him. Cautiously he began moving through the large sitting room, the dining room, the kitchen, which was furnished with every class of modern convenience.

Until he heard a car door slam out on the street and the squeal of tires as a car roared away. She had taken the black BMW, the new Schwarzwalder model with the powerful V-12 engine that cost . . . what? Nearly sixty thousand quid.

Digging out his notebook, where he had copied down the number plate, Ward reached for his mobile phone to call it in.

✝

BY THE TIME McGarr located the chemist over whose shop Dery Parmalee rented a flat in the village of Dunlavin, it was well after midnight.

"This is really quite extraordinary," Joan Daley, the pharmacist, complained yet again, twisting the key in its lock.

Dressed in a housecoat, she had her dark hair studded with hot-pink curlers, and there was something like a meringue of mud on her face. The tops of her bedroom slippers were punctuated with blue pompoms. McGarr's phone call had got her out of bed, she had told him more than once.

Switching on the lights, she stepped back as though to let McGarr enter first.

"Please, lead the way," he said. "The more quickly we get this over, the sooner you'll get back to bed."

All chemist shops smelled the same, McGarr believed—a saccharine mélange of soaps, perfumes, and lotions with a hint of more powerful substances emanating from behind the counter where the prescriptions were made up.

But not all chemist shops contained what amounted to a little shrine in one corner with a barren cross and a devotional rail where waiting customers could kneel and pray.

"You're religious, I see."

"Which is none of your business." Using a key to open a door between the counter and the shrine, the woman switched on another light and again stepped away from the door.

"If you're going up there, you're going up yourself," she advised, her eyes bright with contempt. "You'll not make me a party to any police illegality. If you insist on violating Mr. Parmalee's privacy, you'll do it yourself over my stated objections."

Smiling slightly, McGarr nodded. "Perhaps you'd like to return to your bed. I could show myself out."

Her head went back. "I'll wait right here."

Not trusting him, McGarr imagined, because she knew herself too well.

The staircase up was dark and lined with stacks of books and magazines, one of which was dated six years earlier, he saw as the beam of his pocket torch slid over the cover.

And the flat was dusty. From the cobwebs in the corners and the dust balls on the hardwood floor, McGarr judged that the place had not been cleaned in some long time. At the top of the stairs, he found another switch.

The apartment was two long rooms following the T-pattern of the building, the larger, where he stood, being a work area. Tables, chairs for six, and three desks ran the walls, with what appeared to be a mini–command center in the middle of the space.

The collection of tables held a veritable array of electronic equipment—computers, printers, faxes, a telephone console, and the like. Along with a bank of other devices that McGarr only recognized partially but assumed were the electronic eavesdropping devices that Parmalee had lied about having in his car.

McGarr attempted to activate one of the devices, but nothing happened. Nor with a second and a third. Things were happening so fast in electronics that it was impossible for somebody not involved in the field to keep up with the advances.

It had taken McGarr a good fortnight to master the intricacies of his cell phone—voice mail, call forwarding, messaging, beeping, conferencing, and so forth—and his adolescent daughter sometimes had to help him open files sent via E-mail to his home.

The second room contained only a large, circular bed and a magnificent hand-carved armoire fronted with a tall mirror. Unlike the rest of the apartment, the glass sparkled, its purpose being—McGarr assumed—to present the occupants of the bed with a clear view of themselves. The bed was unmade and, from the arrangement of the pillows, had last been occupied by one person only.

In the armoire, McGarr found only a jacket and several pairs of trousers, with socks and underwear in the lower drawers, which had not been opened in some time. McGarr had to tap them back into place.

Between the mattress and its box spring, where it could still be felt, he imagined, but a pillow would cushion its shape, was a Sokolovsky .45 Automaster, the engraving said. Handguns were something McGarr knew well, and the large, heavy, and powerful gun was something of a rarity.

While its smooth lines probably did not disturb Parmalee's comfort much, it was the sort of weapon that could be pulled out and fired quickly. All controls, including the safety, were contained ingeniously within the trigger guard.

But at what cost. The last McGarr knew, the 3.6 pounds of an Automaster weighed in at close to fifteen hundred quid. Conclusion? The editor-in-chief of *Ath Cliath* slept in Dunlavin in fear of his life.

But since Dery Parmalee could not possibly possess a license to own such a weapon under Ireland's strict gun laws, McGarr removed the clip, checked the chamber, and slipped the gun under his belt.

Back in the other room, he looked for the documentation, all the instruction manuals, advisories, warrantees, and the like that inevitably accompanied electronic devices. Perhaps he could find out how to switch the equipment on.

Finding nothing of the sort in the filing cabinets or desk drawers, he began looking behind the machines for a dealer's sticker or something that might give him a lead.

Again he came up empty, except for a business-sized card under one of the machines that McGarr had switched on. Obviously rather old, with tattered edges, it had been taped to the surface of the table.

On it in tight script, somebody had written: M-J, 1; Duggan, 2;

Breen, 3; guest A, 4; guest B, 5, and so on through many of the rooms of Barbastro, McGarr guessed, including Mudd office, 14; Mudd cottage, 15.

With the blade of his penknife, McGarr cut the tape around the edges of the card and turned it over: "Dery Parmalee, Ph.D.," it said. "Publisher, Editor-in-Chief, *Ath Cliath*." And then in smaller type near the bottom, "Dear, dirty Dublin revealed for what she is—a strumpet and a whore."

Although jaded and over the top like much of what Parmalee's tabloid ran, it was not a new observation, Joyce and Plunkett having given voice to the thought during the last century, and Swift in his own way before that.

Down in the chemist shop, McGarr found Joan Daley waiting by the door.

"How long ago were those machines brought into the flat?"

Her eyes shied. "What machines? I don't go into Mr. P.'s flat. I have no idea what's up there, nor do I care."

"Surely he comes and goes when you're here."

"And when I'm not. He has a key."

"You trust him, then—with your shop?" And all the drugs it contained, went unsaid.

"*He's* a gentleman. Are you through?"

"Is Fred Duggan your priest?"

She opened the door and pointed toward the darkness. "If you mean *Father* Fred Duggan, that's none of your effing business. I hope I'm understood."

At his car, McGarr rang up Barbastro. "Fred—Peter McGarr here. I'll be there in five minutes. I want you to open the gate."

"Why?"

"I take it you're the executor of Mary-Jo's estate." It was a guess, but—

"That's right."

"Her will—you have it there?"

"Yes, but—"

"I want to see it."

"Oh, Peter, isn't this highly unus—"

"Five minutes." McGarr rang off.

IT TOOK WARD several hours to search Delia Manahan's house in Killiney. Beginning in the basement, he worked his way up.

What was plain from the outset was the woman's dedication to sport. Yes, she had two children, a girl and a boy from the look of the bicycles and other outdoor paraphernalia stored in the cellar, but much of the hiking, camping, even technical mountain-climbing equipment had to be hers. Ward counted over a dozen different kinds of hiking boots and climbing boots in the one woman's size.

Also, she fished both saltwater and freshwater, and hunted. Up in a rather large room off the sitting room that was dominated by an enormous television, Ward found heads of an emu, a water buffalo, and a leopard on the wall, all bagged by Manahan, as photos on a nearby table corroborated. There was also a glass-fronted and climate-controlled gun case that contained two large-bore hunting rifles and a number of fowling pieces.

Apart from hunting and fishing, seemingly alone—the men in the sporting pictures all appeared to be guides, from their deep tans or weathered faces and well-worn outdoor garb—her life seemed unremarkable.

She was religious, certainly, with holy pictures, crosses, and replicas of icons everywhere he turned. But that was not unusual in a deeply religious country. Many of the photos showed Manahan visiting Notre Dame, Chartres, Assisi, and the Vatican, with the other woman—Geraldine Breen—also present. In three, Father Fred Duggan had his arms around both, and from the shadow in the Vatican shot, it appeared as though Duggan had taken the snap of the two women.

Ward climbed the carpeted stairs to the bedrooms, hoping to find . . . what? Some telling detail, some memento, perhaps even a sheaf of letters too precious to be destroyed that would reveal who Delia Manahan was. What her involvements had been since—he knew from having questioned her—the death of her husband a decade before.

After all, it was in bedrooms that people spent the most intimate moments of their private lives, where they assembled themselves in the morning and regaled or composed themselves at night.

Among their undergarments, jewelry, family photographs, books, magazines, and sometimes correspondence, there was almost always something revelatory of character or tastes.

But there too, as in the photos on the first floor, only one event seemed to have changed how she lived her life—the death of her husband.

At the time, Manahan had been thirty-two or thirty-three, Ward judged, but the husband much older. Perhaps in his early fifties. While he was alive, all their cars were large, the house appeared to be under construction, and there had been other dwellings as well in some tropical clime where people—could they be servants?—had dark skin.

But after his death, the woman's image changed dramatically. Formerly decidedly chic, with a pretty face and a good figure, she suddenly abandoned stylish clothes and makeup.

Gone was her long, dark, and wavy hair and any attempt at stylishness. Instead she kept her locks close-cropped and almost mannish in cut.

As well, she appeared to have taken to wearing muumuus—what Ward's mother had called the shapeless shifts worn by some of her sister crones late in life. Sacks that concealed the woman's pleasant curves.

Sports bras that tightened her breasts to her chest but yet produced odd high crescents in her clothes became usual, slacks always,
and mannish footwear.

Perhaps it was then that she had entered Opus Dei, Ward
guessed. Geraldine Breen appeared often in those shots as well,
sometimes with Manahan's two children. Hiking, camping, and
climbing were sports that Manahan took up during that period in
her life.

From the look of their bedrooms, Manahan's children had since
grown up and left home. The closets were virtually empty, and the
posters of rock stars on the walls were dated. In the portrait of the
girl's field hockey squad from St. Columba's College, two were holding a banner that read "1996 Champs."

The caption also listed the names of the squad members, but
nowhere was a Manahan listed. Using what appeared to be the girl's
graduation portrait, Ward found her among her classmates, Mar-
guerite Foley being her name in that photo.

The name also appeared on the letterhead of some stationery in
the desk and was burned into the butts of the hockey sticks that were
hung crossed on a wall.

Obviously, Delia Manahan's husband, the father of her children,
had been Foley by name.

But nowhere—not in any of the several photo albums that Ward
had gone through and in none of the correspondence that referred to
the deaths of Manahan's parents, their burials, and the arrangements
of their separate wills—was a son mentioned. Or a Frank. Or perhaps
a stepson by the surname of Mudd.

In fact, Delia Manahan Foley appeared to have been an only
child.

Ward moved to the fourth and final bedroom, which appeared to
have been occupied by Geraldine Breen. An overnight bag was open
on the dresser, and the bedcovers had been turned down.

But Ward had only spread open the bag when he heard the sound of feet behind him and glanced up in time to see something descending at the end of Breen's fist—a sap, he guessed, as it smacked into his skull and filled his eyes with a blinding luminescence. Stunned, he staggered into the wall.

"Shame on your mum," she said. "Didn't she tell you it's not on to be rummaging through other people's belongings? Not acceptable at all."

Ward tried to straighten up, but his balance was gone.

"Did you find what you were after? Or can I relieve you of the need?" She was still dressed in the housecoat, which was tied with a wide sash, rather like a kimono.

As he staggered toward her, her foot came up with great force and struck him in the groin, nearly lifting him off his feet. When he buckled up, she whipped the sap across the back of his head, and he fell hard on the carpet

"So much for the Marquis of Queensberry," he heard her say, before the blinding light faded to nothingness.

FATHER FRED DUGGAN was waiting for McGarr beyond the stout gates of Barbastro, as he had been on McGarr's other visits.

"I've had a chance to think about this, Peter"—Duggan wagged his head—"and really, it's not right. Not by custom, not by law. The will should be sealed and submitted to a court, and—"

"It depends on whose law you're citing, Father," McGarr said, cutting him off. "If it's the law of right and wrong, where murder is wrong and right is discovering who murdered Mary-Jo and Mudd so they can be removed from society, then taking a peek at this will of hers is right, I'd say. Wouldn't you?

"Or is there some higher principle at stake here that I'm missing?" Driving at speed, McGarr nearly had them at the front door.

"I'm not sure it's purely a matter of black-and-white. If we were—if we *are*—called into a court of law, and some opposing lawyer were to ask just how you or I knew how Mary-Jo chose to dispose of her estate *before* the will was actually read, well then, we'd both be in the broth, wouldn't we?"

"You, surely. Me, I'd be condemned by some for being overzealous and applauded by others for my . . . doggedness, which has been said before. But"—McGarr stopped the car and turned to the priest making sure their eyes met, both being skilled in confessional techniques—"you know what's in it?"

It was plain Duggan wanted to look away, but that would be tantamount to an admission.

"You already peeked?"

The dark eyes still did not shy.

"Maybe you can tell me, and we'll avoid your moral dilemma."

McGarr studied the large man as he considered the suggestion—his matinee-idol good looks, with the square head, full shock of wavy dark hair, dark eyebrows, chiseled features, and even a dimple in his definite chin. He blinked once. "I'll agree to continue this conversation only because I believe, since you've just told me, that it will help you in your investigation."

Priest as casuist, thought McGarr, who slid the gearshift into neutral and switched off the ignition. "Good. Who gets the lion's share? Opus Dei?"

Duggan could not help it. As though McGarr had skewered a nerve, his eyes bolted away. "Mary-Jo—you have to understand—was extremely devout."

"What percentage?"

"Well . . . the bulk of it."

"What percentage?"

"Really, Peter—this conversation—"

McGarr let his eyes pass down the serpentine facade of the mansion. "What percentage?"

"I don't know. I haven't worked it out. Maybe eighty-five or ninety percent."

"And who gets the ten percent? How much money are we speaking about here?"

Duggan shrugged and shook his head. As though following McGarr's line of sight, he too was now staring up at the graceful structure. "We'll need a *full*—and I mean *complete*—accounting of that, surely, so as not to rely on estimates or speculation. I'm certain she had nowhere near what has been said, the press thriving on inflation and hyperbole as it does."

"Your estimate?" Landing the big fish of Mary-Jo Stanton's estate would certainly enhance Duggan's stature within Opus Dei, McGarr imagined. And he would know the figure.

Duggan sighed. "Really, I couldn't, I shouldn't say. But"—his hand reached out and touched McGarr's sleeve—"if I had to estimate, and it's just a guess, mind, Mary-Jo was probably a . . . billionaire." On the last word, the timbre of Duggan's voice rose.

"In pounds or dollars?"

"Either. Both."

"How did she come to accumulate such money? Writing books?"

Duggan shook his head. "Not entirely. She inherited this place and a substantial amount of money for the time. Without question, it was invested shrewdly."

"By whom?"

"Financial planners."

"A person? A firm? What are their names? I don't have two shillings to rub together," McGarr joked, "but I'll beg, borrow, and steal whatever I can and put it in their hands."

Duggan wagged his head. "Money gets money, we all know that."

And some more than others, McGarr thought. "A name. Who?"

"Well, there were more than one."

"The one being Chazz Sweeney."

That Duggan did not react noticeably to the name was telling, McGarr judged. He knew about—and he most probably had arranged for—Sweeney's visit to Ilnacullin earlier in the night.

"I don't know who in particular, but Charles Sweeney was a fast friend of Mary-Jo's."

"And Opus Dei's."

Duggan swung his head to McGarr. "That's not a crime, I hope. In your book."

McGarr shook his head. "I have no book, Father. Tell me the names of the others who will share ten percent of a billion pounds or dollars." McGarr turned to Duggan and made sure their eyes met. "You perhaps?"

Duggan nodded. "Mary-Jo wished me to live comfortably after her death."

"How comfortably? What's the number? Twenty-five? Fifty?"

"Well, she left me this house and most of the rest of her estate. But"—Duggan's hand came down on McGarr's sleeve—"she knew, because I had told her, that I plan to leave all I have owned in my life, which up until now has been next to nothing, to a charitable foundation that I'll set up within the Church."

"Meaning within Opus Dei."

Duggan nodded. "Which is to say, the Church."

Not as Dery Parmalee had seen it. "How much of the rest of it?"

"About one hundred million, I estimate. But everything could be higher, given what's happening to Ireland and . . . you know, the boom and all."

"Which leaves fifty million going to whom?"

"Various philanthropies, mainly."

"Geraldine Breen inherits how much?"

"Ten million pounds. She was Mary-Jo's best female friend."

"What about Dery Parmalee?"

Duggan's features suddenly glowered. "Lord knows I argued

against leaving that . . . Puck from the Dark Side a farthing. But M. J. said she respected his intelligence, if not his morals, and perhaps if he were to find himself financially secure, he might turn his talents back to spiritual matters. So I'll see that her wishes are carried out."

"And Father Sclavi?"

"*Nada, niente.* She had only just met him."

"Delia Manahan?"

Duggan shook his head. "I don't know why she left her out of the will, since they had been friendly for at least a decade. But again, it was Mary-Jo's wealth to do with as she liked."

"The gardener—Frank Mudd or Manahan?"

"Of course not."

"What about her literary estate, the books and manuscripts, the royalties and so forth?"

Again Duggan glowered. "I don't know the whys or wherefores of that decision either, because it seemed to me so . . . contrary to what Mary-Jo had striven for in her life, which was to illuminate Christianity with the new light of her intense scholarship and great wisdom. But all of that also goes to"—Duggan pulled in a breath and let it out slowly—"Parmalee."

"Did Parmalee know about the terms of her will?"

Duggan shook his head. "At least, short of her or one of her solicitors telling him or his breaking into the safe here in Barbastro—no."

"Anybody else apart from yourself and the solicitors?"

"Not that I know of."

"Right, then." McGarr pulled back the lever and opened the car door. "Now, I'll see the document, please."

"But . . . I thought you said you required only a summary."

"I'll see the document." Closing the door, McGarr stepped past Duggan.

"Shall I infer from this that you don't trust me?"

Infer anything you please, thought McGarr. "The document, please."

†

WHEN HUGH WARD finally regained consciousness just as dawn was breaking, he found himself sprawled facedown on the carpet in the bedroom of Delia Manahan Foley's house.

The wrist of his left hand had been shackled to his right ankle with his handcuffs. And the key ring, with its key to the cuffs—he noticed, when scanning the room—was looped tantalizingly over a bedpost.

With the use of opposing arm and leg, it took Ward the better part of four hours to crab himself up onto the bed, reach the keys with his free hand, and then—what was the excruciatingly difficult part—insert the small key in the tiny lock and twist the cuffs open.

By that time, he had a splitting headache, double vision, and he hoped he did not have a concussion, after the several others he had suffered in the ring and while on duty. Ward did not wish to spend his declining years punchy, like other boxers he knew.

But more troubling still were the whereabouts of his handgun, billfold, and mobile phone. Gone, of course, was Breen, her bag, and her personal items, which had been scattered around the room.

The phones were dead.

Outside, the tires of his car had been slashed and the radio disabled.

"Ah, shit," he said to the dashboard. His head was throbbing, his vision still impaired. "Shit."

PART IV

ETERNITY

15

NOREEN MCGARR was in the kitchen of Ilna-
cullin early the next morning preparing breakfast when the telephone rang. She answered it quickly, so as not to disturb the rest of
the family, who were still sleeping.

"Noreen, luv. How's by you?" intoned the deep masculine voice
on the other end. "Have you a fair day there, or is it pissing? Here,
it's simply pissing, pissing all over my holiday."

Which was immanent justice, thought Noreen, who despised the
practice of people phoning without the courtesy of announcing
themselves. Sublimely egocentric or, on the other hand, needy of val-
idation, they assumed even casual acquaintances would recognize
their voices on first hearing. If not, you loved them not, and immediately—even before any conversation was begun—you were guilty of a
social faux pas.

"Who is this, please, who believes he can ring up this number
at"—she glanced up at the clock—"seven blessed ten in the morning
and appropriate my first name so blithely?"

There was a pause, then: "Ooops. Noreen, it's Chazz Sweeney. Is
your man about?"

"Yes, Mr. Sweeney. He is about sleep, which is where he shall remain until breakfast. Would you like to phone back at, say, half past nine? I'm sure he'll be able to speak with you then. Or perchance you might provide me with your phone number, and he, my mahn," Noreen pronounced broadly, as Sweeney had, "will get back to you."

"Noreen, perhaps you didn't hear me. It's Chazz Sweeney."

There you have it, she thought. Mr. Control himself.

"I'm in Greece, and the time difference completely slipped my mind."

Was there a time difference? Noreen wondered. "May I take a message?"

"No. I simply must speak to him. It's imperative."

"That's not possible. Peter was up quite late last night and, in fact, for two nights running now, and he needs his sleep."

"Listen to me—I *must* speak with him."

Suddenly, Noreen was nettled, and she fought against the feeling, considering who Sweeney was—the "fixer" of Irish politics. Unfortunately, the Irish police were politicized at the very top of their administration, which inevitably filtered down through the ranks.

McGarr had weathered several changes in government, but so too had Sweeney, whose connections were reputedly potent, in spite of his checkered past. Or perhaps because of it. If Noreen had learned one thing from her well-connected father, it was that political insiders respected—no, they revered—survivors, hoping that they too could overcome their own indiscretions and illegalities.

Sweeney had done that in spades, it was said. But being no politician, Noreen did not have to honor that. "I'm sorry, sir. If you leave your—"

"You're not understanding me, Mrs. McGarr. It's imperative that I speak with him. *Now!*" he roared.

Noreen removed the phone from her ear and looked down at it.

"Do you care for your lives as presently lived?" Sweeney went on.

"Do you value your husband's position? Or are you simply an ignorant cunt!"

Noreen slammed the receiver into its yoke. After Sweeney attempted several other calls, she disconnected the line, which served the house from the kitchen and rang otherwise only in the front hall.

An hour later she plugged the phone back in, and it rang almost immediately. "Don't you dare hang up on me. Get that bastard on the line immediately."

Noreen placed the receiver on the counter, poured a cup of black coffee and a wee eye-opener into a snifter, and carried the two vessels up to her husband in their bedroom. There she woke McGarr and explained about Sweeney.

"Don't hang up, but don't say anything further to him either." Slowly, McGarr roused himself, drank part of each libation, then shaved and showered. After changing into fresh clothes, including shirt and tie, since inevitably the media would be snapping his picture or filming him coming and going, he went down to the kitchen.

There, too, he greeted his daughter and parents-in-law before picking up the phone. "If you ever dare speak to my wife like that again, I'll beat you bloody," he said into the phone. "And if you call here again today I'll file a formal complaint against you for harassment. Now, what is it you want?"

"Ah, shit—let's not stub our toe on this, Peter. I was only after wondering how you're coming on the investigation and if you've announced that the Mudd fella murdered poor Mary-Jo before killing himself."

"Remember my warning about phoning this number again," McGarr said, before ringing off.

Turning around, he found all eyes on him. "Now, shall we have breakfast?"

✝

DRIVING INTO DUBLIN, McGarr switched on the radio, and the news on every station led with Mary-Jo Stanton's and Frank Mudd's deaths, along with speculation that they were a murder and suicide.

Radio Telfis Eireann—the country's state-funded outlet—even featured an interview with a former Garda commissioner who wondered why no announcement had been made declaring the case "what it obviously is," and when that would happen.

Two other stations, which did not possess news-gathering staffs and borrowed stories from the newspapers, mentioned that print media were running the story on page one, and *Ath Cliath* had come out with a special "blowout" edition "splashing" the story.

Commentary included Parmalee's allegations regarding Opus Dei's *pillería*—all their supposed "dirty tricks" in Latin America and with the Vatican Bank—an excoriation of José Maria Escrivá, a capsule of Mary-Jo's biography of Escrivá, and a rather accurate summary of her will. McGarr wondered how long Parmalee had been eavesdropping on Barbastro from the flat in Dunlavin.

At his cramped headquarters in an old former British Army barracks within the gates of Dublin Castle, McGarr found a copy of *Ath Cliath* in the hands of most staffers and one on the desk in his cubicle.

Skimming it before the morning briefing, he wondered if Chazz Sweeney had been in contact with Parmalee before publication and what that conversation might have entailed.

If nothing else could be said about the man, Sweeney had his ear to the ground. He had to have known about Parmalee's planned exposé of Opus Dei and claim that its beatified founder was Mary-Jo Stanton's father. What threats had Sweeney uttered to Parmalee? Or what inducements not to publish?

Bernie McKeon entered the cubicle to take a seat by the side of McGarr's desk, where he would act as interlocutor between the morning-taciturn chief superintendent and the rest of the staff. They now filtered in, taking positions around the periphery of the desk.

McKeon glanced over at McGarr before shaking out the reports on his lap. "Now then, ladies and gents, the first matter of concern, obliviously, is the situation in Dunlavin that is unfolding on the streets of Dublin's fair city as I speak. You've all read the papers, scanned the reports, speculated unprofessionally about same without waiting for the facts that would help make your puerile observations more accurate and less *Ath Cliath*–like."

"Just give us the facts, man," said Bresnahan across the lip of her teacup.

"Nothing but the facts," another added.

"And less of your Ass-*Cliath* verbiage," she added.

McGarr cleared his throat volubly and reached for the cup before him.

"First, we have the complete postmortem report. It says factually that the 'silly-sea-oh' was applied to the poor woman's neck before she died of a massive dose of digitalis that she had drunk sometime earlier. Which opens the question of—"

"Why a murderer who had already administered a fatal dose to his victim would then apply an instrument to her neck that could also have caused her death," mused Bresnahan. She was wearing a puce tank top and sweats that fit her snugly. The stone of the brooch that hung on a silver chain around her neck was the smoky color of her eyes.

"Maybe he just wanted to make sure she was dead," said Swords, who was seated on a table along with two others. Given the size of the cubicle and the nearly dozen staffers, the meeting resembled a scrum. "Murderers, as we know, always try too hard."

"Then why didn't he just throttle her with his hands?" said another.

Said Ward, "Because the murderer was sending a message, and that message was religious."

Maybe Parmalee, thought McGarr, attempting to inculpate Opus Dei with the help of Frank Mudd. How else could he have installed listening devices in Barbastro and Mudd's cottage? Hadn't Mudd said he was banned from the house? McGarr would have to ask his sister, Delia Manahan.

"We can only assume that it was Mudd who removed the water bottle that—we also assume—delivered the digitalis. Said water bottle had the logo and name of G. Bass Outfitters stenciled on the front. A white plastic bottle with a black seal cap and drink nipple."

McKeon sipped his coffee. "As for the jacket with the Stafford label that was placed over the video camera, we only have the word of Father Fred Duggan that it was Mudd's, bought him by his 'sister'—and I use that designation provisionally—Delia Manahan."

"And you should use the name Manahan provisionally as well," said Ward.

"The jacket has not been found."

McGarr made a mental note to question Manahan about the jacket as well.

"Also, Mudd's name *was*, in fact, Mudd and not at any time Manahan. He was born Francis Jerome Mudd in Wexford. He expired the same.

"According to Superintendent Ward"—McKeon turned a page—"Delia Manahan, on the other hand, was also born as she presently bills herself, but for a time lived under the rubric of Delia Foley. That was when she was married to F. X. Foley, solicitor and supposed blackmailer, who was himself murdered a decade ago in his office in Fitzwilliam Square."

McGarr's head came up from his coffee cup.

"You'll remember the case, Chief—the office had been scoured, every trace of his law practice removed. And still unsolved."

McGarr did, it was where he had seen Delia Manahan Foley before—when he had interviewed her about her husband's involvements.

"I believe Brother Hugh has a homily to deliver."

As Ward began a somewhat expurgated version of his encounters with Dery Parmalee at the Claddagh Arms and later Geraldine Breen at Manahan/Foley's, McGarr recalled the details of F. X. Foley's murder, which remained unique—death by CPU. The murderer had disabled Foley, a man in his early fifties, then dashed the central processing unit of the office computer into his head. Several times.

All files—every trace of his law practice—had then been removed. Where his file cabinet had sat, a square of greener carpet was left. And every other scrap of paper, computer floppies in a console, even the waste paper baskets, had been purged.

Also, there had been no indication that robbery was the motive for murder, since in an office closet they discovered an array of pricey photo equipment, including several long lenses that pull in shots from afar.

Foley, McGarr later learned through a tip by an anonymous letter, had been a blackmailer, which his lifestyle rather suggested. With houses on Killiney Bay and in the Azores, a trophy wife and an even younger mistress, two expensive cars, horses, and holidays but no real law practice as documented in any public records that McGarr could discover.

McGarr remembered interviewing Foley's fetching young widow in their Killiney home. She said she knew nothing of her husband's professional involvements. She'd had her children and her houses to take care of, and she'd left "the making of money to F. X.," he could remember her saying.

"He was such a gentle man in the best sense," she had gone on. "Do you know what his hobby was? Photographing songbirds. Tiny, shy creatures that you can only see from a distance. Everywhere we went—Madeira, the Midi—he'd take his binos and cameras. Birding gave him such great pleasure, and I thank God he enjoyed himself while he could."

And McGarr could remember her saying one other thing: "No

sin goes unpunished. Ultimately." Her final words to him as he had walked from her terrace toward his car.

"Breen must have planned an escape route," Ward was saying. "But it was my mistake. I should have requested backup the moment I caught sight of her through the gap in the drapes. She slugged me and took my Beretta, keys, and cell phone. Then she slashed the tires and trashed the radio in the car. And finally"—Ward raised his hands—"she left me shackled with my own cuffs in the bedroom. Opposite ankle to wrist. It took me hours to get free."

McGarr now remembered Dery Parmalee's description of Geraldine Breen—that in addition to managing Barbastro, she provided security there as well. He glanced down at his wrist where she had struck him with the martial arts baton. It was still swollen and sore.

Ward had finished his report of his run-ins with Parmalee and Breen. "I took the liberty of making a copy or two of the key to Parmalee's place, in case we need to interview him again." Ward put two of them on McGarr's desk. "I have the original.

"Granted he'll arrange to have the lock changed sometime soon, but at the moment he seems to be occupied with other matters." Ward settled back in his chair.

"Recap," McKeon continued. "Mary-Jo Stanton was murdered when, supposedly, she drank from a sports water bottle laced with digitalis. Before she could die, a sports jacket was hung over the lens of the security camera, and a—"

"*Cilicio*," Bresnahan offered.

"—yet another sporting item was tightened around her neck to make it appear as though she'd been strangled by that instrument of priestly self-abuse. But she died from the digitalis.

"After the coat was withdrawn, and Mudd, supposedly, went to Mary-Jo's side and found her dead, suddenly the video shows the fatal water bottle missing. Only Mudd could have taken it.

"Mudd, however, in his interview with Peter appeared to be

merely your common agricultural sod with a criminal past who had—"

"If you say *gone to ground*, Bernie, I'll—"

"—buried himself there at Barbastro. His crime? Lookout for an armed robbery team over in the States. In a plea bargain, he grassed on his co-criminals and, knowing them all too well, believed he should subsequently go to ground."

Bresnahan shook her head.

"Permanent, like. We all know his fate—four sheets to the wind in the seed room, having been hoisted on his own come-along."

"*Four* sheets?" somebody asked.

"The three that loosed him onto the rocks that we found in a glass beside his corpse. And the fourth that strung him up."

"Now that's a stretch."

"Questions: One, could he have accomplished the feat on his own in his condition, which was jarred? Two, how could a murderer, not possessed of significant strength, have helped him along? Cranking the lever of the come-along would have required muscle.

"There's the matter of the nifty and appropriately titled 'blood hitch' that was tied to the hook of the come-along. In other manipulations around the estate, Mudd seemed capable of only the half hitch and unimproved clinch knot, according to a memo by Inspector Swords, who sails.

"Also, we have the complications of Dery Parmalee, who seems to know all, courtesy of the bugs he deployed around Barbastro. He, as we know from today's *Ath Cliath* and an earlier report by Peter, is not a disinterested party, pursuing a . . . vendetta, it would seem, against Opus Dei and being capable of every class of troublemaking. I have that on good authority."

McKeon's eyes glanced off Ward's. "Consider, as well, the priests, Fred Duggan and . . . Sclavi, who like all people from his neck of the woods has eyes either like a hangman or a pelota player."

"I beg your pardon," said Sinclair. "My mother is Spanish."

"Really?" McKeon paused dramatically, canting his head to one side. "Which team does she play for?"

The grumbles and complaints were immediate.

"Setup," one said.

"That joke is *older* than yehr mudder."

"In ahn-ny case," McKeon went on in broad Dublin tones, "one of the collars, Duggan himself, stands to gain millions with Ms. Stanton's death. With by far the biggest beneficiary being Opus Dei.

"They were on the premises, Duggan had control of the security system, and again Peter reports"—McKeon shuffled the documents until he found yet another report—"Duggan has no aversion to pork." He looked up and scanned the small room, his dark eyes merry.

Ward shook his head. "Bernie, you've used this before."

"I have? When?"

"Only last year."

"Well, don't ruin it then. You seem to be the only one who remembers."

Said Bresnahan, "The report says that Duggan's demeanor, both when seeming to remember the existence of the security system and its tapes, and later, when telling Peter how he searched his copies and noticed that Mudd had removed the water bottle, seemed rather histrionic. Ergo, Duggan was . . ." She paused so the others could join her.

"Hamming it up," several said together.

"I like yous," said McKeon. "Yous have got potential and a certain . . . shtick sense of humor. Which brings us to Geraldine Breen, who we can conclude is prone to violence and is often good at it. And Delia Manahan Foley, about both of whom we just heard Superintendent Ward speak. Both were present when the Stanton woman was slain. Yet only Breen will benefit from her death. Manahan is not mentioned in the will.

"Finally, Peter has filed yet another report regarding Charles Stewart Parnell—'Don't-call-him-Apeneck'—Sweeney, who, you should know, has tried to butt into the case. It seems said sempiternal bagman and hale-fellow-well-wet has turned detective and knows definitively that Mudd did Stanton and then did himself. Over and out, case closed. We might expect more of him.

"So"—McKeon straightened the reports and, reaching over, placed them before McGarr—"who done it?"

"Acting for Parmalee, Mudd did Stanton, then Parmalee did Mudd," said Bresnahan, doodling on a notepad.

"Why would Parmalee want Mudd dead in a manner that looked like suicide?" Swords asked. "If the purpose of his shrift, as detailed in today's *Ath Cliath*, is to blacken the name of Opus Dei?"

"Two things," said Sinclair, a handsome older man with silver hair and precise features. "To shut him up and also make it look like an impossible suicide, a murder masked as suicide. We're dealing with a smart—perhaps a brilliant, but definitely bent—man in Parmalee. He knew Opus Dei with its Sweeneys would jump on Mudd's supposed suicide and want to wrap everything up in a neat packet to quell any suspicion of their involvement and close the investigation into Stanton's death.

"And from his listening post in the village, Parmalee would have been monitoring both our investigation at Barbastro and whatever went on between Duggan, Sclavi, and Manahan, perhaps phone conversations with Sweeney, and whoever else they consulted. He would have known the level of their concern."

"But how would he have got onto the property to do it."

Sinclair shrugged. "Didn't Duggan tell Peter that he'd deactivated the security system? Parmalee also said he'd spent some time at Barbastro writing a book with Stanton. He hinted broadly that he'd been her lover.

"Given the . . . snoop that he is, Parmalee could easily have discovered Mudd's past and blackmailed him into doing what he wished. Also, he would have known Mudd's weakness for whiskey, and Mudd would have drunk with him, if only for the free liquor. And finally, I think it would have taken the strength of a man to have strung Mudd up."

"You're all wrong," said Bresnahan, whose drawing was that of a corpse hanging from a rafter. "It's the two women, Delia Manahan and Geraldine Breen. They have a relationship, that much is plain, living together in two places, taking trips together, even co-mothering her children when they were younger.

"I don't know what sort of relationship they have, sisters in the spirit or the flesh, but it doesn't matter. They were there and could have worked in concert, orchestrating both deaths."

"But we know Mudd removed the water bottle," said Ward.

"And what's their motive?" McKeon asked.

"Mudd could have been brought into it by Manahan. Didn't Peter say in one of his reports that Noreen noticed evidence of a woman—a brassiere, a lid of birth-control tablets—in his cottage that had disappeared after his death?

"As for motive, the millions of pounds that Breen was bequeathed would be enough for the two women to retire in great comfort for the remainder of their lives."

"But why murder the woman?" Swords asked. "And why in that fashion? She was elderly, she wouldn't live forever. And we can't assume that either woman knew—knows—the terms of the will."

"Also, Breen is a . . . wombat," Ward put in. "A zealot of the worst sort who—Parmalee claims, and Peter and I can tell you—has been trained to enforce."

Silence ensued, and the others looked toward McGarr.

He glanced up at Bresnahan and raised his coffee cup, meaning he'd like more. As the most recent addition to the staff, she was the gofer. It was too early—in the day, in the case—to form conclusions.

"What else have we got pending, Bernie?"

McKeon picked up another folder from the stack on the floor by his feet.

NOREEN MCGARR HAD planned her morning to be anything but dull. First, she would take a long ride with her mother and daughter. Maddie was becoming a fine horsewoman.

Later, she would shoot skeet with her father, who had been an excellent shot himself and was her shooting coach. Noreen harbored ambitions of entering the competition to represent Ireland in the over-forty European women's championship that would be held in Denmark in the fall.

But it was while she was finishing up the breakfast dishes—and she knew the others were down at the stables—that she got the distinct impression somebody was in the room with her.

Turning around, she found Delia Manahan in the doorway. "Ooo—you startled me. How'd you get in here?" Noreen reached for a dish towel.

"The front door was open. I called out, once, but I don't think you heard me. You were busy with breakfast, and I decided not to disrupt you. I waited in the sitting room."

"Really?" It had been a good half hour since breakfast. "And how may I help you?"

"I'd like to have a confidential word with you, if I may. Which is why I came here. Barbastro really isn't secure, if you know what I mean."

"A word regarding what?"

"My relationship with Opus Dei and my . . . friend, Geraldine Breen. I rather got off on the wrong foot with your husband yesterday and thought perhaps you and I might chat more easily."

Which sounded reasonable to Noreen, having been with McGarr

during that painful noninterview. "Let's go into the den where we won't be disturbed if my family comes in."

As they passed down the long hall to the other end of the house, Delia Manahan admired several of the furnishings. "Has Ilnacullin been in the family long?"

Noreen shook her head. "My father bought it as a near ruin from a family who had squandered their fortune on race horses."

"Hence the vast stables where I parked my car."

Noreen nodded. "Actually, they've come in handy now that so many more people can afford horses but have no place to board them."

"What about all this weaponry?" Manahan swept her hand at the gun cases that lined one wall of the den.

"Actually, the guns are mine and my father's."

"Oh, that's right. I read it in the papers. You're the left-handed gunwoman."

The word, which had been used in decades past to describe women members of terrorist organizations, made both of them laugh.

Noreen gestured a hand to a chair and sat across from the woman. "So."

"So." Manahan drew in a breath, her hands twined at her waist in a way that emphasized the expanse of her bosom. "So, I entered Opus Dei almost a decade ago, after my husband was murdered."

Noreen's eyes widened.

"Gerry, who had been a client of F. X.—my husband was a solicitor—came to the wake and funeral and was very helpful to me and my children. And later, when we were grieving. She was an assistant numerary, as she is now, and very religious." Her light gray eyes met Noreen's. "Belief, you know, provides the only solace."

Noreen nodded, imagining that belief could be a great help during trying times.

"And over the years, Ger' and I have become the closest of friends. She even has her own room in my house in Killiney."

"And you at Barbastro."

"*But*—don't get the wrong idea. The relationship is strictly platonic and religious."

Manahan could be a pretty woman, Noreen judged, studying her. *If* she didn't insist on such a severe image.

She was wearing a plain gray suit with what looked almost like a clerical collar. On her feet were a pair of silver Mary-Janes. The plucked eyebrows and absence of makeup or jewelry only added to the effect. On her wrist was the sort of functional watch that you could buy in an electronics shop.

"Now, this is what I came to tell you, so you can pass it on to your husband. Dery Parmalee murdered Mary-Jo and—I suspect— Frank Mudd."

"Your brother."

Manahan's eyes canted off. She shook her head. "He's not my brother, either. But it's because of Frank that I know Dery killed M. J. You see"—she paused dramatically, raising one of the crescents of flesh that had been an eyebrow—"Frank told me in confidence that Dery had forced him—blackmailed him—into helping him do it."

Noreen waited, as she knew McGarr would in such a situation. The woman had more to tell her.

"You see, after my husband died and before Opus Dei came into my life, I needed . . . I don't know what I needed, but holding on to somebody of a night seemed like at least a temporary answer. And there was Frank, whom I hired to do all the things around the house that I couldn't. I was so . . . needy I even grasped at the straw that he had the same first name as my husband." She shook her head, as with shame and regret.

"Fortunately, he emigrated to America and I discovered that it was belief—and not a man—that I truly needed. But when he returned about five years later, he told me his tale and how he was afraid for his life. He begged me to take him in, and when I wouldn't because of my religious commitment and my children, he begged me to help him in some way.

"I thought immediately of M. J., whose gardener had just passed away. It was Frank's trade, and behind those walls he'd probably be safe. Well"—the eyes rose again—"I admit I lied to Mary-Jo, telling her Frank was a half brother, a by-blow of my father. Being a by-blow herself, I knew she'd fall for it.

"But that utter . . . bugger, Dery Parmalee, found him out and used him first to plant listening devices in the house, and then to murder M. J. in an attempt to lay the crime on the doorstep of Opus Dei—that's what the *cilicio* was all about.

"Frank told me he disabled the camera with his jacket and on Parmalee's instructions wrapped the ghoulish thing around her neck, twisting the clamp down until she was dead.

"How Dery murdered Frank, I can only guess. But as his *Ath Cliath* tells it, *somebody*—meaning somebody from Opus Dei—got Frank drunk, then made it look like he cranked up the come-along himself and committed suicide."

"*Ath Cliath?*" Noreen asked. "That paper doesn't come out until Friday."

"Special edition. It's all over town today, a thick thing both literally and figuratively, with allegations that we Opusians murdered Mary-Jo to keep her from revealing that she was actually the daughter of José Maria Escrivá, our founder. Then we made Mudd's death appear to be a suicide.

"He even claims he possesses the manuscript that Mary-Jo was about to submit to her publisher—a biography of Escrivá in which she documents his paternity. Parmalee says he'll be publishing a chapter of it every week, beginning this coming Friday."

"Does he say how he got ahold of it?"

"It's right on the front page—she gave it to him, he says, because she feared for her life. He claims he's even got a letter from her to prove it."

Surely a publishing coup, thought Noreen. And what an irony.

Considering her will, instead of Opus Dei's garnering another huge windfall by publishing an expurgated version of the book, Parmalee himself—Opus Dei's bête noire—would certainly reap thousands, if not millions, while hoisting the religious order on the petard of its founder's supposed sin.

Add in her murder and Mudd's either staged or actual murder/suicide and . . . well, the drama of it all was delicious. But perhaps too good to be true, were Parmalee found to have murdered them both and stolen the manuscript, as Manahan's allegation seemed to suggest.

But somebody had been present in Mary-Jo's quarters on the top floor of Barbastro when McGarr had entered to investigate. It was then that Geraldine Breen had attacked him, allowing the other person to escape. The place had been searched and the painting of Escrivá stolen along with all files dealing with him and supposedly the manuscript of the biography.

Could it have been Parmalee?

"When did Mudd tell you about Parmalee?"

"After you interviewed me yesterday."

"How?"

"I rang him up at the cottage. I admit that he wasn't entirely coherent, he sounded a bit drunk. But I have never—make that I never, *ever*—heard Frank Mudd utter an untruth."

Although evidently Mudd had lied to Peter more than once, Noreen thought. "Why did you phone him?"

"Because, after the questions you asked, it occurred to me that he had to have something to do with her death. Nobody else on the property would have had any cause to be anything other than grateful for Mary-Jo's beneficence."

Without doubt a holy thought but innocent in the extreme, given the will, in which millions of pounds of motives for murder abounded. "May I ask one other question?"

Manahan nodded.

"Did you ever give Frank Mudd a Stafford jacket?"

Wide-eyed, Manahan shook her head. "I did give him a Burberry with a matching hat. But that was years ago, before he emigrated. I should imagine it's history by now."

16

THE DOOR OF THE chemist shop in Dunlavin was standing open at noon when McGarr and Ward arrived with an order to search and/or confiscate the listening devices that were illegally monitoring Barbastro from Parmalee's flat.

After perusing the document, chemist Joan Daley handed it back to McGarr. "I can't make head nor tail of that gobbledegook. All I know is—I let the flat to Mr. Parmalee, who pays the rent like clockwork, and neither of you is him. End of story." Her makeup was only somewhat less obvious than the cosmetic mask she had worn on the night before.

"As far as I'm concerned, you go up there, you're breaking the law. Again."

McGarr was already halfway up the stairs with Ward in his wake.

"I'm going to ring up Mr. Parmalee this very moment, as I should have last night."

"Do that. And ask him to join us. We've a few questions for the man."

At the table that held Parmalee's array of equipment, McGarr let Ward take over, electronics being rather a generational pursuit.

"As I suspected, Parmalee recorded what he picked up on flash cards." Ward pointed to the several slots on what McGarr supposed was a recorder, then held up one of the recording cards. "As you can see, they're tiny, eminently portable, and easy to conceal.

"But because Parmalee couldn't be here all the time, he probably used this computer here"—Ward pointed to the CPU that had been placed on the floor beneath the table— "to monitor key words."

"You're coddin' me."

Ward shook his head. "It's done all the time, has been for . . . at least the decade since voice recognition was perfected. We can get some yoke from the Tech Squad to come out here and figure out which words, but I'd bet some were all those things he claims to know about Opus Dei and Escrivá, the founder."

McGarr made a mental note to notify the Tech Squad. "For the moment, let's see what we can pick up."

Flipping several toggle switches, Ward soon located voices—several people at prayer. While they chanted, McGarr had Ward run him through the procedure of switching between the monitors in the rooms of Barbastro, before saying, "I think I'm okay now. See if you can locate Parmalee."

"But how will you get about if I have the car?"

"Noreen. I'll ring her up. Failing that, I'll walk. It's only just up the road. And remember—what we want is a copy of the letter from Mary-Jo that Parmalee said accompanied the manuscript and a copy of the manuscript itself, if possible.

"If he won't give you that"—and McGarr had little hope Parmalee would allow anybody to copy the biography that he planned to run chapter by chapter in *Ath Cliath*—"you at least want to eyeball it, feel its heft, turn the pages."

"Examine the bibliography, footnotes."

McGarr nodded. Since she was renowned for her scholarship, any book of Mary-Jo Stanton's would be laden with attribution.

They had gone over the plan in the car on the drive out from Dublin: Ward would find Parmalee and demand he display the letter and manuscript. It would give Ward some idea of where Parmalee was storing the items.

Later they could obtain a search warrant. Had Parmalee been the person who tossed Mary-Jo Stanton's quarters on the night of her murder and stole the portrait of Escrivá—to say nothing of the manuscript—he might keep the two items together in some safe place. That way he would have *art*, as journalists termed graphic representations, when he began running the biography in his paper.

"If you suspect it's nearby, bust him. We'll toss the place and take our chances." With the law, which the highly litigious Parmalee was sure to invoke.

After Ward had left, McGarr removed his jacket and loosened his tie. As he'd been shown, the channels could be controlled with a clicker, meaning that he did not have to sit by the controls.

Pulling back the heavy drapes that kept the room in near darkness, McGarr raised the shades and discovered that the windows provided a rather fine view of Barbastro: the cottage in the copse, the garden where Mary-Jo Stanton's corpse had been discovered, with the large chalk-white house in the distance across an expanse of chartreuse lawn. Fountains plashed at four separate sites, and a wing of eider ducks, pausing on their northward migration, alighted gracefully in the pond by the stables.

As he listened for the first hour, McGarr conducted a second exhaustive search of the premises, discovering nothing additional other than a Swarovsky spotting scope and tripod that Parmalee had hung from a hook high up on the wall of a closet off the main room.

Positioning it in the window that looked out on Barbastro, he found that the most powerful of its three lenses placed him virtually on the front steps of the large white house.

Meanwhile, he listened to Fathers Duggan and Sclavi conversing mainly in Spanish about the arrangements for Mary-Jo's wake and funeral. Most phone calls were conducted in English.

Because of the autopsy, the casket would be closed, McGarr

learned during one call. "But only the faithful will be allowed in, the faithful alone," Duggan mused. "By invitation. I'm drawing up the list to be taken round by messenger." Silence ensued, and then, "I know, I know—it's hugely distressing. But, as you're wont to say, no sin goes unpunished. Ultimately."

McGarr turned his head and glanced at the bank of electronic gear. Duggan was probably speaking with Delia Manahan. The conversation was soon completed.

And then, about two in the afternoon, as McGarr was tracking Duggan's voice from room to room, he heard Sclavi inform Duggan that he had a call, *"en el teléfono seguro."*

Duggan waited until the door closed, McGarr could hear, before picking up. "Hello." And then, after listening for a rather long time, "I know, Chazz. I know. There was nothing we could do, no way to stop him."

Another pause. "You have to understand, Parmalee has been chewing on this since we convinced Mary-Jo to banish him. Given how . . . erratic and vindictive he is, it was inevitable that one day it would come to this. Didn't we discuss this before Mary-Jo's death?"

Yet another long silence reigned before Duggan said, "Well . . . I don't want to know how that could happen. Also, I think this conversation should come to an end. I'm a man of the cloth. . . ."

After still another lengthy pause, Duggan added, "I should remind you whom you're talking to." A few seconds went by. "I'm going to hang up now. I'm hanging up. I think we should speak at some other time, when you're more yourself."

And after McGarr heard the receiver hit its yoke, Duggan roared. It was a deeply masculine burst of displeasure. Before—could it be?—he began to cry.

McGarr aimed the clicker at the equipment and jacked the volume to the max.

Yes, Duggan was bawling uncontrollably. "How did we get into this?" he asked through his tears. "And *why*? Why couldn't Mary-Jo have lived out her life as God intended? Mary-Jo—dear heart in heaven—can you forgive us?"

McGarr heard a knock, and Sclavi asked, "¿*Cómo puedo ayudarte?*"

"You can't!" Duggan barked in English, his voice cracking. "I'm inconsolable. How could we have strayed so far, so quickly."

Obviously advancing into the room, Sclavi said something else, but McGarr did not hear what it was. His own mobile phone was ringing.

The party on the other end seemed to be having trouble steadying the phone. McGarr heard rustling, followed by a thump.

Then: "Peter?"

The voice was so thin yet shrill, McGarr did not recognize it at first.

"Noreen?"

"Oh, Peter—there's been a terrible accident. We were out shooting, and the gun—my twelve-gauge? It jammed or . . . it wouldn't fire. Fitz, my da' . . . dy took it. You'd better come home. We need you."

"I don't have a car. I'm down in the village over the chemist shop. Can you collect me? Where's Fitz?"

"By my feet. He's bleeding and . . . not well. It blew up in his face. Metal sprayed everywhere."

"Where's Nuala and Maddie?"

"Up at the house."

"Have you phoned anybody else?"

"No . . . I . . . you." From that, McGarr knew she was not well herself.

"I'll be right there."

Hanging up and making for the stairs, McGarr phoned his headquarters in Dublin, and when McKeon came on, he said, "Bernie—Fitz has had an accident at Ilnacullin. Noreen says a gun, a shotgun they were firing, blew up in his face. I want you to get all available help to him."

"Including the chopper?"

"Yes. And whatever ambulance brigade serves Dunlavin. Dr. . . . O'Connell, I believe his name is. He practices in Naas. I'm going to see what I can do."

Now down in the chemist shop, McGarr folded up the phone and slipped it into a pocket. "D'you have a car?" he said to Joan Daley.

"Of course I have a car." She was counting out pills on the counter.

"What kind of a car?"

"A Ford, an Escort. It's brand spanking new."

"What color?"

"Blue. No, midnight blue."

"It's outside the shop?"

"Yes, that's it there." She nodded toward the open door.

"Those the keys?" McGarr pointed to her purse, which was hanging from a peg nearby. The zipper was open.

She glanced up at him. "Yes, those are the keys. Why do you—"

Having to reach over her, McGarr snatched them from her purse. "I'm commandeering your car. You'll be compensated."

With the shrieking woman on his heels, McGarr wrenched open the door of the automobile, started it up, and bolted up the street.

At Ilnacullin, he did not stop at the house or stables but instead drove across the lawns and through the chip-and-put course that Fitz had installed after his long game left him.

McGarr caught sight of them in the distance by the shooting blinds, Noreen down on her knees with her father's head—looking like a bright red berry—in her lap. His arms were stretched out, his legs splayed.

She did not rise to meet him, and once out of the car, he could see it was serious. It seemed as though the older man no longer had half of his face. One eye was untouched. It was open and staring up at her. But his brow, his other eye, his cheek, and even most of his left ear looked like it had been wiped away with one pass of something sharp.

There was blood everywhere—on Fitz, on Noreen, in a puddle on the ground around her knees. She looked up at McGarr, her green eyes glassy. "Is he gone?" she asked in that strange, disembodied voice. McGarr then noticed a black and cratered spot the size of a ten-P coin just behind her right ear. It looked like a splotch of dried blood, although he knew it couldn't be.

Now he was hearing the steady, distant thump of rotors. He had to get back in the car and drive to a clearing where the helicopter could land safely without further troubling either of them.

"Oh—where are you going, Peter? I'm not sure I can support his head much longer."

When he glanced back at her, he saw she was not speaking toward him, as though she could neither turn her head nor follow him with her eyes.

McGarr despaired, realizing he had heard that voice, seen those distanced eyes before. Choosing a landing site that was at least three hundred yards away, he hoped the helicopter was capable of carrying more than one victim and was equipped with litters or gurneys and personnel strong enough to carry the large man. There was no closer site.

In a vortex of wind and clamor, the large military-looking craft landed.

Out of the car now, McGarr opened all the doors and shouted, "This way! This way!" at the four EMT personnel dressed in green-and-orange coveralls. Each seemed to be carrying what looked like a suitcase. After they piled into the car, McGarr slammed it through the fields toward the shooting blinds.

Now both Noreen and Fitz were down, and out of the corner of his eye, McGarr caught sight of Nuala and Maddie entering the field that led to the house. They were about two football fields away.

"J. Hatch, M.D.," the nameplate pinned to the medic's chest said. Late thirties, slight, short blond hair. McGarr hoped she was competent.

Kneeling by Fitz, she took his pulse while scanning his injuries. Seizing the plackets of his shirt, she ripped it open and checked his chest, before turning to Noreen.

Whose eyes were still open. "I seemed to have tipped over. How's my daddy?"

Pushing back her hair near the wound behind her ear, the doctor stood suddenly. "She's first, and hurry."

The two largest men snatched Noreen up and strapped her into a litter that the third man had unfolded from a case. And they left with her, the doctor running beside them toward the helicopter.

"Do you think you could help me?" the third man asked McGarr, taking another litter out of its case.

Fitz weighed at least fifteen stone, which felt much heavier as dead weight, McGarr could not help but think, again examining the gross injury to his father-in-law's face. Jesus God, please let them live.

Hearing Maddie now, crying out for her mother, he snapped his head toward the end of the field and saw Nuala holding her back.

"Ready now?" the other man said. "If we can get him even a step or two closer, the sooner we can take off, the better. The others will relieve you the moment they get her aboard."

They ran as well as they were able, until the two others appeared by McGarr's side, each taking a handle of the litter.

But McGarr was not allowed aboard. "Sorry, Chief Superintendent. You know how it is. Not enough room, and—" Only medical personnel, who would deal with Noreen and Fitz unemotionally.

The crying seemed louder now, and McGarr turned to find Maddie rushing down the hill toward the helicopter. Pivoting, he lowered his head as the bay door closed and the engine cranked over. And with arms out he caught her, so she couldn't move beyond him.

"What happened?"

McGarr lifted her into his arms. "I don't know, exactly. One of your mother's shotguns wouldn't fire, and when your grandpa tried to make it work, it exploded." But how, he wondered—an obstruction in the barrel?

A shell that somehow got packed with too much powder? No. And even if it did, the barrel—modern barrels, forged barrels—would hold for a shot or two. There had been a time when Fitz had packed his own loads, but long ago. And commercial shells were produced automatically, by machines with strict quality control.

The helicopter began lifting off, and Nuala joined them, also asking, "For the love of God, Peter, what happened?"

McGarr explained it again without convincing himself any further.

"How bad is it?" Nuala asked.

McGarr shifted Maddie to one arm and pulled Nuala into them. "They're in good hands. Good hands."

With a burst of power the helicopter rose slowly above the trees, tilted forward, and was suddenly gone, leaving only the staccato beat of its rotors.

"Come, we'll go back to the house," McGarr said, directing them up the hill.

Maddie had quieted, and Nuala was only mumbling something, probably a prayer. But McGarr remained unsatisfied with the explanation. "Tell you what—you two go back. I'll be with you in a jiff. Pack up some clothes, Nuala. You can stay in Rathmines till they're well."

He turned back toward the shooting blinds.

"Where are you going?" Maddie asked.

"To pick up the guns."

"Ah, to hell with the blasted guns," Nuala said to his back.

At the site, McGarr found the shattered gun with only the end of the barrel and the stock remaining intact. The breech, upper barrel, and even the small of the stock were ripped apart.

What force that must have taken, McGarr could not begin to guess. But it had to have been more considerable than a single shotgun shell, unless the gun itself had been defective.

But the gun was new, given to Noreen by Fitz himself as a Christmas present only two years earlier.

McGarr squatted down and with a finger began probing through the debris and blood for the shell casing, which he found still slotted in what was left of the shattered breech.

Twelve gauge. Curiously, it was still bright and brassy, seemingly unscathed. If the shell had been the cause of the explosion, would it have remained in the breech without damage?

McGarr did not think so. He picked up the end of the barrel, holding it up to the sky. It was not plugged, whatever obstruction might have caused the explosion having been ejected. *If* there had been an obstruction.

Tossing the barrel down, his eye caught another bright bit of brass. He picked it up: a flattened, pitted, and frayed disk of metal. It was the case head of a shell with a 2 1 still plainly visible in the middle.

McGarr spun around and examined the several other guns that were stacked neatly in the gun rack behind the shooting station. Not one was a 2 1 gauge. In fact, McGarr did not think either Noreen or Fitz owned a gun with such an unusual caliber.

McGarr raised his head and again looked up at the sky. And he allowed himself to consider for the first time since he had come upon them what had happened to his beloved wife and her father, who had been for nearly two decades perhaps his closest friend and would not—McGarr knew—survive. To die, like that, with half of your face blown off.

But Noreen. Noreen! If there was a God in heaven, he averred, she would survive. She *had* to survive.

His eyes suddenly brimming with tears, McGarr glanced back

down at the blasted case head, and it occurred to him what had happened.

Somebody—could it have been Noreen herself or Fitz by accident?—had chambered a 21-gauge shell into the gun. McGarr knew from his own weapons training that a 20- or even more so a 21-gauge shotgun shell could pass through the chamber of a larger 12-gauge shotgun and would lodge in the bore just forward of the forcing cone area.

That done, the following 12-gauge shell would still fully chamber, with the smaller shell having created an obstruction in the barrel that would almost surely cause a catastrophic failure upon firing.

But both Fitz and Noreen were veteran shooters and did not own a 21-gauge weapon and would not have any reason to possess a 21-gauge shell.

Perhaps the 12-gauge shell had not chambered completely with the 21-gauge round stuck in the barrel, McGarr thought, trying to reconstruct what had occurred. Or, because of the obstruction, the firing pin had not struck the primer exactly enough to fire the cartridge. Noreen had then handed the gun to Fitz.

Breaking open the action, he must have pushed the cartridge in farther, snapped the gun shut, and holding it up to the sky, squeezed the trigger.

The blast of the 12-gauge shell struck the smaller 21-gauge shell, which also exploded, pushing its shell casing backward and preventing the emission of the larger 12-gauge shot and exploded gases.

Result? The gun barrel itself erupted, spewing shrapnel and shot. One large shard took off half of Fitz's face. One small bit entered Noreen's skull.

"Oh, *why?*" McGarr said aloud. Noreen being the kindest, gentlest, most compassionate person McGarr had ever known.

Could somebody have purposely . . . *spiked* the barrel to . . .

what? To send *him* a message? Of? Caution, perhaps? As in, it could happen to him too? He wished it had, being more deserving.

Or perhaps to distract him with the catastrophic injuries that the explosion and shattering of the barrel were sure to cause.

"Ah, Noreen!" he said aloud. To think he had caused this—killed her father, perhaps killed her too.

Who could have spiked the barrel? The possibilities were many, given the years that he'd been a Guard and the enemies he'd made. But who recently had access to the guns, which were kept in cases in the den? Unlocked. There was no need for locks in such a family.

Parmalee. When McGarr had gone into the kitchen to phone his headquarters two nights earlier. Or, having stayed the night, he could easily have stolen downstairs in the large house and nobody would have known. Even if somebody had heard him on the stairs, they would have thought he was going for a drink or something to eat.

Of course, Chazz Sweeney had also shown up in the den, Fitz supplying him with a surfeit of drink until McGarr returned. Surely Fitz had been called away to the phone throughout that time. Or by Nuala to do this and that. He had not remained with the man for the several hours that Sweeney had occupied the room.

As well, Sweeney had been both up front with his wishes and confident that McGarr would carry them out. There had been no need for such a . . . barbaric warning.

No. It had been Parmalee, who was the joker, the literal *vice* in all that had happened since Mary-Jo Stanton's death. Or who was responsible for her death. Slipping a smaller shell into the breech of a gun belonging to McGarr's wife, just to send him a message, put a gust of wind up his britches, was surely just the sort of sneaky, nasty, impersonal, and—in the present instance—cruel act of which he was capable, McGarr did not doubt.

Glancing back up at the sky, which was freighted with high, puffy clouds, he roared, "Parmalee!" And was suddenly lost in rage.

At the car, he found his mobile phone. "Bernie—find me Parmalee."

"What about Noreen and Fitz? We're worried sick here."

"Find me Parmalee!"

"Peter, how can I help you? Where are you?"

"I'll not say it again—find me Parmalee."

"Hughie's been trying to do just that for the last five hours, but—"

McGarr rang off.

17

AT THE HOSPITAL, the most that the resident physician in charge would reveal was that both Fitz and Noreen were in surgery and would be for some time.

When McGarr asked for the official status of their conditions, the man's eyes shied to Nuala and Maddie, and he wondered if he could speak with McGarr alone.

"Your father-in-law, Mr. . . ." He glanced down at his clipboard.

"Frenche."

"As well as your wife, Noreen, are gravely injured. In Mr. Frenche's instance, it would take a miracle for him to live. The trauma to his face and head are extensive, he's lost blood, and—as you know, he's rather elderly."

The man seemed to sigh before meeting McGarr's eyes. "Your wife has a rather large piece of metal lodged at the base of her brain."

"Your prognosis?"

"I have none, and there is none at the moment. The surgeon, whose specialty such injuries are, is flying in from the west, as we speak, in a Garda helicopter that a Superintendent"—he glanced down at the clipboard—"McKeon arranged.

"Another of your staff, I assume, Inspector Bresnahan, will meet him at a heliport about two miles distant from here. It's the best that we can do, I'm afraid. *Better*, in fact, given the help that you've been able to provide. Given the circumstances.

"But her condition has been stabilized, and she'll suffer no further damage."

"And what's the extent of that—the damage?"

He shook his head. "Again, we'll just have to wait for the specialist."

"What's his name?"

"Wichman. An American. He's highly regarded."

Thanking the man, McGarr went back out to the foyer, where Nuala and Maddie waited, worry lining their faces.

"Well?" Nuala demanded.

McGarr shook his head and relayed the information, leaving out Fitz's probable fate. It was, he realized, the life-changing event in her and Maddie's life more than in his.

Nuala would lose a husband and perhaps her only daughter; Maddie might lose her mother and her only living grandfather. McGarr would only lose a great, good friend but—please, God—not the love of his life.

A wave of guilt and anger welled up in him again; and he knew he must—but he could not—just sit there and comfort them. Not when he knew who had brought the tragedy to pass. "You take this, I have another in the car." He handed Nuala his cell phone. "I'll phone you every hour or so."

"What—you're not going to stay with us?"

McGarr considered taking Nuala aside, but Maddie should also understand why he was leaving. "It was not an accident."

The older woman looked away, obviously trying to understand how the accident could have been otherwise.

"Think how careful Fitz was—*is*—about his guns, how he taught

Noreen. I'll tell you the details later, but I really should follow this up while I can."

"Ooooh! Really?" Her voice sounded to McGarr like the keening he had heard his own grandmother utter upon the death of her husband. Years ago. "Has it anything to do with Mr. Sweeney?"

"Could be."

"Then you be very careful. He's . . . a bit of a chancer, I'd say. And ruthless."

"Daddy!" Maddie said through further tears and rushed to him. "Oh, Daddy—don't leave me. Don't leave me!"

Saying, "He'll be all right, he'll be all right," Nuala had to pry her away. "And you will too."

Brimming with a mix of emotions too distressing even to contemplate, McGarr went back out to the car.

DERY PARMALEE WAS nowhere to be found, McKeon reported when McGarr reached him at Murder Squad headquarters.

"Hughie put in six hours trying to run Parmalee down. But he was knackered after his busy night last night, and he's gone home for a wee snooze."

"I've got Rut'ie, Swords, and Sinclair on him now, and I've been phoning both his residence and *Ath Cliath* steadily. Busy signals at both places."

Every news organization in the world with a Catholic readership would be wanting to interview him about his claim that Escrivá was Mary-Jo Stanton's father, thought McGarr.

And/or buy the rights to the manuscript, *if* it actually existed and Parmalee had possession of it, as he claimed.

"Wait," McKeon continued. "Here's Swords. I'll put him on." There was a pause and then, "Chief—they've got security on every door, and I'm afraid I had to muscle a bloke. But he's either not there or hiding under a desk. And I heard definite concern in the voice of his managing editor. I think it's true—they don't know where he is. And if *Ath Cliath* can't deliver after the claims he's made—"

Their credibility would be ruined, and the paper might not survive, thought McGarr, who had his own issues with survival.

"Where does he live? What's his address?"

McKeon came back on. "Are you all right, Peter? Where are you now?"

"The address, please."

McKeon gave it to him—a commercial building off a laneway in the Liberties, not more than a short walk from where Ward and Bresnahan now lived.

"Do you need help?" Now there was concern in McKeon's own voice. "I could meet you there."

"I need you where you are. And thanks very much for the helicopter and the surgeon."

"How are they?"

"Not good. I'll be in touch."

When McGarr got close to the Liberties, he speed-dialed Ward, whom he woke and asked to meet him at Parmalee's.

"You have the key I gave you?" Ward asked.

"Of course."

"I'll be there as soon as I can, Chief."

An old brick commercial building of four floors, it had a wide cargo door beside the front entrance. There were no lights on, even though the day was declining. Not even around back, where McGarr discovered a raging guard dog that would be inside the building, McGarr reasoned, were Parmalee away.

"Laughlin & Sons," a faded sign announced. "Corn Factors: Barley, Rye and Other Grains." There was no other advisory, not even a nameplate, and McGarr imagined that Parmalee—as a successful publisher—owned or rented the entire building.

When his insistent ringing met with no response, not even from the intercom, McGarr used the key that Ward had provided. Once in, he switched on the hall lights, leaving the door ajar for Ward.

McGarr did not know what to expect of Parmalee's digs, given who the man was and his background—ex-Jesuit and book writer, now tabloid journalist/publisher. But what he found rather amazed him.

The first floor was one large open room painted a stark white, with brilliant fluorescent lights lining the ceiling. Apart from a beechwood floor that gleamed like blond ice, there was not one stick of furniture or any other appurtenance.

Recently installed heating vents and circuitry had been left exposed and conspicuous, as was the recent trend in rehabbing former commercial buildings.

The second floor was the same and smelled of fresh paint and even fresher varnish. Its restoration had just been completed. Had Parmalee been planning to move *Ath Cliath*'s newsroom or some other aspect of its operations here? he wondered.

The door to the third floor was equipped with a stout, modern lock, but when McGarr tried the handle, it swung in to expose a view far different from that on the antiseptic lower levels of the building. Obviously his living quarters, it looked as if Parmalee had scoured antiques shops and estate sales and furnished the flat like a smaller version of Barbastro.

The foyer, which seemed to be a duplicate of that in Dunlavin, had handsome carved double doors complete with fanlight, opening into a reception hall with a splendid double staircase leading up to the final floor.

McGarr slowly made his way through other rooms that contained sculpted plaster ceilings, inlaid mahogany doors, a magnificent carved white-marble Adam fireplace. Most of the rooms were hung with tapestries, portraits, and ornate mirrors in heavy gilt frames. There were burgundy velour wing chairs in the sitting room, butter leather overstuffed chairs in the drawing room, and an enormous crystal chandelier in the central hall.

The kitchen was Barbastro's too—an enormous Victorian work space stacked with multipaned cabinetry and flagged with heavy stone. A deal table sat near the door to what proved to be a set of back stairs.

From there, McGarr could hear the dog barking again. At Ward, he assumed. But as a precaution, he drew out his Walther and checked its action.

The grand staircase had been solidly constructed and was new, with no spongy steps or squeaks. At the top, he found himself on the floor of the building that contained the bedrooms when he switched on lights.

Here too, McGarr imagined, the ornate model of Barbastro was repeated. But it was the house that Parmalee had lived in when he had been working with Mary-Jo—the house that McGarr had visited as a guest—and not the house that had evolved after Father Fred Duggan arrived ten years ago, the house with locked "quarters" at the top of the building.

And what was he smelling—something strange and harshly . . . metallic. Or sweetly metallic. McGarr had smelled that odor before, and he knew where.

But sensing somebody on the stairs behind him, he stepped back into a shadow and caught sight of Ward climbing the stairs two at a time. There was somebody behind him.

Ward explained, "This is . . . what's your first name again?"

"Enda."

"Enda Flatly with the Drug Squad."

Flatly raised the Garda dogtag ID that hung from a lanyard around his neck. Like McGarr and Ward, he too held a gun.

"I couldn't help noticing the lights and open door, Chief Superintendent. Thought I'd poke my head in, have a look around." He was youngish—middle thirties—with short-cropped blond hair and a brace of rings gilding his right ear. Wearing a leather jacket and jeans, he had black gloves studded with large brass buttons on the knuckles.

"Good man," said McGarr. "But we have the situation in hand." He pointed toward the stairs. "This is our operation."

"Begging your pardon, sir—I think I'll stay."

McGarr waited.

"Well, I was on stakeout and saw you use a key to get in here. How is it that you have a key? We've been investigating Parmalee as well, you see." Flatly's smile was brittle, but his light eyes were bright. There was a large space between his front teeth.

"Are you a friend of Mr. Parmalee, or did you just happen to come by the key that Superintendent Ward took from Parmalee two nights ago when he beat the piss out of him, opened the door, and carried him inside?"

"You're investigating Parmalee for . . . ?" McGarr asked.

"Ecstasy. Like the tablets Superintendent Ward filled Parmalee's pockets with and scattered around the ground outside. I have it all on infrared film.

"Tell you what—" Flatly jerked up his weapon and punched the barrel into the back of Ward's skull. "I'm tired of your shit. You two gods with a badge.

"Both of you—drop your weapons. Nothing burns my arse more than two fucking corrupt cops! Drop 'em!"

Shoving Ward forward into McGarr, Flatly assumed the half crouch of a shooting position with both hands on his large-caliber handgun. "Try me?"

Setup, McGarr thought. Parmalee had been watched from the moment he had surfaced as a threat to Opus Dei, McGarr had refused to play along with their low-profile scenario of Mary-Jo's death, and this was the result.

No, this was part of the result. The other part was being played out at Richmond Hospital, and McGarr could only blame himself. Why had he taken Chazz Sweeney—the man who had supervised political corruption for over two decades—so lightly?

"I'd love to whack two arseholes like you. We have all our ducks in line, and it would be so easy. So right. In the circle that counts, I'd be a hero."

Hearing the slight thrill in Flatly's voice, McGarr knew the man would shoot them if he believed he could get away with it. And he obviously thought he could. It was the thrill of really big death, even bigger than what McGarr now realized he had been smelling since he first began climbing the stairs.

But Maddie would need at least one parent, if Noreen did not pull through, and Nuala would need him as well. He dropped his Walther. "Hughie."

Ward let his fall to the carpet too.

Flatly kicked them down the stairs. "Now then, Corrupt Cop One—you walk to that doorway and throw the light switch."

Flatly meant McGarr, who complied. "Now both of you enter the room and sit on the bed."

Where Parmalee was positioned on his stomach with his left wrist attached to his right ankle with Garda-issue handcuffs. The same way Geraldine Breen had left Ward at Delia Manahan's house in Killiney. Less the bullet wounds.

At least six were grouped at the back of Parmalee's head, with the bright shell casings sprinkled over his blue blazer and the bedcover.

McGarr thought of the other shell casing. And of Chazz Sweeney, who, to his knowledge, had been the only other guest recently left alone in the den of Ilnacullin in Dunlavin where Noreen's shotguns were stored.

"What have we here?" Flatly asked histrionically. "An example of Corrupt Cop Two's handiwork? It wasn't enough just to thump the fucking yoke, after he abused Whore One and threatened to expose your immoral 'marital' situation with Whore Two. No. You had to run him up here and dispatch the gobshite as well.

"Check the shell casings, Corrupt Cop Two. Go ahead." Flatly nudged Ward forward. "Pick one up."

Ward did. Examining it, he glanced up at McGarr and began extending his arm, before glancing at Flatly.

"That's okay. All right. The 'Chief'—I believe they call you, Corrupt Cop One—should see it too."

As Ward handed McGarr the casing, their eyes met and a thought passed between them. If Flatly was alone, it was bad police strategy—one gun on two suspects. In such a small space, there was no chance of patting them and cuffing their wrists. And even if Flatly wasn't alone, it was still unwise not to show the second man.

Flatly hadn't, because there was none. Flatly was alone, doing Sweeney's dirty work singularly. Which also was not smart, ultimately, Sweeney being Sweeney.

"And what caliber proof of your corruption might that cartridge be, Corrupt Cop One? Can you see it? Or have your eyes deteriorated along with your morals?"

McGarr stared down at the small shell casing, knowing it was his chance. Now that Noreen and Fitz had been attacked, it was total war. He would not abide by the law while Sweeney and Flatly practiced their *pillería* with—how had Parmalee himself phrased it?—with God on their side.

McGarr stepped toward the lamp by the side of the bed. "I'll need me cheaters."

"Tut-tut." Flatly quickly moved to the other side, where he would have two clean shots at them without having to swing the barrel much. "Open the jacket and show me."

McGarr complied.

"Now slowly draw the glasses out."

Again he complied, feeling the frames slip by the concealed

special-purpose pistol that he kept in a pouch of the pocket. He released the jacket and slid the frames of his half-glasses over his ears.

After examining the shell, he would remove the glasses and ask to return them to the pocket. Maybe then he'd have a chance, with Flatly having seen that he was not wearing a shoulder holster.

Reaching the shell casing under the lamplight, McGarr looked down. "It's a thirty-eight."

"Bingo! Right you are, Corrupt Cop One. Now tell me, Corrupt Cop Two—what was the caliber of the gun you lost last night to a woman, no less?"

Ward only looked at Flatly.

"Thirty-eight, I'm guessing. Could this be the very weapon?" From a pocket of his leather jacket, Flatly pulled a handgun shaped like a Beretta with the long grip/magazine that could contain thirteen cartridges. It was a model 84, Ward's weapon of choice.

"No need to chat on. It's your gun, the one you used to whack poor publisher Parmalee here, just when he was reaching the heights of celebrity. Why? Because he threatened to expose you and your whores and your whorish 'family.'

"All it now needs are fresh prints." Flatly tossed it down on the bed near where Ward was standing. "Pick it up."

Ward did not move.

"Pick it up, or I shoot him." Flatly raised his Garda-issue Glock and pointed it at McGarr's forehead. "You returned to the scene of the crime for Corrupt Cop One's idea of how to dispose of the body. Exposed by me for who you are, you put up a fight. I, me—Enda Flatly—saved bloody fucking Ireland the anguish of a costly fucking trial. Pick it up!"

It was then they heard a door slam below in the house, and the sound of whistling came to them.

"Who's that?"

McGarr hunched his shoulders. "One of yours, perchance?"

"Or a Parmalee 'friend,' " said Ward. "Pity the gun's not loaded." He pointed to the Beretta on the bed. "Or does Gerry Breen do all your killing for you? What now, Righteous Cop? What's God's plan for you now?"

"Maybe that's Him on the stairs."

Plainly, Enda Flatly did not know how to proceed. The whistling was growing louder now, as heavy steps climbed past the empty floors toward the living quarters.

"Know that song?" McGarr continued, removing his half-glasses. "It's 'You'll Never Walk Alone.' You know, *'When you walk through a storm, keep your head up high, and don't be afraid of the—'* "

"Shut your bloody gob!"

"But you're too young to have heard it much and *copped* onto its message. An important message, wouldn't you say, Corrupt Cop Two?" McGarr's eyes met Ward's again, and a far more important message passed between them. They had heard Bernie McKeon sing "You'll Never Walk Alone" countless times. It was his party piece.

And a deep, orotund, but rather gravelly voice now came to them in loud echo, as the man opened the door to the second empty floor.

"You'll never walk alone! You'll ne-ver walk alone!"

"And, of course, killers like you and Gerry Breen always walk alone. Or is it *work* alone, as in *Opus* Dei. But maybe killing isn't work for you. It's just *pillería*."

"Shut the fuck up!" Flatly hissed.

"May I put my glasses away? I would hate my family and friends to think I died myopic." There was no way that Flatly would shoot either of them any time soon and give away his position.

"Down on the floor, the both of you. Arms and feet spread-eagle. Now. Now!"

As McGarr turned to squat down, kneel, and then comply with Flatly's order, he opened his jacket as though to put away his glasses. But with his body shielding his hand, he grasped the grip of his Advantage Arms model 422.

"The old legs aren't what they used to be."

"Shut up, cocksucker!"

When Flatly swung his head to the door and the singing, which was loud now, McGarr pivoted on his heels, raised the small powerful gun in both hands and fired its four .22-magnum chambers simultaneously. At Flatly's head.

The report was stunning, and the concussion kicked back McGarr's arms.

On his feet now, Ward rushed toward Flatly, who had reeled toward the open door. But there, two other shots, fired from below, staggered his body and kept it from tumbling down the stairs.

Having fallen from Flatly's hand, the Glock lay on the carpet. McGarr snatched it up.

"It's all right. It's us, Bernie," Ward hollered out the door. But they heard nothing except the sound of feet on the carpet, somebody heavy retreating down the stairs.

"Go after him, but be careful."

Rushing down the stairs, Ward picked up his own weapon—the Beretta that Flatly had made him discard—and McGarr moved quickly toward the front windows.

From there, a few moments later, he saw Chazz Sweeney lumber out of the building and climb into a waiting car that sped off.

Obviously, he had come to take care of Flatly, who had shot Parmalee with the gun that Geraldine Breen had lifted from Ward.

Flatly's corpse could then have been dumped in any side street— a zealous cop, the media would call him, this week's victim of the drug trade. Where Breen was, was anybody's guess. But she and Sweeney were linked, that much was now plain from the way Parmalee had been trussed on his stomach, wrist to ankle. Her signature hold.

"Ring up Bernie and get the Tech Squad to document all of this. You write the report, just as it happened." McGarr tossed Flatly's Glock on the bed, then moved toward the stairs and his own Walther.

"Also, issue an all-points for Sweeney. Armed, dangerous, and wanted for murder.

"Then I want you to search this place thoroughly. You're looking for the biography, the painting, and any connections you can make between Parmalee and the other principals in the case—Sweeney, Flatly, Duggan, Sclavi, Manahan, and Geraldine Breen."

If Parmalee had not killed Mary-Jo Stanton himself but had known through his illegal voice surveillance that she would be killed, and if he had subsequently induced Mudd to wrap—or had himself wrapped—the *cilicio* around the woman's neck in an attempt to lead the investigation to Opus Dei, then he had also known who killed Mary-Jo.

He had told Ward that it was Geraldine Breen, but only after a beating. And Parmalee had been fixated on damaging Opus Dei any way he could.

"Where you headed?" Ward asked.

"Sweeney's office on the quays."

"You'll need some help. He had a driver, he wasn't alone."

Somehow, McGarr didn't think Sweeney would want to lead him and a contingent of Garda to his office. Also, Sweeney's office had been raided before by court order, the files sequestered, examined, and returned—with the famous apology and huge cash settlement.

And what McGarr was looking for was at least ten years old, something that Chazz Sweeney—fixer, bagman, and Opus Dei avatar—would not have thrown out and would now consider innocuous.

But that would make him eminently indictable.

18

UNUSED TO THE mobile phone, Nuala fumbled with the device until McGarr heard, "Hello?"

"It's me, Maddie, your dad."

"Oh, Daddy—when are you going to get back here? Terrible things are happening, and . . ." Like a surgeon's scalpel, her sob cut through McGarr.

Nuala's voice then came on. "Peter?" There was a long pause, as if she had to summon the strength to speak. But then her voice was strong.

"Fitz is dead, and better off, from what the surgeon here tells me. The explosion ripped him apart. He would have been blind and under the knife for countless operations just so he could breathe and chew and talk normally. And, sure, we had a great life together."

In emotional shock, her voice was matter-of-fact, as though she were discussing the weather or something that had occurred in the course of the day. It might take a week for the reality to set in, and then she'd need help.

Until McGarr asked, "What about Noreen?"

"They still have her in there. A whole team of them. And"—her voice cracked—"I wouldn't get your hopes up. He said, 'It's most delicate,' extracting the blasted thing. So whatever you're about, you should work away. Because she'll be . . . unconscious when and if they're ever through with her." There was a pause, and then, "God bless and save our great, good young woman." Upon which Nuala broke down.

McGarr then heard, "Daddy?" It was Maddie again. "I know you have to do what you're doing, but . . ."

"Ring off, luv. He's only doing what he should," said Nuala through her tears.

"Bye-bye, Daddy."

With tears in his eyes, McGarr looked down at the phone and could not keep himself from thinking how much like her mother she sounded. And he thought—if there was any God in the universe, He would let Noreen live.

LOOKING LIKE A decrepit tooth in an old mouth, Sweeney's building sat alone on the quays in a swath of vacant lots slated for redevelopment as a harbor-area mall.

Sweeney would repair its crumbling cornices, McGarr had read. He would replace the old paned windows, rehab the interior, and wind up with the one authentic period building in some architect's *monde nouveau* scheme.

How the man had engineered that was an indication of his power. *Before* tonight, when he became a gunman and murderer, and perhaps a double murderer, having sat in the den with the shotguns for hours—by Fitz's report—before McGarr had arrived at Ilnacullin. Fitz, who was no longer a witness who could be sworn.

But *why* would he have spiked the barrel? What reason would he have had then—before he had appealed to McGarr—beyond distracting McGarr from his investigation of Mary-Jo Stanton's death? And would he have done such a thing himself?

McGarr thought not. Dispatching a surrogate like Breen or Flatly to do the dirty work was more his style, although he had not been beyond ridding himself of Flatly when needed.

Seeing no visible signs of an alarm system on the building, McGarr moved round to the back, where he had caught sight of a window boarded up with peeling plywood. After a brief search through the surrounding rubble, he found a length of iron pipe and soon had the plywood off.

Rearing back, he smashed the window and its sash bars so he could step in, his halogen torch casting a bright cone of achromatic light into what proved to be a storage room. It led into a hall and a flight of stairs, off which McGarr found Sweeney's office.

But McGarr ignored the office and instead climbed the stairs, suspecting that what he was after would have long since found permanent storage on one of the three floors above. And it took him the better part of two hours—during which he phoned the hospital twice more only to learn that Noreen was still in surgery—before he came upon what he was seeking:

An old green file cabinet that had been battered in moving. Much of the paperwork contained inside was yellowed with age, and some of it dated back to the 1960s. But the letterhead on much of the photocopied correspondence was Francis X. Foley, Esq., Solicitor.

It was the cabinet that had been removed from Foley's office after his murder a decade earlier, the one that had left the patch of greener carpet on the floor. Sweeney would not have destroyed such useful information, McGarr knew—piecing through the folders and noting the celebrity and/or wealth of the names he came upon.

There was a photograph taken from afar of the wife of a still popular politician, on a beach on her back, with her legs wrapping the thighs of some dark-skinned younger man, her head back and eyes closed in obvious sexual thrall.

Another—taken through the windscreen of an automobile—

pictured her husband performing what appeared to be fellatio on the same man, who looked bored, a cigarette dangling from his mouth as he peered out the side window.

Other files of other people contained tapes labeled "Phone Conversations, 6/6/66 to 9/10/66" or "Bedroom Tape, Enhanced—See Transcript." From what McGarr saw in one drawer alone, Foley must have been blackmailing dozens of people simultaneously. Little wonder he could afford the several houses, the flash cars and lifestyle.

Until he was found out by Sweeney and whoever murdered him, McGarr remaining convinced it would not have been Sweeney himself.

But there was nothing in the folder labeled "Mary-Jo Stanton/ José Maria Escrivá," not even a scrap of paper.

McGarr closed the drawer and moved down the stairs to Sweeney's office and the large old safe with the gold-leafed door that he had seen there. Removing his hat, he pulled over a chair and set about cracking it, which was yet another skill that he had learned during his first stint as a policeman—with Criminal Justice in France during the late sixties.

At the time, Marseilles had been awash in drugs, and what was needed were young, tough, undercover cops who could infiltrate the drug rings and/or pose as buyers. Being demonstrably Irish with red hair, gray eyes, and execrable French was a big plus, and McGarr proved himself in shamrocks, coming up with a bust of over four metric tons of cocaine along with the entire chain of command behind the sale.

But more valuable to McGarr was the training he had received from a cadre of French criminals who mentored the recruits in exchange for shortened sentences. Everything from stealing cars to second-story work to breaking into bank vaults was on the curriculum. And McGarr had proved an able student, who could now pick or crack almost any standard lock or safe.

But all that was B.N., "Before Noreen," as he would say to her in partial jest, now losing his concentration as a wave of worry and grief washed over him.

Closing his eyes, he wondered if he could make contact with her if he thought hard enough, consciousness to consciousness, brain to brain, because of all the years—nearly twelve now—they had been together daily in the most intimate contact. In so many ways, they had become like two halves of one whole person, she certainly being the better part.

Of course, she was neither conscious nor was her brain intact, but would that matter? he wondered. Was there, could there be a kind of consciousness that transcended any mere grave injury, such that even after death a person—that person whom you loved beyond the love in dreams—would remain with you in your life, like a kind of companion and helpmate? A presence who could continue to share your experience, your joys, sunsets, little pleasures, and quiet moments?

That he was actually thinking such a thought now frightened McGarr rather more than his mobile phone, which began vibrating in his pocket.

"Chief?" It was Ward. "Bernie and I are still at it here at Parmalee's, but I just came up with something on his computer. Late last year, on the nineteenth of December, he composed what appears to be an anonymous letter to, I think, Delia Manahan. Shall I read it to you?"

Still seated with his shoulder and head against the old safe, McGarr grunted.

"There's no salutation, no date, nothing up top. It begins: 'You should know that Gerry Breen murdered your husband, who had been blackmailing Mary-Jo Stanton with the claim that she was the daughter of José Maria Escrivá. Truth is, she *is* the daughter of Escrivá, who met M. J.'s mother in Spain when he was appointed chaplain of Madrid's Patronato de Santa Isabel.

" 'Your husband, who was an accomplished researcher if a heinous man, discovered her birth certificate and other particulars in East Germany before the Berlin Wall came down, and for years he bled Stanton and Opus Dei. In fact, he put the notion that Escrivá was her father into M. J.'s head, causing her to begin writing the biography of Escrivá which, as you know, is her present project and nearing completion.

" 'But when the Berlin Wall finally fell, STASI files became public, and Opus Dei numerary Geraldine Breen was sent there to (1) find the file and destroy it and (2) find out who had earlier accessed it. And there was your husband's name; they made him pay 20,000 pounds for the privilege but insisted he show his passport.

" 'Breen then flew directly back to Dublin and broke into your husband's office, where he discovered her going through his files and made the mistake of trying to stop her. Gerry, as you well know, holds black belts in several martial arts and is a crack shot.

" 'Did you ever ask yourself why she keeps honing those skills when she never competes, why she periodically goes away solo on holidays? I understand you two have fought over that very issue. Gerry has even sought out the advice of Father Fred on the subject of your quarrels—how to mollify your complaints while she's taking care of Opus Dei *pillería* any way she can. They talk about that too.' "

And you listened, thought McGarr.

" 'So, after Breen murdered your husband, she befriended you, saying that, unbeknownst to you, whenever your husband took his many "business trips on legal matters"—could that be the way he phrased it?—he had actually been doing the work of Opus Dei. Which I find, well, the cruelest of stealthy ironies.

" 'Subsequently, she helped you with the wake, the funeral, the house, the kids, the car, the dog throughout that trying time. She became virtually your guardian angel and could have been more had your mutual religiosity not got in the way, she's confessed to Fred.

Meanwhile she was scouring your house whenever you were away. Monitoring your phone calls. Making sure no hint of Mary-Jo's paternity got out.

" 'Bringing you into the Opus Dei fold? Perhaps you believe you came to God purposely, designedly, intentionally. Fair play to you. But purposely, designedly, intentionally they brought you there, just in case your husband had left copies of his files in one of his many offshore safe deposit boxes or other repositories.

" 'With malice aforethought and malice in deed, I write this because I think it only just that you should know how your husband died and why he was taken from his young children and you just when you needed him most.

" 'I'm certain it was a struggle. But, then again, you had God in the guise of Opus Dei on your side.' "

"There's no signature, Chief."

"Where is Delia Manahan now?"

"I thought you'd ask that, so I checked. She just returned to Barbastro—the house in Dunlavin."

"Thanks."

"You going there, Chief?"

"Yah."

"What about Noreen and Fitz?"

McGarr told Ward, and there was a long silence on the other end. Then, "I can't tell you how sorry I am for you. How's Maddie taking it? And Nuala?"

"They're together there—at the hospital." Where, McGarr knew, he should be. But at the moment his own sorrow had taken the form of anger.

In fact, it was a cold, considered rage that he had never felt before.

As he had dealt with Flatly, he would discover those who were responsible for the catastrophe that had occurred to his family, and serve them the same.

19

BUT MCGARR DID not proceed directly to Dunlavin. Instead, he drove due south to Killiney and Delia Manahan's house.

There he lowered the visor with his Garda shield pinned to the other side. He found the front door—which faced the Irish Sea and had been kicked in by Ward the night before—slightly ajar. McGarr stepped in and began his search in the basement, where Ward had reported Delia Manahan kept her outdoor gear.

Finding the camping equipment hung neatly in organized rows from the wooden floor joists so it wouldn't mildew, he began searching through the rucksacks and backpacks, the zippered pouches and compartments. But he did not find what he was after until he remembered that Noreen kept their water bottles—the several with the pop-up nipples that she took with her when shooting or riding, or on a hot day she brought out to him in the garden—in the kitchen.

Which is where he found what he was looking for—not one white plastic water bottle stenciled with the logo "G. Bass, Outfitters" but five. Why five?

In passing up the stairs, he had also noted, that all the climbing ropes lining the stairwell had been looped, then tied rather professionally with noosed knots.

The photos that he came upon in Manahan's bedroom—again because of Ward's earlier reconnaissance—showed Manahan, Geraldine Breen, and a girl who, McGarr suspected, was Manahan's daughter.

They were standing near a large wooden sign that said "San Juan Wilderness Area." In back of them were red pines and aspen trees, and, in the far distance, towering gray stone cliffs imposed on a crystalline blue sky dotted with puffs of cumulus cloud. The Rockies, McGarr assumed, where at elevations of ten thousand feet and greater, hydration was essential.

Each of them was toting a rucksack with water bottles similar to the G. Bass model in pouches to either side. Total of six. McGarr tucked the photo in his jacket.

Back on the ground floor, he located the room that Ward had dubbed the "television room." In a wall case behind glass were the "fowling pieces." Not finding the key in either of the two drawers below, McGarr broke the glass.

The gun with the smallest bore was a 21-gauge Czech-made shotgun with a carved stock and a hunting scene engraved on its German silver receiver.

Again he searched the drawers below. The only box of 21-gauge shells that he could find had two loads missing. The thin shells had yellow plastic jackets.

Placing the five water bottles in a carton, he left for Dunlavin.

AS USUAL, FATHER Fred Duggan met McGarr at the front door of Barbastro. "Isn't it rather late for a visit? I would have thought you would be with Noreen and Fitz. By the by, how are they?"

"How'd you hear about that?"

Duggan's head went back, and his blue eyes studied McGarr's

face. "Wasn't it all over town with the helicopter and all? Some of your neighbors rushed over and found the house wide open. The local Guards, of course, knew the story."

One call from you—a recently bereaved priest—and they told all.

Duggan's eyes fell to the carton McGarr was carrying. "Whom do you wish to see?"

God, McGarr thought, for Whom he had two questions named Noreen and Fitz.

"Delia Manahan here?"

"Up in her room. By that I mean, up in the room she usually occupies when she's here. But I don't think she wishes to be disturbed, since she's at her prayers."

McGarr pushed by Duggan and mounted the main staircase two steps at a time.

There was light under Delia Manahan's door, but it took at least a minute of rapping to get her there.

"I hope this is important," he heard her say before she opened the door a few inches to look out.

Thrusting his weight into the carton, he shoved open the door, knocking her back into the room.

"What's this?" she demanded. "I'm at my prayers. Get out! Get out!"

Spinning around, McGarr saw Duggan in the open door, and he kicked it shut. Before grabbing the woman by the back of the neck and shoving her toward the room's only easy chair, into which she fell face first.

Ripping open the carton, he dumped the five G. Bass, Outfitters white-and-black plastic water bottles over her. "Don't say a word, not a word," McGarr hissed into her ear, before spinning her around and stuffing her down into the chair.

To calm himself, he then walked toward the window that looked out at the garden where Mary-Jo Stanton had been found. And he checked his mobile phone to make sure Nuala had not phoned him and he had not heard the ring during his . . . ruckus.

He began speaking to the dark window, knowing that if he looked at her again—the shaved eyebrows, the severe, ascetic, *religious* image that she had honed—he might not be able to control himself.

"I don't know when you got the letter from Parmalee. Rather, the anonymous letter that you sometime later figured out was from Parmalee. But it enraged you. As well it might.

"For ten years, a cunning, duplicitous enormity had been worked on you. After murdering your blackmailing husband, the father of your two children, who you did not know was a blackmailer, Gerry Breen had ingratiated herself with you. Helped you with the wake, the funeral, the house and kids.

"You became fast friends who, it turned out, had something in common—an abiding religiosity that Breen stoked, given her extreme commitment to Opus Dei. Which seemed like the answer to you as well. So after completing your studies—financed in part, I should imagine, by them—you came aboard. God—or at least, a life dedicated to God—seemed like the answer.

"And your relationship with Breen also became deeper. You traveled, hiked, camped, and perhaps even"—McGarr could hardly bring himself to say it—"*shot* together. Skeet, perhaps big game—I don't know how or when those heads appeared on the walls in that room in your house—and maybe even at targets, given Breen's special office with Opus Dei, that of enforcer/protector. Security. It was what she had been doing at Barbastro all those years—keeping guard over Mary-Jo Stanton, whom Opus Dei did not know what to do with. But you didn't know about that. As yet.

"No. All you knew was that Gerry Breen and you were the closest of personal friends, and you also shared beliefs and interests. I don't know what else you might have shared, and I don't care. But when the letter arrived, you decided to get back—at Breen and at Opus Dei.

"How better than to get rid of Mary-Jo Stanton, to whom Gerry seemed more completely devoted even than she was to you, and who appeared to be a personage within the Opus Dei fold. I'm not sure you understood why—that she was the fleshly daughter of Opus Dei founder José Maria Escrivá—and I'm not sure it would have mattered or increased your rage.

"In any case, you decided to employ an intermediary to exact revenge. You had already placed Frank Mudd—your former lover—here at Barbastro as gardener, and you knew it wouldn't take much to recruit him. What you didn't know was that Parmalee had already turned Mudd into his own mole and informant, threatening to expose him to his erstwhile co-criminals in the States, on whom Mudd had informed.

"He had Mudd place bugs in every bedroom and public room of this house, and, most likely unknown to Mudd, he also placed a bug in Mudd's cottage."

In the reflection off the glass, McGarr saw Manahan raise her head.

"Monitoring and recording the voices from a flat over the chemist shop down in the village, Parmalee heard every little squeak and sigh that you two made in the bedroom, to say nothing of your proposal to Mudd.

"But the strategy that you chose wasn't sufficiently pointed to suit Parmalee—digitalis being a bit too anonymous for the ex-Jesuit who blamed Opus Dei and Duggan for removing him from Mary-Jo, whom he claimed to have been bedding, and for ending their collaboration in the writing of books. Duggan might call in a country doctor, who would declare the elderly Stanton's a death from natural causes. So Parmalee developed his own plan.

"Prepping the water bottle with digitalis—the sixth of your six with the G. Bass, Outfitters logo stenciled on the front"—McGarr flicked a hand at the five around her chair—"you either gave it to Stanton yourself before she went out, or you had Mudd place it by her as the two were gardening in the hot sun. Mudd's job was to retrieve it after the old woman drank from the bottle and expired.

"You could not have known that Mudd and Parmalee—or perhaps just Parmalee himself, given the label in the jacket that was placed over the surveillance camera—waited, most probably in the garden haggard, for the digitalis to begin to take effect, then obscured the lens and wrapped a barbed *cilicio* around Mary-Jo's neck, tightening down the clamp enough to draw blood but not enough to cause death. The point being to inculpate those who either used or had access to such a device, namely, Opus Dei, whose founder, Escrivá, had been known to use one himself.

"Which brings us to Mudd, who—you believed—was the only person who knew how you . . . worked Mary-Jo's death. Not the most intelligent man and an episodic drunk with a criminal record, he could be leaned on and made to tell the truth. So he had to be taken care of in a way that would make it look as if he killed himself as penance or in remorse for having killed Mary-Jo.

"Getting him drunk was the easy part, stringing him up something else, given his size. But for a climber like you, tying a secure blood hitch to the beam in the feed room and then attaching a come-along to the noose were skills that you'd practiced before. And the come-along with its crank handle could make it possible for somebody to hang himself, even while drunk.

"You then scoured the place, removing the brassiere that had been hanging in the toilet"—again McGarr watched Manahan react. Shifting her feet, she turned her head toward the door, as if thinking of fleeing. "And all other traces of your presence.

"You probably even went to Father Fred and owned up to Mudd not being your brother as you had originally told him and Mary-Jo when you pleaded they take Mudd on as gardener." McGarr was winging it here, merely supposing she had done so. "And now you had your doubts about him. Maybe Duggan should reexamine the tape of Mary-Jo gardening right before her death.

"Duggan bought the suggestion, reviewed the tape, then came to me, making no mention of your admission about Mudd's not being your brother. If Mudd and Mudd alone were believed responsible for Mary-Jo's death, with no Opusian complicit in any way, then Opus Dei would remain guiltless for her murder. Just something done by a crazed drunk. End of story. The crime wrapped up neatly even before it hit the press.

"But you couldn't have that, even though it was in your interest as far as suspicion of murder was concerned. Although you had removed Mary-Jo from Gerry Breen, Opus Dei and Breen herself would remain unscathed. In fact, both would be massively rewarded by her demise. The biography of Escrivá would either go unpublished or be expurgated by some Opus Dei scribe, and Opus Dei would end up with the bulk of Mary-Jo's fortune. Even Breen would suddenly find herself a wealthy woman.

"But you had the manuscript of the biography, didn't you? It was you in Mary-Jo's quarters when I climbed up there to investigate. And, as with the *cilicio*, in cutting the painting off the wall your intent was to put the police on the trail of an Opusian zealot.

"But the manuscript was something else, wasn't it? It was dynamite. Placed in the proper hands, it would blow the myth of Opus Dei's beatified founder sky-high. Linked to the other allegations about the order, it might do much to knock them from the preferential position they enjoy in Rome.

"And the proper hands were Parmalee's, which is how he obtained the manuscript, shortly after the murder. I don't know if by then you had connected the letter you had received with Parmalee. But who else could it be? Who seemed to know as much about Opus Dei and some of the priests themselves?

"What you did know, however, was that I'd surely be questioning Parmalee about the manuscript. That I'd want to see the letter from Mary-Jo that he wrote about in the paper and, when he couldn't come up with that, that he'd need to throw me and my staff some sort of bone.

"So you sent him the same sort of revelatory letter that he'd sent you, telling him where Gerry Breen was.

"Endgame? It must have seemed that way to you at the time. Breen would be hunted down and arrested, Parmalee would publish the manuscript, and Opus Dei would have to go on the defensive. And Breen might even be charged with Stanton's and Mudd's deaths, when and if it came out what role she had played in the order over the years.

"Little could you have known how capable your erstwhile friend and co-Opusian is." McGarr turned from the window and regarded Manahan directly. "Which is something you should heed."

As though steeling herself, she had folded her arms across her substantial chest, and her gray eyes were bright. "I'm afraid I don't understand. Why *heed*?"

"Because she's not a woman given to half measures, and she's no longer under our control."

"I've less reason to fear Gerry than I have to be concerned with any of the . . . bullshit that you just uttered. May I speak candidly as a solicitor?"

McGarr waited.

"You don't have a scrap of evidence, otherwise you wouldn't be here trying to get me to—could it be *confess*? My opinion? You're delusional. Shouldn't you be somewhere else? Out actually looking for Gerry or back at the cop shop massaging paper. Or even better, from a human perspective—at the hospital with your wife and her father. But maybe not even they need you in your present state of mind."

Suddenly McGarr found himself hunched over the woman, their

faces inches apart. "I don't know how you *worked* that, but there are two ways I can *work* you. One is the usual way, the legal way. But that's far too easy and good for the likes of you.

"What you need is pain. Not the pain of losing a husband who was a blackmailer and thief. No. And not the pain of having been misled even for a decade by a group of conniving clerics. Not that either.

"What this situation demands—and I will serve you up—is pain of the sort that my father-in-law, whom you also murdered, felt. And my wife is presently feeling.

"I could and should"—from inside his jacket McGarr pulled his derringer with the four barrels and slammed it into the space between her eyes, knocking her head back into the cushion of the chair—"pop you right here and now. You vicious, heinous, frightful piece of work."

Loading his weight into the stubby pistol as he pushed himself to a stand, McGarr stepped away from her. "But that would be far too easy. I know somebody better suited to the job, somebody who will make your pain linger."

"Who?"

"Why, your bosom buddy. Your pal, your friend—Gerry Breen."

"She'll never believe you. Because you know, as I do, it's not the truth. You have no proof."

"We'll see." McGarr slipped the derringer back into his jacket and moved to the door.

HE FOUND FATHER Fred Duggan in the hallway not far away. "Ear to the door, could it be, Father?"

"Me?" the cleric said archly in a way that confirmed his guilt.

Taking the larger man's arm, McGarr reached for the handle of another door off the hall and opened it. Shoving the priest inside, he said, "Either sit down or I'll sit you down."

Like the other bedrooms that McGarr had been in at Barbastro, this too was supplied with plain, if expensive, furnishings designed for the contemplative life.

Attempting to compose himself, knowing that somehow he really should try to dismiss his anger at what had happened to the person he loved most and her father, McGarr suddenly realized he had already passed beyond that. He had already decided that he would seek his own revenge. And in that way he would cross a line that he had promised himself he'd never cross.

Glancing at himself in the mirror of the armoire as he turned to Duggan, he saw a short, squat, aging man whose face was drawn and whose eyes were cold with fury. And it occurred to McGarr that he should have long since abandoned the occupation that had now proved so disastrous. But out of selfishness or self-will he had contin-ued to work, when all indications—his countenance alone!—dictated that he should have quit.

And would now, after having crossed the line.

Turning to Duggan, he regarded the fit, dark, and handsome priest who had not only enriched his order enormously but had been enriched himself beyond the wildest dreams of any ordinary person. Or priest.

But then again—McGarr reminded himself ruefully—priests were no *ordinary* persons. They were ordained.

Could Parmalee have been right?

Noreen. McGarr wondered how Noreen was at the moment and if, in pursuing the cause of her distress, he was trying to ignore and deny her injuries. And Maddie and Nuala—what were they feeling?

Did they need him? Of course they did. But.

"Father—can you appreciate that I'm a bit exercised here, per-sonally? And because of my . . . extremity, I will put to you candidly a few questions that I want you to answer candidly. Am I under-stood?"

Wearing clerical garb, with his hands now clasped in front of his chest, the priest nodded, his brow furrowed in—could it be?—feigned concern. "Of course, Peter."

"Before you pointed out to me on the videotape the water bottle that Frank Mudd removed from the murder scene, did Delia Manahan come to you saying that Mudd was not her actual brother and that she was worried about what part he might have played in Mary-Jo's death?"

Duggan's eyes canted off toward the door. "I'm not sure what you know about Opus Dei, but we have a policy of keeping things like that intramural."

"Tell me!" McGarr roared.

Startled and with widened eyes, Duggan nodded. "She came to me."

"Did she tell you Mudd was not her brother?"

Duggan nodded again.

"And that you should review the security videotapes."

Yet again, Duggan nodded.

"You did that and came to me."

"Yes, she made a . . . clean breast of the matter, confessed the error of her ways, and I forgave her. Of course, she also made a complete formal confession followed by communion."

If McGarr had not been completely satisfied that Delia Manahan had murdered Mary-Jo Stanton, Frank Mudd, Fitzhugh Frenche, and possibly Noreen McGarr, he was now.

"But not a complete confession." Plunging his hands into his trouser pockets, McGarr turned his back on the priest and moved toward the little shrine that had been placed against an otherwise bare wall. It pictured a Sienese Jesus with a long, slightly bearded, sallow face, touching his exposed sacred heart with one hand while raising the other in a graceful gesture of beneficence.

McGarr had once heard a nun explain that the picture, which was a common feature of churches and homes countrywide, symbolized God's love. He loved mankind so much that he sent His perfect son to earth to teach imperfect man that in goodness and purity of heart, there is life after death.

At the time, McGarr had wanted to believe that. But he did not then, and he did not now.

"How do I get in touch with Geraldine Breen? I know you know, and I want you to tell me." He turned to Duggan.

"I'm sorry, but I don't. The last I heard or knew about Gerry was the night of Mary-Jo's death. Up in her quarters when she attacked you and your men took her away."

"You're lying to me."

"What?" Duggan unclasped his hands and sat up in his chair. "I'm a man of the cloth, and—"

"Perhaps. But you're a liar, and you're lying in front of this." McGarr waved a hand at the shrine. "And in that." He pointed at Duggan's clerical collar.

"Let me tell you a few things, Father. Maybe it will improve your memory.

"Ten years ago, Gerry Breen murdered Francis X. Foley, the solicitor, in his office in Fitzwilliam Square. She murdered him because—among dozens of others—Foley was blackmailing you and Opus Dei, using Mary-Jo Stanton's probable paternity as the basis. He claimed he had proof that she was the daughter of your José Maria Escrivá."

"Escrivá de Balaguer," Duggan corrected.

"You paid him, and you paid him for many years. Why?"

"Who says we paid him? I don't. This is the first time I've heard any of this."

Now glaring at the man, McGarr had to struggle to contain himself. "Breen, who functioned around here as security and is obviously well trained, discovered who Foley was and, after slaying him, made off with his files. I found them tonight in Chazz Sweeney's office in town, where, I'm sure, he put the information to use over the years."

Duggan hunched his shoulders and again twined his hands across his chest, confident that the files did not contain any information about Mary-Jo Stanton's paternity.

Or so McGarr read the gesture.

"I'll admit that Mr. Sweeney is friendly to us, but I don't see how his possessing those files in any way incriminates him. I know for a fact that he's a collector. That building of his is chock-full of things he purchased at estate sales, auctions, and the like."

Again McGarr had to return his hands to his pockets and turn away. "Worse than the murder itself, you compounded the crime by having Breen work at befriending Delia Manahan, Foley's widow. Breen helped her with the wake, the funeral, the children, the house, and eventually duplicitously brought the woman into Opus Dei.

"Why? To keep her close, just in case her husband might have made copies of his files and put them aside in one of the offshore banks he had used to conceal his identity. Think of it—for over ten years now, you and she and Opus Dei lied to the woman, allowing her to follow your rules, do your bidding, work for you, and—I'm sure—contribute to your coffers when, all along, you had murdered her husband, the father of her children, and disrupted the course of her life."

"It couldn't have been much of a course, living with a black-mailer, as you say. But"—Duggan's hands came up—"in no way do I admit or even acknowledge any of what—"

"Until, *until*"—McGarr spoke over the priest—"Dery Parmalee overheard you and Breen discussing Manahan, laying out all the sordid—"

"You don't know that."

McGarr spun around on Duggan. "Oh, yes, I do. I also know that you and Sweeney conspired in all of this, and that bothered you, Father, because you knew—you *know*—it's more than simply wrong. It's evil.

"See this?" From a pocket, McGarr pulled out a small square piece of plastic.

"What is it?"

"A flash card. A recording disk. It can store photographs, words, even voices. Small, eminently portable, cheap. For over a year, and with the help of Frank Mudd, Dery Parmalee used these to record every conversation that you had here in Barbastro."

Duggan's head went back slightly, as though he now understood the source of Parmalee's information.

"He had Mudd place listening devices in every room he could, until you—correctly suspecting that Mudd's presence in the house was unusual—banned him from the place.

"Granted, Parmalee had his own life to live, so he couldn't monitor all that was said. Instead, he let a computer do it, screening key words, such as Foley, Manahan, Fitzwilliam Square, Escrivá—get the picture?"

Duggan only stared at him.

"I myself am computer-illiterate, so I had to listen from Parmalee's flat over the chemist shop down in the village. Granted, I didn't hear you discussing how and why you murdered Foley, but I did overhear this conversation.

"Shall I play it for you?"

Duggan still said nothing, but his eyes were hooded.

Holding the device in his hand, McGarr turned up the volume and carried it only a step in Duggan's direction, not trusting himself to get any closer to the priest.

They heard:

"Hello." Some silence went by, and then, "I know, Chazz. I know. There was nothing we could do, no way to stop him." It was Duggan's voice, recorded early that afternoon at Parmalee's flat in the village.

Another pause. "You have to understand, Parmalee has been chewing on this since we convinced Mary-Jo to banish him. Given how . . . erratic and vindictive he is, it was inevitable that one day it would come to this. Didn't we discuss this before Mary-Jo's death?"

Another long silence. "Well—I don't want to know how that could happen. Also, I think this conversation should come to an end. I'm a man of the cloth. . . ."

Another lengthy pause. "I should remind you whom you're talking to. . . . I'm going to hang up now. I'm hanging up. I think we should speak at some other time, when you're more yourself."

"This is the part I like most," McGarr said to Duggan, pointing to the recording machine in the palm of his hand.

With force, the receiver hit its yoke and Duggan roared his displeasure, following which he began to cry.

McGarr turned up the volume yet higher, as the man could be heard bawling uncontrollably.

Then: "How did we get into this? And *why*? Why couldn't Mary-Jo have lived out her life as God intended? Mary Jo—dear heart in heaven—can you forgive us?"

Then a knock, and Sclavi asking "*¿Cómo puedo ayudarte?*"

And Duggan's "You can't! I'm inconsolable. How could we have strayed so far, so quickly."

McGarr switched off the recorder. "Can I tell you this? I don't completely understand what that was about, since I know you and your order played no part in Mary-Jo Stanton's or Frank Mudd's deaths.

"But shortly after this call, Dery Parmalee was shot and killed execution-style in his digs in the Liberties tonight, where sometime later, Sweeney shot and killed Detective Inspector Enda Flatly before two witnesses."

Duggan's eyes widened; plainly the last bit was news to him.

"And this"—McGarr pointed to the recorder—"makes you—a holy priest—a party at least to Parmalee's death."

Duggan opened his mouth, as though to object.

"You! Knew! *Before* Sweeney had Breen cuff Parmalee's wrist and ankle together in her signature fashion and then empty a magazine into the back of his brain. You could have saved the life of another human being, regardless of his flaws and failings. And yet you did nothing but indulge yourself in an emotional display."

Duggan wrenched his eyes away.

"I wonder if you felt that deeply when you had Breen or Sweeney spike my wife's shotgun, killing Fitz and maybe Noreen too."

The eyes, which were now brimming with tears, returned to him. "Now that, I swear . . . No, not us."

McGarr slipped the recorder into his jacket and pulled out his mobile phone. "What I want from you now is simple and easy for you to accomplish without violating any of your . . . scruples."

He handed Duggan the phone. "Ring up Geraldine Breen—I know you know where she is—and tell her I wish to speak with her. And speak only. I don't want to know where she is. The call is not being traced. I just want to chat."

"I don't know. I—"

"Do it!" McGarr roared. "Or so help me, I'll splash you and your order across the front page of every paper in the country."

Now very much looking his age and having to wipe the tears from his eyes, Duggan fumbled with the phone. "I—I can't see. My spectacles." But he punched in a number, then: "Gerry? I want you to listen to me and do as I say. I have somebody here who wants to speak with you. You know who he is—"

"And hear him out, don't ring off no matter what he says," McGarr prompted.

Duggan repeated his words before handing McGarr the phone.

"Miss Breen—it's Peter McGarr. Miss Breen?"

Finally, he heard a voice.

"I'd like you to hang on for a moment. I've something to tell you, but I need some privacy." And to Duggan: "You stay here. Don't move from that chair."

Out in the hall, McGarr shut the door and stuck a nearby chair under the knob. At the door to Delia Manahan's room, he knocked and waited until he heard her approach the door and ask, "Who is it?" before he began speaking into the mobile phone.

"Geraldine Breen, are you there?"

He heard another acknowledgment.

"Geraldine Breen—I'm phoning you because I want you to know several things. First and foremost, I know who killed Mary-Jo Stanton and Frank Mudd, and it was not Dery Parmalee."

McGarr then heard what amounted to a shriek behind the door, and the key rolled over in its lock. "You can't!" Manahan yelled.

"Why not?" McGarr asked.

"Because it's . . . it's tantamount to signing my death warrant."

McGarr managed a thin smile. "As you said, I have no real evidence, evidence that would stand up in a court of law. But you and I know you killed Mary-Jo Stanton, after Parmalee learned who killed your husband and wrote you an anonymous letter. You murdered Mary-Jo to get back—"

With her eyes widened and her wan face suddenly flushed with fear, Manahan reached for the phone, but McGarr batted her hands away.

"Gerry, it's Delia!" she shouted. "Don't believe him! He lies. He thinks I tampered with his wife's shotgun and—Give me that fucking phone!" Manahan lunged again, but the second swipe of McGarr's left arm caught her on the side of the neck with such force that her shoes flew off her feet as she fell hard onto the hall carpet.

Bending down so he was only inches from her face, McGarr proceeded to tell Breen how the two murders were accomplished: the G. Bass, Outfitters water bottle, the come-along secured by the fancy knot, the theft of the manuscript that was mailed to Parmalee so he could run it in *Ath Cliath*, the duplicity that matched Breen's own in every way but duration.

As McGarr spoke, he watched Manahan's light gray eyes work, darting here and there but never—not once—meeting his own.

"Are you there?" he had to ask when he had finished what he had to say. But Breen had rung off.

McGarr straightened up, closed the phone, and slipped it into his pocket. Turning, he made for the staircase.

"Where are you going? You can't leave. Not now."

Nearly stopping to go back and do what his hands were telling him he should, McGarr instead forced himself down the wide staircase, passing under the crystal chandelier toward the formal entrance of Barbastro.

"Arrest me! You have to arrest me!" Her voice echoed in the foyer.

Turning back to her, McGarr made sure their eyes met. "No sin goes unpunished. Ultimately." With all the force he could muster, McGarr slammed the door shut.

Ward was waiting, parked in a rental car behind McGarr's Rover.

Explaining the situation, McGarr added, "Don't let her leave the country, here or in the North. But do nothing. Just follow her. After the fact . . . well"—his eyes met Ward's—"Breen should be stopped."

Ward nodded. "And you?"

"Hospital."

20

FOR TWO DAYS, Ward, Bresnahan, and McKeon followed Manahan, who first tried to fly out of Dublin Airport.

Denied that privilege because of the phone call Ward had earlier placed to Customs and Immigration, she then attempted to board the ferry to Wales from Dun Laoghaire. Failing that as well—and nearly getting arrested for trying to bribe a port officer—she abandoned her Mercedes at a car rental agency and in a new Audi drove north to Aldershot Airport outside Belfast.

There too, however, she was told that her traveling privileges had been revoked, and she panicked. Driving at a furious pace throughout the afternoon and early evening, she reached Killarney in distant Kerry around eight-thirty. Finding a room at the Great Southern Hotel, she appeared in the bar of the old and ornate Victorian edifice as if transformed.

Gone was the severe look with the stark white hair pulled back in a ponytail and the plucked eyebrows. In fact, gone was the white hair, courtesy of a dark brown wig, and certainly Manahan was the mistress of makeup. Somehow she had given herself quite credible eyebrows, at least from the distance of about thirty feet, and her entire coloring made the forty-two-year-old woman look at least five years younger.

Wearing black spandex slacks and a sleeveless marled-silk turtleneck that made the most of her ivory shoulders and large breasts, she surveyed the bar before sitting next to a handsome man in his early fifties who appeared to be alone. When he proved to have a companion, Manahan carried her glass of white wine out into the lounge, pretended to glance at a promotional magazine, then returned to the bar and a seat next to another man.

In changing her own position, Bresnahan passed by the bar and heard her say, "Is that an American accent I'm hearing?" Leaning back against the bar, Manahan had propped her elbows on the edge to present a provocative view of her breasts.

In a nasal twang, the man replied, "Ain't me with the accent, darlin'. But I sure as hell cotton to yours." His eyes were riveted on the marled silk.

Out in the unmarked Garda car, Bresnahan slid into the backseat and closed the door. "She's in mufti at the bar, about to pick up an American."

"She'll dump the Audi and go off with him tomorrow, like husband and wife," said McKeon.

Ward shook his head. "I'll bet an evening of pints she's out of there with him by"—he glanced at his watch—"closing time."

Which was two hours away.

Said Bresnahan, "She's obviously got the cash, and she'll leave the bar to freshen up, then feed him some line like—'Just got a phone call, and I have to be in Galway City tomorrow early. Tell you what, cowpoke. I like the cut of your . . . er, jib. What say we take a little side trip. On me.' "

"Literally. And off they go. If she stays away from her credit cards, her disappearing act may well be complete," McKeon put in. "But I'll take you up on the timing, Hughie. She must be dead tired, and he'll want a brief exploration of possibilities, so to speak, before getting off more regularly."

McKeon lost the bet.

Around midnight, Manahan and her cowpoke left the hotel, bags in hand. Climbing into his rental car—with small American flags on the bumpers, placed there so tourists could be waved through checkpoints in the North—they drove off into the night.

"Tell you what," McKeon said, wheeling after them. "I'm sick of this driving about."

"Wherever they put in next, I'm ringing up Father Fred Duggan and grassing on the bitch."

"Making you what? An accessory."

"Are you daft? After what she's done? How many has she murdered—three and counting?"

There was a pause before Bresnahan said, "Maybe we should phone Peter. Find out how Noreen is." Bresnahan was one of Noreen's closest friends.

"No," said McKeon. "The last thing he needs is chat from the likes of us who've got this necessary job of work to do. And if the news is bad, I swear to you, I'll whack the bloody bitch myself, Breen or no Breen."

Two hours later, when Manahan and her American companion pulled off the dual carriageway into the Clare Views Hotel near Ennis, Ward turned to McKeon. "Why not make that phone call to Duggan, Bernie. I'd hazard our Yank and his yank-ee will be sleeping and so forth for some time."

"Her feeling safe, at least for the moment."

Being careful not to be seen by Manahan, who might remember her from Killarney, Bresnahan got out of the car and stepped into the hotel.

The Clare Views was far different from the Victorian-style Great Western; it was a large, modern hotel alongside the dual carriageway leading to nearby Shannon Airport.

In the bar, Bresnahan waited until the pair had gone upstairs before identifying herself and asking for a room on the same floor as the couple who had just checked in. "Adjoining, if possible."

Around daybreak, Ward and McKeon watched a Land Rover move slowly past the hotel before parking in the lot in back. The "man" who climbed down from behind the wheel was no man.

Wearing a cloth cap—over what looked like a shaved head—and a leather bomber jacket with wide shoulders, Geraldine Breen surely looked mannish, apart from the way she carried herself.

"It's all in the hips," said McKeon. "Notice how they roll. You can't unlearn that."

"What do you think she's got in the bag?"

McKeon hunched his shoulders. "But I'm considering her armed and dangerous. And sure we know she's a killer thrice over." He pulled out his 9mm Glock and checked the clip.

Moving straight to the back door of the hotel, Breen unzipped the bag and pulled out a small device that she inserted, it seemed, into the electronic security lock.

"What's that?" McKeon asked.

"A superkey, I think. It reads the security code for the day and spits it back into the lock. Presto, the door opens."

McKeon shook his head. "And we call that progress. Give me a six-inch dead bolt any day."

The moment the door closed, Ward stepped out of the car. After disabling the Land Rover, he would cover the front of the hotel. "What about the American?"

"What about him?"

"She can't afford to leave a witness."

McKeon smiled slightly. "You can sum it up in two tunes. The first is titled 'Never Up, Never In.' And the flip side is . . . ?"

Opening the back door, Ward pulled out one of two Steyr-Mannlicher model Ms mounted with a nightscope. It was a target rifle preferred by many professional shooters and a sapper's weapon with few equals.

" 'What Price Gorey?' "

"Give it up, Bernie—this is serious."

McKeon swung his head to Ward, and their eyes met. "Don't I know it."

Ward closed the door. Through the orange glow of the cadmium vapor lamps in the car park, he moved toward the Land Rover.

McKeon reached for his radio to warn Bresnahan, who had earlier advised them that she was up in a room next to the couple. "You should know that Breen seems to be equipped with what Hughie calls a superkey. It can—"

"I know."

"What about the two in the room?"

"They seem to be sleeping now," she reported in a whisper.

"No more oos and aaahs?"

"*Bernie!*"

"Which is my dilemma altogether. These days, it's all thought and no—"

Switching off her set, Bresnahan opened the door just enough to see down the hall. At length a figure appeared and moved toward her quickly, like a fleeting shadow, but passed right by both doors. Less than a minute later, the lights in the hall went out.

In fact, the power in the hotel went out, as Ward could see from a position across the street.

Ditto, McKeon from the now darkened parking lot out back, where he got out of the car and retrieved the second rifle. In the darkness, the night-seeing capability would be essential.

In the hotel, Bresnahan closed her door. Given the superkey and all the electronics at Barbastro, Breen might also possess night-seeing eyeglasses of the type that Bresnahan herself had used on stakeouts.

What to do? Let her simply enter the room and dispatch two human beings, one of them utterly unaware of the situation and the danger he was in? Granted swift, sure justice would be done in regard to Manahan, but Bresnahan now decided that she could not abandon the American. She could not live with herself were she to do nothing to save him.

"Rut'ie—you okay?" Ward now asked from his position across the street from the front of the hotel.

With her Glock out and her ear to the door, Bresnahan heard what she thought was the rustle of somebody again passing by the door. But she couldn't be certain, until she picked up the soft click of a latch sliding back as a door swung in, followed almost immediately by a much softer click.

Slipping in, thought Bresnahan. Perhaps enough sound to rouse them briefly, but not enough to put them on their guard and wake them completely.

Breen would now wait for a while, listening to their breathing, allowing the pair to fall back into deep sleep, scanning the layout of the room.

Given the darkness, which in Bresnahan's room was near total, and given who the woman was—enforcer, assassin—Breen would surely have equipped herself with the ability to see in the dark.

Also, there was the matter of the bag she was carrying. What could be in that?

Time to act. With Ward covering the window and its narrow balcony, there was only one way out of the room for Breen. And one way in.

Slipping the Glock under the waistband of her slacks, Bresnahan used both hands to open her door, making sure her fingers caught the latch to minimize any noise. She would have to be in position before she made her move.

Out in the hall, she removed her shoes, which would make her fleeter of foot on the deep carpet, and propped one shoe between the door and the jamb. The room would provide her with a refuge should she need it.

It was an American-style hotel with stairwells at either end of the floor. There Bresnahan could see bands of achromatic light leaking from under the doors, produced by the emergency lighting that was required by the building code. At least she would have two bearings in the darkness.

Which was when Bresnahan heard a deep woman's voice shout, "Billy!" followed by a thud and another dull sound and a woman's shriek.

Bresnahan rushed toward the door and fumbled for the handle, but it was locked.

Suddenly a light appeared under the door, and the same voice—obviously, Manahan's—continued, "Now, Gerry—I know what that bastard, that godless cop, told you on the phone. I was there and tried to stop him. He's wrong, dead wrong, and just trying to complete what Parmalee began. He's trying to smirch—"

The sound of the blow was loud, even through the door, and was followed by a whimper. "Ah, God, no—don't do that again. Not there."

And louder still.

Glock in hand, Bresnahan could shoot at the door, which would surely stop what Breen was about. But it might also bring on an ugly hostage situation that would result in the death of the American, if he was still alive.

Instead, Bresnahan stepped away from the door as the blows and cries for mercy continued. Reaching for the radio, she said, "Hughie—Breen's in the room, and the American doesn't seem to be conscious. And she's beating the piss out of Manahan or Foley or whoever the feck she is.

"Could you place a shot someplace high on the window? You know, like shatter the thing. Maybe that will flush her out here into the hall."

"We don't want hostages," said McKeon. "We want her to continue."

"Do you know where they are in the room?" Ward asked.

Bresnahan stepped back to the door, the better to hear. Maybe she could pick out where they were.

Yet another shriek, still louder. Then, "Ah, Christ, Gerry—not that. That wasn't me. Why would I have used something like that? It was Dery, trying to rub our noses in Mary-Jo's death."

Bresnahan then heard another voice that she could barely make out, saying, "Did you kill her? And I want the truth."

Evidently Manahan nodded.

A mumble.

"Why do you think? To get back at you and Duggan and the rest who murdered my husband, destroyed my family life, and then codded me into actually *joining* you and *working* for you and *dedicating* my stupid fucking life to your cause. You must have had many a sneering, ugly, forked-tongue laugh at my expense, you fucking bunch of hypo—"

The sound of the slap was audible, and something crashed at a different place in the room.

"Well?" Ward demanded. "You there, Ruthie? Where do I fire?"

"I don't know, I'm trying to—"

"Just shoot me! *Shoot* me, you hypocritical bitch!"

More mumbling followed, then some rustling noises, and finally, "You promise?"

"Have you ever known me to break my promise?" said Breen. Obviously they were approaching the door, which Bresnahan now backed away from, Glock in one hand, radio in the other.

"Just shoot, someplace high on the window and over to the right," if the room was anything like her own.

But before Ward could slip the radio into his jacket pocket and raise the nightscope to his eye, the light in the room went off, and Bresnahan heard somebody gag or choke. And then: "You promised!" in a strange, high voice that was followed by a strangled cry.

Suddenly the door burst open.

Down in the street Ward squeezed off a round that bucked through the double-glazed window, shattering both panes, which crashed in a cascade of glass onto the narrow balcony and spilled into the street.

Hearing the report, McKeon raised his weapon and sighted on the rear door of the hotel.

Backlit now by the ambient light from the street, a figure with wide shoulders and wearing a hat rushed from the room directly at Bresnahan, who dropped down into a shooter's crouch and squeezed off four quick rounds, the muzzle blasts strobing the dark hall.

Yet the figure did not stop. She cut right, making for the door at the end of the hall.

Standing to pivot, Bresnahan had raised her arms to fire again when a blinding flash seared her vision and her body slammed into the wall.

The rear door of the hotel did not open quickly but rather in jerks, as though the figure behind it were testing the strength of its closing spring.

But when McKeon saw the black leather cap peek out, followed by the wide shoulders of the jacket, he squeezed the trigger, and the figure reeled out from the open door, falling to one knee.

As she tried to rise up, a second shot to the chest slammed her back into a sitting position against the wall.

Having heard McKeon's fire, Ward had raced around the building and was the first to reach her, followed almost immediately by McKeon, who said, "Shit—it's not Breen, it's Manahan. And what's that around her neck?"

It was a *cilicio*, whose long sharpened spikes had been screwed into her neck.

Looking up, their eyes met. "Rut'ie," Ward said, pulling his Beretta from its holster. "Cover the front."

But it was too late. The door of the hotel had nearly closed, and McKeon only caught a glimpse of the person fleeing into the trees that bordered the dual carriageway. Beyond, he could see the lights of a waiting car.

Raising the rifle, he tried to sight her in. But the copse was dense, he could no longer see her, and he would not risk firing at the waiting car with others passing on the highway now as early morning came on.

Leaving the wood, Breen had slowed her pace, not wanting any of the drivers passing by to see her running to the escape car and perhaps taking note of it.

And there was no hurry. As she had set the hit up, she'd change cars thrice and drive over back roads through the Clare countryside to find herself in a safe house near Killaloe in an hour's time.

She could see as she reached for the handle of the door that the car was going, the lights were on, and the driver was poised behind the wheel. Wrenching the door open, she slid in and turned her face to the driver and the barrel of a short, four-chamber handgun.

"Why did you spike my wife's shotgun? What did that gain you?"

Breen said nothing since there was nothing to say. She had been acting under orders.

"Sweeney tell you to do it?"

Orders. Or, rather, order. Now that he knew, there was only one course of action. Breen's hands reached for the gun, all four barrels of which exploded in her face.

Having heard the muffled blast, McKeon watched as the car started moving, turning onto the exit ramp toward the hotel.

McKeon again raised the rifle, but he soon saw it was McGarr at the wheel. Geraldine Breen was slumped in the passenger seat, her head resting against the window. Blood was flowing from a massive exit wound in her shaved head. It was the size of a small red fist.

"I thought you might need a hand. Pulling in, I saw him parked by the side of the road, using binoculars to scan the hotel."

Sprawled in the backseat was a young man with his hands cuffed behind him and a tight scarf gagging his mouth. A small silver cross studded with bright stones hung from one ear.

"It wasn't much of a leap." McGarr's face was drawn, there were dark circles under his eyes, and he was in need of a shave.

"Where're Hughie and Ruth?"

The car park was now swarming with uniformed Guards, two EMVs, a fire brigade, and hotel guests and management.

"And you are?" asked a sergeant who was standing by Manahan's body near the rear door of the hotel.

"The bad fairy," McKeon replied, brushing by him. "And this is my magic wand." He hefted the Steyr-Mannlicher. "Just look at the evil it's done."

In stepping over Manahan's body at the back door of the hotel, McGarr scarcely looked down. Why give her even so much as a thought, he said to himself climbing the stairs. She's already consumed far too much of your life.

Ward was crouched beside Bresnahan, whose forehead was swollen and red. Three EMT personnel were standing nearby. There were others in the bedroom, tending to the American, who was conscious.

"I think she might have a concussion," said one of the medical team. "That's a mickey of a bump. We should take her to hospital."

"No. No concussion, no hospital. I can see, I can talk. All I have is a splitting headache. What about Breen?" Her eyes swung up to McKeon.

Who pointed to McGarr. "Deus ex machina, exactly."

"And you? What are you doing here?"

McGarr only returned her gaze.

"How's Noreen?"

"Coma. They're doing some tests, trying to understand why."

Bresnahan's brow furrowed and tears flowed from her eyes. She sobbed.

"Now we really are taking you to hospital," said the most senior of the medical technicians. "Policewoman or no policewoman."

"Just because I'm crying? You don't know *why* I'm crying."

McGarr turned and walked into the room where the American lay in a bed covered with glass. "You're a lucky man," another technician was saying.

PART V
NEW LIFE

21

ON THURSDAY, day two of Noreen's coma, McGarr received a call while sitting at her bedside. He had to remove her hand from his to open the mobile phone. He heard:

"Peter, Chazz here. How's the boy? Not well, I should imagine. Understandably, understandably.

"Listen—guess where I am? Ach, you couldn't, not in your wildest dream, so I'll tell you. I'm sitting in Dery Parmalee's seat here in the newsroom of *Ath Cliath*, because—are you ready for this?—I'm the bloody, feckin' publisher. No shit.

"I don't think I told you about D. and me, but we were tight. Very tight, especially after closing."

It was supposed to be a joke.

"Peter, are you there?"

McGarr still did not reply.

"The deal. I imagine you're interested in that. So, the deal was consummated . . . at least a good week before D., God love him, ran that fallacious carry-on about Mary-Jo Stanton and Opus Dei. I think he thought he'd need some travelin' money, don't you know. Given how scurrilous, downright wrong, and un-Christian it was. It's such a pity that he wasn't fast enough in his removal.

"Are you still with me?"

McGarr knew Sweeney knew he was.

"Shall I cut right to the chase? I'm sitting here in me office with the editorial board surrounding me, so you can question them about just when and how the deal with Dery was done. That is, if you don't believe me, and there's no reason you should.

"Add to that, bucko, I'm staring down at a proof of the front page that will run tomorrow. It's another special edition, don't you know, since the last was such a circulation smash.

"Before we go to press, however, I'd like you to sign off on some of the facts, since they concern you and those near and dear to you. But don't think this is a read-back by any means. No, we don't do that around here anymore, do we, boys and girls?"

When there was no response, Sweeney roared, "Say something, you arseholes, so he knows you're for real."

"No read-backs," McGarr heard a voice say.

"I'll be waiting. And—one other thing—come alone, so we can deal in private." Sweeney rang off.

Deal. There would be no deal; Sweeney had shot Flatly. Ward and he had witnessed the crime. Also, Sweeney was in receipt of the files that had been stolen by Geraldine Breen after she had murdered F. X. Foley.

And it had been Sweeney—bagman, power broker, Opus Dei zealot—who had controlled whatever other mayhem Breen was responsible for, like the signature death of Dery Parmalee.

Sitting on a chair beside the hospital bed, McGarr leaned forward and kissed the narrow patch of pale skin on Noreen's brow that was not swathed in bandage.

If only, somehow, he could perform a miracle and fix the damage that the small shard of shattered gun barrel had caused. Not for the first time, he thought: If only there really were a God actively at work in the world, He would acknowledge Noreen's goodness, her exemplary life, and all the good works she had performed daily.

And make her whole and sound again, she who had been so charitable to all she dealt with. She who had a bereaved mother to comfort and a young distraught daughter to raise. She who had been in
the fullness of her life. She whom McGarr had loved with his whole
heart and soul.

Taking her hand again, he raised it to his lips and felt the cool—
no, cold—skin.

It had been his prayer for the days that she had been unconscious.
His ritual in leaving her.

Placing her hand back on the bed, McGarr stood and turned to
Maddie and Nuala, who were sitting in more comfortable chairs
behind him. With brow furrowed and eyes narrowed in concentration, Nuala was knitting furiously, as she had since Fitz's death.

Maddie was using the light near the window to complete her
homework. "Your mother would want you to keep up with your
studies, no matter what," he had told her. And perhaps they'll keep
your mind occupied, he had thought.

Mind, if by some . . . if by the grace of God Noreen pulled
through, McGarr would not want her—and she would never have
wanted—to be grossly disabled. No. Please, let her survive as she
had been.

"I'll be back."

Maddie's head came up. "Where're you going?" Since the "accident," as they were calling it, she had been utterly solicitous of his
company. The one night they had slept at home, he had to doze in a
chair by the side of her bed. She would awake every time he tried to
leave the room.

"A wee matter."

"When will you be back?"

"By and by."

"You said that last time, and you were gone for a day."

"This is right here in town."

"What *time* will you be back?"

McGarr scanned the auburn tresses and turquoise-colored eyes that she had inherited from her mother and thought, as tears welled up in his own, Well, at the very least Noreen was leaving him this fine girl.

"In time for dinner. I'll take us all for a good dinner."

She only stared at him, her eyes vacant, her thoughts—he imagined—spooling back on what it had been like, only a few days earlier, to have her beautiful, vivacious, intelligent mother, who had been interested and involved in every class of thing, in the kitchen, quickly, deftly preparing a meal that was usually better than could be had in any restaurant.

Which is something Maddie had said when she had been younger, adding, "I don't want to go out to eat. Everything you get *out* is greasy or the taste isn't quite right."

Nuala raised her head. "I'll cook, if you do the shopping, Peter. I don't think I could face a market yet."

McGarr scanned her time-worn face, looking for Noreen in it and feeling guilty that he was. Nuala, whose loss was doubly his own but who was carrying on. Nuala who had not once alluded to the fact that it had been McGarr's occupation—the choices he, and nobody else, had made in life—that had caused the death of her husband and perhaps her only daughter.

"I'll try to make it quick. Phone me." If.

Before leaving the room, he scanned Noreen once again, as if trying to lift a permanent visual impression of her there, alive, in the bed.

THE DUBLIN NEWSROOM of *Ath Cliath* was housed above a row of shops off Thomas Street West in the Liberties, not far from Parmalee's residence.

In fact, movers were carrying out desks and chairs, and McGarr had to wait on the stairs while a cordon of navvies trundled by carrying CPUs and stacks of keyboards.

"Is *Ath Cliath* moving?" he asked the man with the clipboard at the top of the stairs.

"Not far. Just up the alley and a street away."

"Be finished soon?"

"After we lock up the paper, the whole shebang goes."

"Over to Dery's?"

The man glanced up at McGarr, his eyes hooded. "You'd best speak to Mr. Sweeney about that."

"And where is he, presently?"

"Corner office." His chin pointed the way.

Seated behind the room's only desk, Sweeney did not get up when McGarr appeared in the doorway. In fact, the immense man did not lower his feet, which were propped on the windowsill. With a phone to one ear, he was writing on a pad that was positioned on his considerable paunch.

Sweeney had rolled up his sleeves to expose forearms larger than the thighs of most other people; they were covered with a mat of graying hair. Under bushy brows, his eyes were so bloodshot and rheumy they looked like glowing coals.

Seated with him in the room was a younger man who was also in shirtsleeves. Maybe forty, he was thin and blond with punky twists in his hair and a gem-studded cross hanging from one ear. It was an exact duplicate of the one Geraldine Breen's wheelman had been wearing out in Clare.

Sweeney lowered the phone slightly and rumbled, "The door—close it."

Neither the other man nor McGarr moved.

"I said—the door! Close the fucking door!"

Reluctantly the other man rose from the chair and closed the door.

"Run him through the documents, while I finish up here."

"You're who I think you are?" the other man asked.

McGarr said nothing. And wouldn't. It was all he could do to keep himself from pulling out his Walther, holding it to Sweeney's head, and maybe even squeezing the trigger.

"I'm Chazz's solicitor. And these are the terms and conditions of the sale of *Ath Cliath* to Chazz." The document was a sheaf of legal-looking papers with a stamped seal on the final page, which the man turned to. "It's duly notarized and witnessed. There's my signature there. I was one of the witnesses."

Neil Dougherty, Esq., was the signature.

"And here is the deed to Parmalee's building where *Ath Cliath* is moving as we speak. All of this was accomplished two days ago, including the registration of the deed."

"Where's Parmalee's signature?"

Dougherty pointed to it.

"And the amount paid?"

"Here." Dougherty turned to an interior page and pointed to the amount, which was three million pounds. "A nice round figure."

"What was the method of payment?"

"Cash. Parmalee insisted on it."

"How did Sweeney finance it?"

"He didn't. No need.

"He withdrew some funds and paid the man. Here's the record." From another manila file, Dougherty pulled a Bank of Ireland withdrawal slip that said Sweeney had withdrawn the money in one-thousand-pound notes.

"It was a traveling case stuffed with money. Parmalee came alone." He shook his head, as though still marveling at Parmalee's courage or stupidity.

Nowhere at the murder scene in Parmalee's residence—in fact, nowhere in his building—had any money been found. Not a pound note nor any other valuables, like jewelry or a wristwatch. Flatly or Breen, McGarr assumed, having removed everything after Parmalee's death.

"I made you a copy of all of this." Dougherty reached for another folder. "You'll find it all legal and aboveboard. No judge in the land would find otherwise."

Apart from the money. Sweeney could simply have withdrawn the money with no actual payment made to Parmalee, dead men telling no tales. As well, Parmalee's signatures, if genuine, could well have been penned under duress.

Still standing by the door, McGarr slipped the folder under his arm as Sweeney droned on. "Go over there and stand beside Sweeney," he said to Dougherty.

"Sorry?"

"I said, walk around the desk and stand beside Sweeney."

"Why? I don't understand."

"I want you where I can see you."

"But—"

"Just do it." And as Dougherty moved around the desk, McGarr barked, "Hang up the phone." Sweeney's ruined eyes swung to him. "Hang up the phone!"

When Sweeney's eyes returned to the notepad, McGarr took two quick strides toward the desk, picked up the telephone console, and ripped the wire out of the wall.

Sweeney's legs and feet came next. Rearing back, McGarr kicked them from their perch on the windowsill. "Stand up and place your hands behind your back."

Sweeney only regarded him. "Aren't you the bothersome, pissant little cunt. Touch me again, and I'll have you taken care of, if I don't do it meself."

In one motion, the Walther came out of McGarr's jacket and was stubbed into Sweeney's meaty forehead, right between his eyes. The blow knocked back his head. "Stand up. If you so much as move your hands, I'll blow your brains out."

His heavy features drawn with anger, Sweeney still did not stir. "You should know you've been warned. And maybe you should look at this before you make yourself more of an arsehole than you already are." Now on the desk, the fingers of his right hand found what looked like a tear sheet or page proof.

The latter. It was the front page of *Ath Cliath*, or at least a prospective front page, since there was no date on the folio line.

"BIGAMIST COP SPAWNS HAREM IN LIBERTIES LOVE NEST." The photo showed Ward walking between Lee Sigal, who was pushing a baby in a pram, and Ruth Bresnahan when she had obviously been in her last month of pregnancy. Having turned to the side, she appeared hugely swollen, with her large breasts splayed to either side.

"Neil, here, preferred 'COP ON COP SHOPPING: HOW FRATER-NIZING, ADULTERY, AND BIGAMY CAN LEAD TO ADVANCEMENT IN THE GARDA SIOCHANA.' I told him it was too long." A hand came up and pushed the gun barrel away. "Now, step away from me so we can talk."

Lowering the handgun, McGarr moved to the other side of the desk and scanned the body of the story, which had been written by Parmalee, or so the byline said.

It detailed Ward's life:

His childhood in Waterford, his long, successful career in the ring and as a Guard who had "mustanged" his way from walking a beat to becoming "the anointed successor to Murder Squad top cop, Peter McGarr, who is due for retirement."

Then came his "reputation as a 'swordsman,'" his "rather pub-lic" involvement with Bresnahan beginning around five years earlier, and more recently the revelation that he had sired a son with "former university professor and wealthy Jewish heiress, Leah Sigal," four-teen years earlier. "Days after that," Ward had been "near-fatally wounded in a shootout with a drug dealer," and it was "Leah who nursed him back to health after he left hospital." And who had become pregnant by him. "Again! Proof that 'love' doesn't die. Or at least lust.

"But the fact that Ward had a ready-made family and tried to break off with Bresnahan meant nothing to the vivacious copette—said to be the hottest number in the Garda Siochana—and while on assignment with Ward early last year, she managed to get herself pregnant, she says, by him.

"Now the three of them—correction, the six of them—live in bigamous splendor in Sigal's newly remodeled digs, rumored to contain at least fourteen rooms, in the now-fashionable Liberties. When Ruth goes to work, 'Lee'—as she is known—has no problem taking care of both babies, sources say. But no Mormons they!

"The theater? The symphony? Nightclubbing? The finest restaurants in Dublin? They go often. Why not? Lee pays the other bills, and the eighty grand Hughie and Ruth are paid to uphold public morality is mere walking-around money.

"Which they do in style. Bresnahan and Ward are rumored to be . . ." McGarr glanced up from the proof sheet.

Sweeney's smile resembled more a baring of large, uneven, and yellowed teeth. "You should know, if anything in a legal way happens to me, Dougherty here—or some of my crew—will make certain that this stunning piece of investigative journalism at its finest is splashed all over the country."

Sweeney's smile became more complete. "Do you play chess, Chief Superintendent? Is this check? Or don't you care about your anointed successor and the lives of his wives and children?"

Which would be ruined, at least in Dublin, where no fault or frailty was forgotten or forgiven, McGarr knew. Especially indiscretions by public figures charged with upholding the law who openly flaunted their disdain for "public morality."

Both Ward and Bresnahan would have to resign, and they would have a tough go of establishing themselves in any sort of security or investigative work, which was all they knew. Both had been cops all their working lives.

But it would be their innocent children who would suffer most. "Oh, you know who they are . . . ," would be said behind a hand. The "better" people and schools would shun them, and their possibilities would be diminished.

"Put that thing away." Sweeney waved a hand at the Walther. "And never bring it out again in my presence."

McGarr's mobile phone was vibrating. Slipping the weapon into its jacket holster, he pulled out the phone and glanced down at the lighted display. It was Nuala.

"Peter—they asked me to call you. It's imperative that you return."

"Why?"

"Just come, please."

Closing the phone, he turned to leave.

"McGarr!"

He stopped in the open.

"Catch." Sweeney threw something that struck McGarr in the chest and fell to the floor. He picked it up.

It was a 21-gauge shotgun shell with a yellow plastic case.

"See? You shot the right woman after all."

Sent by a man who could not be more wrong. And who would not go unpunished. Ultimately.

22

DR. WICHMAN, the American surgeon who had operated on Noreen, was waiting for McGarr when he entered the hospital, and his eyes told the story.

The news was not good.

"Shall we speak here? Or up in the room where your daughter and mother-in-law can take part?"

"Take part in what?"

"In discussing . . . strategies." He was a tall man with gold glasses and light-brown hair.

"Here."

Wichman squared his body to face McGarr directly. "You're a policeman, I understand."

McGarr nodded.

"And you've probably had to say to others what I'm going to say to you now."

McGarr's heart sank.

"You know that we ran some tests late yesterday."

McGarr nodded.

"To confirm our findings, we repeated them an hour ago. And we're now sure that a catastrophe has occurred. As we tried to repair the damage to your wife's brain, we had to place a clamp on a major artery that has subsequently ruptured, we think, beyond the clamp. But only an autopsy will confirm that.

"The rupture, however, flooded the brain, and your wife no longer has any brain function."

Wichman waited for a few moments. "Do you want to sit down?"

McGarr shook his head.

"Shall I continue?"

He nodded.

"We could continue to keep her on life support, but . . ."

What was the point?

"Or . . ."

You could say your good-byes and switch off the machine.

HOLDING HANDS, the three of them entered the darkened room together, where the only noise was the sound of Noreen breathing.

Stopping at the side of her bed, Maddie, Nuala, and McGarr looked down at her—untouched apart from the bandages that swathed her head.

And in an overwhelming, smothering, blinding wave of remembrance, McGarr seemed to recall every vivid moment that Noreen and he had shared together.

From the first time he met her in Nuala and Fitz's picture gallery in Dawson Street, and he tried to kiss her, and she slapped his face. Through the early, heady infatuation he felt for her that in some ways never truly stopped. To their marriage, which had been profoundly happy without ever being . . . tritely happy, and the deepening of their love.

Which had everything to do with Noreen, McGarr believed. She had been courageous, truthful, loyal, passionate, fiery about the causes that mattered to her—and so many did—and never petty. But mostly she had been loving through the daily trials and tests that, added up, reveal who a person truly is.

Leaning down toward Maddie, McGarr whispered, "What you've got to say to yourself is that it's only your mammy's body that is leaving us here today. But her spirit is carrying on in each of us and will live in us just as strongly as we're living ourselves for the rest of our days. Say it to yourself, Maddie—say, 'Mammy, come live and be with me, now and forever.' "

A sob racked the child, who, turning her head into McGarr's chest, said, "Oh, Mammy—Mammy, come with me. Be with me, always." Before she broke down, and McGarr had to take her from the room.

Where Nuala stayed for the better part of an hour, saying prayers.

When she could sit with Maddie and comfort her, McGarr moved to the desk, where Wichman was waiting. "I want to be the one to throw the switch or whatever. I couldn't have anybody else . . ."

McGarr remained by the side of Noreen's bed for the day and a half it took her strong heart to stop beating.

EPILOGUE

THE MORNING OF Noreen's burial was stormy.

In Dublin, waves rolling in from the bay were washing over the granite blocks along the Liffey. Hugh Ward had to hold tight to the brim of his fedora as he moved from his car to the battered front door of Sweeney's building.

Ringing the bell, he glanced up. Overhead, the sky was freighted with lines of dark cloud, rather like an armada, that was sweeping to the west.

A woman opened the door as far as a chain would allow. "Yes?"

"Charles Stewart Parnell Sweeney—I understand he's here. May I see him?"

"And you are?"

"Detective Superintendent Hugh Ward, Garda Siochana." From under his mac, Ward pulled his photo ID.

"I'm afraid Mr. Sweeney can't see anybody this afternoon, he's—"

"This isn't a social call. I have warrants for his arrest." Ward displayed these as well.

Her eyes widened. "May I ask on what charge?"

"Charges. One count of murder. Four counts of conspiracy to commit murder."

"Can you wait a moment?"

"No. Open the door."

"I can't, Mr. Swee—"

"What's that arsehole want?" Ward heard Sweeney boom from the top of the stairs.

Stepping back, Ward raised a foot, stomped on the lock stile, and the old door sprang open, knocking the woman to the side.

Sweeney was gone from the top of the stairs that Ward charged up two at a time, his Beretta drawn. He caught Sweeney in his office, fumbling with a lower drawer of his desk, and a second kick— delivered at speed—sent the large man sprawling into a corner of the room.

"What have we here?" By the tip of the barrel, Ward drew an old handgun out of the drawer. "Could this be my lucky day? Is this the gun you used to shoot Flatly?"

"Who'll believe you after I run the story in *Ath Cliath*? You planted the bastard. I never saw it before in my life.

"You know"—picking himself up, Sweeney began to laugh— "in many ways, I'm going to like this, especially after I sue you, the government you represent, and your fucking whores into the next generation. One million pounds? Pah—this time it'll be ten million."

With everything he had, Ward sank his right fist into Sweeney's upper stomach, collapsing the massive man across his desk. Wrenching Sweeney's arms behind him, Ward cuffed his wrists.

And at the top of the stairs, Sweeney tripped, when Ward stuck a foot between his legs. After a brutal tumble that broke the banister, the large older man slammed into the edge of the door.

Ward waited until Sweeney finally opened his eyes. Bending— ostensibly to help the man up—he whispered so the woman would not hear, "That's only the beginning of your accidental life, Mr. Sweeney. You want to run that story about me and my family? Go ahead. But cops talk, and you're a cop killer. Like you, we take care of our own."

AT SWEENEY'S ARRAIGNMENT in Central Criminal Court, Lee Sigal, Ruth Bresnahan, Maddie McGarr, and Nuala Frenche sat in the front row.

Behind them were McGarr, Ward, McKeon, and nearly the entire personnel of the Murder Squad, less the few needed to answer phones.

And behind them were dozens of other Guards. In fact, the courtroom was packed with police. Word of mouth being what it is in police circles.